# A PERFECT YEAR?

Ollerford
PUBLISHING

*Ruth Foster*

# A
# PERFECT
# YEAR?

## RUTH FOSTER

# CONTENTS

Author's Note

# Author's Note

This story is the product of many stories. They have come my way every December for years, dropping out of greetings cards in the heart of the festive season.

Round robin letters are a literary one-off. A sheet of A4 crammed with a year's news paints a picture of real life like nothing else. Everyday events sit alongside momentous achievements. The summer's holiday catastrophe rubs shoulders with the cat's unexpected kittens; the painful loss of a beloved relative gets equal billing with a garden makeover. But look further, read between the lines and there is always more.

What if these separate life collages could be combined into a single story? The thought sneaked up on me one grey day in early January as I was about to consign that year's round robin letters to the recycling. The thought became an idea that germinated at the back of my mind – and eventually, here is the result.

Ali, Caroline, Robert and their families are fictional people living a particular drama. Upley Rising does not exist, though there are places in the UK that look quite a lot like it. Their yearly letters (including those penned by pets, small children and more) tell their own interconnected story, as well as the story of Britain through the 1990s and 2000s.

With heartfelt thanks to everyone who has supported me in making this unusual book a reality: family, friends, and everyone who has ever sent me their annual newsletters. As Caroline says in her 1987 letter: you know who you are.

# Prologue: December 1997

**15 Paradise View**
**Upley Rising**
**Thameshire**

Dear Friends

Christmas again already. Choral muzak in the supermarket, snow in tins, chocolate at rip-off prices. And the annual newsletter. Be warned: our 1997 review is not for anyone with a weak stomach. It includes a family holiday tragedy, a bloodsucking insect invasion, a dental extortion scandal – and the mysterious case of the missing Berlin Wall …

\* \* \* \* \*

*Paradise House, Paradise View*
*Upley Rising, Thameshire*

*Dear Everyone,*

Can life get any better? I'm delighted to announce another outstandingly successful year for the Wright family.

Starting with me, I have devoted 1997 to my thrilling new business start-up. Back in January, mapping out revenue projections in my walnut-panelled home office while the nanny collected the children from horse riding and fencing, I must admit to the tiniest flicker of self-doubt. Chewing on my Mont Blanc pen, I asked myself how I was going to meet this daunting new challenge. But defeat is not in my vocabulary and I can report that my new venture is exceeding all expectations …

* * * * *

### 14 Paradise View, Upley Rising, Thameshire

There is normal life and there is life according to the newspapers. This year the two converged: 1997 was agreed by all to be momentous, heartbreaking, gamechanging. We lost a people's princess; gave up British Hong Kong; learned that a sheep had been cloned. Some say we came perilously close to losing our monarchy. The national net curtains were drawn back, to reveal extraordinary public outpourings of joy and grief. In August people wept as they laid wreaths on the same streets where in May they had cheered the youngest prime minister in living memory.

It is somehow reassuring that here in Upley Rising national events never threaten to eclipse routine. Everyday business has rumbled on, at present with seasonal overtones …

* * * * *

# PART ONE 1987–1990: ALI, CAROLINE

## December 1987

**2b Bellavista Road,**
**London N8**

Dear Friends

Don't throw this card in the bin! It's not an anonymous blackmail letter. The mad scrawler is me, with my arm trapped in a humungous plaster cast. My right arm, the writing arm. I'm actually quite cosy here at home on a Saturday afternoon, curled up in front of the gas heater in my corduroy armchair. But it's a different kettle of fish battling to work through the London commute two weeks into December with what the hospital called a minor injury. Apparently a 'non-displaced fracture of the ulna' doesn't get me time off work with sick pay. Everything from putting on a cardigan to locking the door takes twice as long, and those lucky folk with seats on the Tube just avert their eyes from my greying sling. Never have so many commuters studied The Times crossword with such concentration.

But in every cloud lurks a knight in shining armour. My knight is Antonio, who has given up the rent on the cupboard in Clapham we laughingly referred to as his bedsit and moved in full time. Neither of us is sure if this is because – cue violins please – we could no longer live without seeing each other every day, or whether he just got fed up with me playing the sympathy card. I was phoning him most nights to come over and help me run a bath or open a tin of tuna. In the end it was easier for him just to stay, instead of setting off in the dark with his collar turned up against the rain on the off chance that the night bus might arrive.

Ant also says it's good for him to change address regularly given his background. At first, every time the doorbell rang he jumped, but he's getting slowly more relaxed as it's usually just the TV licence people or the Jehovah's Witnesses.

Living together means we've both had to make sacrifices. Antonio has to pay towards the mortgage, and in return I have cleared out my tiny, much-loved spare bedroom. I had to pack up my paperback collection (who knew 150 Penguins could fit into four boxes?) and do a serious cull of my LPs (Melanie out, Joni Mitchell stays). Oxfam picked up the spare bed, my guitar is wedged behind the fridge and we've moved the Swiss cheese plant to the bathroom, where it seems much happier. Defying all the laws of nature, Antonio has managed to squeeze into bedroom two – now called the Tardis – an old decorating table, four huge sacks of gravel and cement, some industrial-quantity cans of paint, a sinister black container labelled HAZCHEM and some sort of chainsaw.

Having an artist in residence is, I have discovered, not a romantic garret existence. There are endless practicalities, like unblocking a bucket load of half-set cement from the bathroom sink. Ant reminds me how Henri Matisse famously said that 'creativity takes courage'. Funny how he didn't mention anything about plumbers.

We hope we'll see some of you in the new year. Weekend guests are always welcome, though staying over will mean a return to my infamous saggy futon in the living room. And it will be moussaka and chips at the taverna round the corner until my arm is mended and my so-called cooking skills are back to normal. But before I forget: jokes about stepladders, librarians and Gibbon's Decline and Fall of the Roman Empire (three volumes of which catapulted off the shelf at the wrong moment) are strictly off the agenda. Work it out.

In the meantime excuse the xeroxed greeting, writing this lot out 34 times was not an option.

Festive Greetings to you all, and have a very happy new year,

*Alison and Antonio*

## December 1988

**2b Bellavista Road,
London N8**

Dear Friends

Another Christmas on the way, and where would we be without Cliff to sprinkle a bit of festive spirit into our meagre lives? Every shop here is playing Mistletoe and Wine all day on repeat. You have to wonder about the impact on the staff.

But fear not, Art has triumphed over kitsch in our corner of North London. I can say this on good authority having spent a full year living at the gritty coalface of creative activity. One freezing Tuesday evening last February, I got home from work after a long and lunchless day to find the fridge empty but for a lone open bottle of Asti Spumante. Antonio, halfway through the contents, was shouting down the phone in a mixture of Spanish and English. I worked out from the English bits that he'd been chosen by the Old Sidings Artspace trustees as a finalist for their Young Artists' Summer Show. This is – genuine quote from the judging panel – 'an exceptional platform (sic) for the best emerging new talent'.

At last, the breakthrough we'd been waiting for. If you haven't heard of the Old Sidings (and have you been living in a cave?) it's Harringay's most talked about new arts centre: a soot-blackened cavern of a building that could swallow most art galleries whole. Its trustees inspire terror across the contemporary Art World, and getting exhibition space there makes gold dust look cheap. It was a make-or-break moment for Ant's career.

There was just one snag: how to prepare a groundbreaking installation on an epic scale in a humble Victorian conversion flat with artex ceilings? Antonio was undaunted. For the next few months we put what was passing for normal life on hold while he worked up his Vision. This started with experimentally painted giant hands all over the living room wall, followed by endless hours of hammering, punctuated by chain sawing, drilling and swearing. The noise screeched through every flat in our building.

So much for my dreams of being a Muse, sitting strumming my guitar by the open window while Ant gazes at me and washes pastel colours onto sunlit canvasses. Instead I had to cook a compensatory supper for Mrs Smith in the flat next door and the elderly couple who live downstairs (deaf, except when it comes to hammering).

Preview Night arrived, the date clashing with the big Nelson Mandela birthday concert – the highlight of my year. After a token tantrum, I gave up my seat at Wembley – it was right at the back in any case, and we could videotape the whole thing. And the exhibition opening was just as entertaining. I'd invited all my family down just in case not enough visitors showed up. But the great and good of the Art World turned up in taxis all the way from Mayfair and piled through the gigantic doors of the Old Sidings, all blah blahing away. There were hundreds of them – possibly because of all the free plonk on offer. I've not seen so much alcohol changing hands without cash since someone smashed the offie window down the road last year. The papers were there too, probably for the same reason.

My main job was to keep a watch out for the Chilean secret police: Ant had a last-minute panic that he'd be bundled out of the exhibition and into a waiting car by plainclothes detectives masquerading as art lovers. I think it was just nerves: I told him that no artist can have fame and anonymity at the same time; he had to get on and charm the guests.

My other job was to circulate and make sure that none of the reviewers missed Ant's installation – all 600 square feet of it, transported in numerous trips by hired van and reassembled on site. There was a dodgy moment when I had to steer my dad away from the London Arts News reporter. Dad was holding forth with some choice comments about getting the slow train all the way down from Sheffield just to look at an engine shed which had been tarted up with public money when it could have been put to proper use if it weren't for the Beeching cuts. Meanwhile Ant, resplendent in an outfit he'd compiled from the charity shop's discount bin, had his official photo taken with my sister Gill. 'The artist with his intriguingly bohemian wife' was the caption in the paper.

Anyway, the reviews were mostly good, if you can work out whether art critics like something or not*. Antonio is quietly proud in a reflective way; it's a right shame his mother didn't live to see his success. The secret police thing seems to have subsided for now and he is busy reapplying many coats of magnolia – a colour he says should be banned – to the living room wall, where the hands remain visible in ghostly form behind my stripped pine shelving.

Now all we have to do is wait for the big commissions to roll in, while we eke out my salary on tins of beans.

In the rest of our news, my job too has had its moments of high drama. I should have smelt trouble when the Head Librarian called me in with a steely smile, gesturing for me to sit down before announcing he had a very special project for me. 'Special' being one of those words that comes with an invisible health warning. The project in question is nothing less than transferring our entire catalogue onto a new computer system. Now this may not keep you awake at night, but it means that tens of thousands of pink, yellow and green index cards, which for decades have held the key to all knowledge, will shortly vanish from the face of the Earth to be replaced by invisible bits of electricity.

It's a terrifying responsibility – and to carry it out I have been allocated three impoverished, sleep-deprived postgraduates. Picture me not too long ago. I bribe them to keep going at their consoles with endless mugs of coffee, which keep getting spilled over the cards, and on one terrible September afternoon all over a computer keyboard. The cards dried out on the radiator but the keyboard sizzled dramatically before entering computer oblivion. This does not bode well for the technological future.

I coped with all the stress by joining the Sunday Times Fun Run work team. Run plus fun being my athletic equivalent of diet plus donut. Being overtaken by a small terrier halfway through a two-and-a-half mile jog was not part of the plan, but the dog's owner donated £25 saying she hasn't had such a good laugh in years.

So that's our year. We are going to my parents for Christmas. Antonio is taking them an offcut from his installation (which didn't quite get a buyer) as a present; he's somehow under the impression that this will endear him to them.

Festive Greetings to you all and wishing you a happy new year,

*Alison and Antonio*

*Edited highlights from the London Arts News:

> *The extraordinary installations created by Antonio Garcia Cortinez are offered as a ring-fenced arena representing both the security and the banishment of the refugee … "as one of the 'escondidos'," explains Antonio, "you may simultaneously hide and be hidden." People and walls are seamlessly represented by a series of continuous concrete mounds, deeply scored and randomly scuffed, spray-painted with human hands*

*and embedded with broken television aerials evoking the need to communicate amid the desire to escape ... A powerfully innovative conceptual project, 'Nuevo Mundo' is thrown into sharp relief by the sombre halls of the Old Sidings space. People are starting to talk about the work of this young Chilean refugee, who won the Clapham Young Artist's prize at the age of just 20.*

\* \* \* \* \*

## December 1987

*10 Mansion Court*
*Dukes Gardens, London W6*

## Dear Everyone,

What a perfect year it's been. And how better to end it than with our very own Christmas Message, in this inaugural letter from Charles and me as a married couple.

Beginning with what the East Berkshire Listener singled out as 'the standout county event of the year'. Charles and I were delighted to welcome 238 of our closest friends and family to make our special day truly memorable.

I will treasure forever the view from the top table in our 2,000 square foot marquee gracing the stunning grounds of the Royal Devereux Hall. So many people commented on our brainwave to have a nautical-themed wedding party in one of England's most landlocked counties. The First Class cruise liner theme definitely went down a storm. With the cream canvass billowing in the autumn breeze, and our three-foot-high lighthouse wedding cake, we really could have been in the grand dining room of the Queen Mary. Full marks go to all the guests who followed our fun dress code. So many handsome captains! And the women tried so hard too. Charles was resplendent in his Admiral's uniform as we opened the ball to Rod Stewart's Sailing, and everyone danced the night away to our Titanic-style orchestra. I have stored away the naval bunting for the future, as Charles loved it all so much he has promised to buy me a yacht one day.

Having a real rock star on the guest list was the icing on all five tiers of our wedding cake. We had insisted to Ditch that he was there strictly in his capacity as Charles's brother and best man – so what a complete and utter surprise it was when he burst into a preview rendition of his new single, Put the Ring on her Finger. I hope you all bought a copy; it was so exciting having a song dedicated to me, then seeing it get all the way to number 53 in the charts.

Doesn't every wedding have its moments: Ditch has since reassured me that his banter about Charles and my cousin Clara in his very amusing speech was strictly a joke. And dear Uncle Walter redeemed himself from his comment about bridesmaids and puddings by recording the entire reception on his camcorder, starting with the receiving line and running right through to the last dance. So now, every time we rerun the video of our wedding day, we can have a small chuckle at the guest (from Charles's side of the family) who slipped away early with three unopened bottles of Bollinger. You know who you are!

I have enclosed individual handwritten slips acknowledging our appreciation for the many wedding gifts we received. Particular thanks are due if you made a choice from our list at Selfridges. But to those of you who bought toasters, there is no need to feel guilty, many of them have gone to good homes via the charity shop. We have kept three as backups, as the cheaper makes tend not to last too long. The same goes for the four thoughtfully chosen fondue sets.

I had intended to write thank-you notes from our Caribbean honeymoon in October. But every time I sat back in my palm-fringed hammock with pen and paper at the ready, I just drifted away into tropical bliss as the waves gently lapped onto the white sands. How lucky Charles and I were to be sipping pina coladas and watching a glorious sunset over the bay while a hurricane was wreaking havoc across the United Kingdom, causing misery and untold damage to all of you at home.

My mother has invited us to spend our first Christmas as a married couple with her. She will finally allow us to share a bedroom: she's charmingly old-fashioned, and had never quite believed Charles would tie the knot, even when I told her how he had whisked me off to Rome and gone down on one knee at the Trevi Fountain in front of hundreds of applauding tourists. Now we are looking forward to crisp Christmas weather, country walks, chestnuts roasting on the fire, mulled wine and carols on the village green.

It will be perfect; I will make sure it is.

Wishing you all a very Happy Christmas,

*Caroline and Charles Wright*

# December 1988

*10 Mansion Court*
*Dukes Gardens, London W6*

## Dear Everyone,

We hope that your 1988 has been as richly rewarding as ours.

Charles and I have devoted our first full year of wedded bliss to building our dream future together: one where every dinner out is candlelit, holidays always come with miles of private beach, and a taxi pulls up just as you emerge from Harvey Nichols laden with essential purchases.

We both know that to get on in life there is no substitute for honest hard work; not unless a shortcut is the quickest way. So Charles, my hunter-gatherer, has been dedicating himself to procuring as many international airmiles as possible. It's exhausting work, navigating the globe from one hotel minibar to the next, and passing tedious hours in business-class lounges finding creative ways to fill out expense forms.

And though I miss him when he's away, my own feet have barely touched the ground this year. Imperative Events is going from strength to strength, and my skills have been needed all over the country, making sure that we live up to the company strapline: *Precision is our Definition.*

It's never a dull moment sorting out all those last-minute hitches that crop up at the most important events.

One week it was a genuine bomb scare: the Chief Executive of one of our biggest clients was about to give a headline speech at a big business convention in Birmingham, when screaming alarms went off. I had to employ all my charms to persuade the police to turn off the noise until he'd finished talking. Then there was the sheep episode at a county wedding in Wiltshire. A gaggle of grubby livestock blocked the entrance to the private chapel, all bleating at the bride just as she stepped out of the Bentley in billowy white chiffon. I made an emergency decision and grabbed the bishop's staff to chase them away. He was very understanding; I think he was just as worried about his own vestments.

With Imperative Events growing so fast, I now have my own PA based at head office. Jessica clearly sees me as a role model, and has settled in well, though catastrophe was narrowly averted in her first week. I asked her to order some executive toys for a senior management awayday, then found in the nick of time that the catalogue she was about to use was totally unsuitable for a reputable company.

With all this work pressure we needed a break, and Charles, romantic as ever, came up with the perfect way to celebrate our first wedding anniversary. Imagine my surprise when he whisked me off to New York at two hours' notice, where he had booked the best seats in the house for the Broadway production of Phantom of the Opera. It was absolutely stunning, even better than the London production. Afterwards we celebrated with dinner at Joe Allen's, as you do, and who should we see but Sean Connery having a quiet dinner out. He very graciously signed my programme, even though he's not in the show, and Charles took the opportunity to have a chat with him about the agency. A business card pressed into the hand never goes amiss.

We rounded the trip off with a totally indulgent night at the Plaza. You may be wondering how we could afford all this, given we are saving for a house deposit. But the agency is doing well, and Charles managed to charge almost the whole trip to a client account.

The other event of note this year was experiencing the big Nelson Mandela birthday concert in June from the luxury of the VIP section. Charles's brother Ditch, the rock musician – who won this year's coveted Broken String award – got us the tickets. Just as I was sitting down, a man who I think was part of George Michael's entourage swooped over, exclaiming 'Darling, you look ravishing!' and wrapped both arms round me. I was hugely flattered (though not completely surprised) at being mistaken for someone famous, but Ditch stepped over and insisted on rescuing me. He's such a gentleman behind the raunchy rock star image.

The concert was a fabulous experience, though with my professional hat on I felt that some of the political speeches went on far too long. At work events I usually advise clients aiming for impact in presentations to stick to just three key points.

Although he's so busy and famous, Ditch still puts family first. He has included us in his Christmas plans this year. In an exciting break with tradition, we have been asked to join him and some of his select music industry contacts at a *chic* restaurant in Kensington. Mother has been invited to some of her bridge circle friends and says she will be quite happy to settle down later to watch the Queen. So Charles and I are looking forward to a very grown-up urban celebration this year, with posh crackers, one small thoughtfully chosen gift each, and plenty of good wine and good conversation.

How I love living in a sophisticated city like London. Who could want to be anywhere else?

Wishing all our friends a very Happy Christmas,

*Caroline and Charles Wright*

\* \* \* \* \*

## December 1989

### 2b Bellavista Road, London N8

# Dear Friends

Hoping it's been a good year whatever you've been up to.

I've reached a new decade, and taken on more work for the same pay. Ant has sold some art. We've adopted a cat – or it has adopted us. We've had one big surprise. And we are car owners …

In May I made it to 30. Antonio gave me breakfast in bed and a crumpled paper bag from a stall in Camden Market which he said contained a creative *homage* to my career. Inside was a shapeless brown knitted cardigan, massive enough to engulf three librarians. Luckily for Ant this turned out to be a joke. The real present, parked round the corner with a purple ribbon round it, was our first car! And not just any car but a genuine, if elderly, Citroen 2CV which even starts if there hasn't been an overnight frost.

Have car will travel. In June with the sun finally coming out we stuffed the tent into the boot and my guitar into the back and sputtered along the inside lane of the A303 to the Glastonbury Festival. Halfway into Somerset the air turned blue when I asked Ant where he'd put the tickets and he looked vague then said he hadn't actually got round to picking any up from Virgin Records. He suggested climbing over the fence but I paid for us on the gate as all the money was going to CND. While Ant hung out in the Arts Village I tried busking wherever anyone would listen to me. My most attentive audience was two undercover drug squad officers with creases ironed into their jeans who had the brass neck to question me when they heard me singing Alice Cooper's Aspirin Damage.

There was more mud, more rain and more people than the average person gets to see in a lifetime – but I wasn't part of the December 1982 demo at Greenham Common for nothing. Mind you, it may be something to do with hitting 30 but if you ask me, the organisers will have to put in proper loos if the festival is to carry on.

Ant has spent a big chunk of his working year on a pub crawl. Some people get all the luck. He won a grant for an arts project called Emblems of Urban Decline. He was paid – yes paid – to spend long hours 'forensically reconstructing the essence of the London public house'.

The project trustees were clearly expecting ceramic pump handles, painted pub signs and suchlike. Ant's end result was Acid Tongue – a series of glass jars featuring pickled onions dyed assorted colours and in various stages of atrophy. It went on show at the Whitechapel Gallery and both my parents flatly refused to get the train down for this one. I was more than a bit sniffy too – it took weeks to get the smell of vinegar out of the flat. Even Salvador, a mangy mog who started slipping in through our sash window and has ended up moving in with us, stayed away.

This was just as well as he has a habit of leaving cement pawmarks in Ant's work; and on one occasion a dead mouse, which ended up part of a gallery exhibit where it got some admiring comments.

There is a happy ending to Emblems of Urban Decline. Some rich banker type bought Acid Tongue for a mind-boggling sum to display in his converted Limehouse studio. There's no accounting for taste but we aren't complaining since we finally have bank statements that we ostentatiously leave lying around instead of stuffing them behind the sofa.

We spent some of the cash on a summer holiday in Brittany: a trip back to its roots for the car, and an adventure which included two breakdowns, vast quantities of cider and one late-night arrival at a campsite which when we climbed out of the tent in the morning was exposed in full glory as a nudist colony.

Which brings me to the big surprise I mentioned: I'm pregnant! Unplanned, unexpected. And unthinkable, say my parents who are under the mistaken illusion there will be a swift, discreet wedding. We are both over the moon. I've got morning sickness most of the day, which on the upside means I've had to give up running. I crawl through the working week and spend weekends on the sofa in my big brown cardigan, studying drawings of rubbery pink foetuses in parenting books. This week it has fingernails! Next week it can open and close its little fists! Soon it will be able to make me a cup of tea before it's off to university … Antonio, meanwhile, is using some spare bits of old metal to design and build a crib.

She or he is due at the end of May. So I am looking forward to two whole months' paid time off to enjoy the summer, sitting in the park writing articles for the

Liberated Librarian journal while baby dozes peacefully on a rug in the sunshine, before I go back to work and normal life resumes.

Festive greetings to you all, and a happy new year.

*Alison and Antonio*

## Christmas 1990: NOTE NEW ADDRESS!

**15 Paradise View**
**Upley Rising**
**Thameshire**

## Dear Friends

Buy one get one free. Two for the price of one. Double trouble – and half the amount of time for anything. I'm writing your Christmas update propped against a door on a packed commuter train, in the fragment of my day which I call my quality time. In case you hadn't heard, Ant and I became the proud parents of Eleanor and Felipe, on April 1$^{st}$ this year. Before midday, and nobody thought to say 'white rabbit'.

Even the radiographer thought she was seeing double when my 18-week scan showed not one but two little bodies waving gleefully at the camera. "Ah," remembered Antonio all of a sudden. "Yes, there have been many tweeens in my family, have I never mentioned this?" No he hadn't, at least not in English. The radiographer tried to calm me down by explaining that fraternal twins are not necessarily to do with Antonio's genes. Anyway, the scan did at least explain why I was so strangely large. Not fat, just doubly pregnant, which felt like some sort of result.

The eagle-eyed among you will have spotted our scary new address. Once we'd got over the shock of expecting twins we thought we'd better get ourselves organised. Beginning with a review of our possessions crammed into the flat: Ant's studio full of solvents and sharp tools; all eight meandering feet of my Swiss cheese plant; our stereo and merged collection of about 200 LPs taking up most of the living room. Not enough space to swing Salvador the cat. Clearly something had to go.

In the end it was the flat. On the market it went: 'Stunning two bed. Victorian conversion – original features – inventively enhanced by well-known North London artist.' We got three offers in the first week. The highest was from a local left-wing journalist, which I reckon validated us profiting from the evil property market.

Who was it who said that moving house and giving birth are two of the most stressful life events? Not us. We had everything sorted, a completion date of mid-April for the house and the babies not due until the end of May. My Sasco wall planner was the personification of order and control. Piet Mondrian himself couldn't have slotted so many coloured boxes alongside each other so satisfyingly.

So on March 31st, I made the entirely rational decision to go and do my bit for democracy at the Poll Tax protest in central London. The weather was dry, Antonio was deeply immersed in an entry for the Tapworth Prize. I was feeling fine. Here was a real chance to make a difference, to take a stand against the monstrous bid by You-Know-Who to exploit the masses with an evil tax that defied the laws of morality. What could possibly go wrong?

I found out what, the moment I got off the Tube. As I walked up the steps I got sucked into the throng, people pressing in on all sides, everyone moving in the same direction and chanting for the same cause. At first it felt exhilarating, like we could achieve anything through sheer force of numbers. But as we got closer to Trafalgar Square the atmosphere changed. The chanting turned to shouting and I started to feel claustrophobic and dizzy. Turning back was not an option; I was hemmed in more and more tightly. Police on horseback started charging at us randomly. What was I doing there? Why hadn't I stayed at home with my feet up, knitting bootees? How could claiming our right to free speech in this country feel so threatening and visceral? It was more like Tiananmen Square than Trafalgar Square.

Surrounded by 100,000 angry demonstrators, my labour pains started. Not the polite introductory pangs they tell you about in antenatal classes: breathe gently and count slowly to 50 while thinking about clouds. This was massive, two babies on the way, searing agony. There I was bent over double in the crush, trying to call for help above the megaphones and the shouting. I grabbed onto the man nearest me and gasped, "I'm in labour!" but he just gave me a thumbs-up and shouted, "Great, so am I love!"

Sometimes only a miracle will do. A nameless angelic woman saw that I was in trouble, gripped my arm and shielded me with her Maggie Out! placard while she got me through the crush to a shop near the National Portrait Gallery which was trying to close up but let us in to call 999. The rest is the apocryphal blur – blue ambulance lights flashing through the crowds, arriving after an age at University College Hospital, an endless night of tubes and monitoring, then Antonio white-faced agreeing to a

Caesarean while I was still gabbling on about a birthing pool and scented candles. Though to be honest by then I was really looking forward to as much anaesthetic as they could pump in.

Eleanor Margarita and Felipe Alexander were delivered at 11.30 and 11.32am on the Sunday morning, April 1st. Full marks to our National Health Service – even though they didn't let me give birth in my Axe the Poll Tax T-shirt. The babies' low birthweights (3.5lbs and 3.8lbs respectively) fast-tracked them into the Special Care Unit where they spent a month clinging to each other in a single incubator, intertwined baggy blue and pink bundles. We visited every day, and 'celebrated' Antonio's 30th birthday on April 14th in a Chinese restaurant round the corner from UCH, with me charging back to the hospital between courses to the milk expressing room.

Under strict hospital instructions to rest after the Caesarean, I spent the next few weeks packing up removal boxes in between baby visits. By the beginning of May the babies were strong enough to come home to the new house.

\* \* \* \* \*

So here we all are in Upley Rising, suburban England's best kept secret. You've probably heard the name but thought it was from a sitcom. So did we, until we decided to drive through it for a laugh on the way back from visiting my parents, and because I remembered that my old friend Vanessa had moved there.

And reader, we fell for it at first sight. Think chocolate box picturesque, but not the fudgy Devon-thatched-cottage kind, more dark chocolate mints that you'd take to a dinner party to impress. The village centre is all early Victorian gothic with quirky features, pleasingly arranged round a willow-fringed duck pond. There's a truly weird clock tower that could be straight out of The Hobbit; a butcher, Fox & Sons, in the same family since 1834; a gentlemen's milliner; and even – for essential shopping – a doll's house and miniatures shop, where you can browse for a miniscule Chesterfield should you feel so inclined.

Vanessa, thrilled to see us, gave us a quick tour. Antonio was half bemused, half creased up with hysterics – but two weeks and three viewings later we had somehow spent the rest of the Acid Tongue prize money on a deposit for our new house, which was on the market for a price we could actually afford only because the previous owners wanted a quick sale.

To outward appearances we are now a typical nuclear family in a respectable outer London suburb. Ant claims it is the perfect place to hide in plain sight from the Chilean secret police, who will never think to look for him here. Our leafy road could be a model for Victorian respectability; it's even got a class system. There are terraced houses at one end, followed by semis (ours is the last in the row), then much posher upper-class detached villas. What's more, we live round the corner from the sort of tennis club that's probably got a drawbridge to stop People Like Us getting in – should we be insane enough to apply.

But that's as far as it goes: behind our front hedge (and yes, it's privet) lies our hidden world of chaos. Boxes of nappies stacked to the ceiling; Calpol and colic; jumbles of babygrows bursting out of cupboards. And noise. How can two small babies produce so much washing or cry so loudly?* I phone my mum for advice but she's at the wrong end of a 31-year timeline, talking down a wire from a world where fluffy nappies dry in neat rows on the washing line and babies are put to bed at 6pm prompt where they sleep the night through.

Antonio and I operate a sleep rota where communication means blearily signalling to each other when we pass in the night. Ant calls the babies Los Anarquistas. My year planner is about as useful as a lettuce in a fish and chip shop. But every time it all gets too much, Felipe smiles his first smile or Eleanor suddenly frowns exactly like my grandmother used to. And I remember that I did my bit to bring down the most notorious prime minister in living memory.

We will surface from all this soon. Somewhere under the loads of dirty washing languish our plans for restoring our new home to its former glory. Out will come the monstrous electric fire blocking our genuine Arts and Crafts living room fireplace. Off to the tip with the avocado bath blotched with dark-brown stains. We will restore the carved covings in the hall and bring the Edwardian floor tiles lovingly back to life.

In the meantime it's been a quick coat of brilliant white and lots of cleaning. But we do have three bedrooms, a massive living room (welcome back my paperback collection), a garden where the twins occasionally fall into a peaceful slumber, and – best of all – a side passage leading to a garage which is Antonio's new studio. Landed gentry or what!

I went back to work at the end of September. What the government calls maternity pay is their way of having a laugh at women's expense, with not a penny extra for twins or early babies. And the bills don't pay themselves. The Head Librarian gave me three new projects and a bottle of gin. He is (half) human after all. Antonio, who missed the deadline for the Tapworth Prize because he was busy becoming a father, is trying to work again between nappy changes.

This time next year we will be back in control of our lives. In the meantime, this Christmas we are off to Yorkshire. The minute we arrive I plan to hand the twins to Mum and Dad then spend as much of the break as I can asleep.

Festive Greetings to you all,

*Alison and Antonio*

*\*A baby's cry reaches 115 decibels, which is noisier than a vacuum cleaner or a power saw (the average library is 40 dB). We have an ongoing argument about whether two babies crying at once produce double the amount of decibels. Answers on a postcard please.*

\* \* \* \* \*

*December 1989*

*18 Everspring Road*
*Upley Rising, Thameshire*

*Dear Everyone,*

I am beyond thrilled to be sending out this year's Christmas cards from our enchanting new country abode.

Our change of lifestyle followed Charles's promotion to Senior Client Business Relations Manager earlier this year; I am enclosing his embossed business card for your files. His new role came with a well-deserved pay rise, and shortly afterwards I found him leafing through a stack of glossy sports car catalogues. We had a little chat and I made the joint decision that we needed to move on from 'boys' toys', and the time was right to spread our wings and move up the property ladder. The capital in our flat had already tripled; what a clever investment it turned out to be.

I got out the A to Z and drew a big circle round the whole of London to start my research; and here we are, living in the heart of the English countryside. Upley Rising has been mentioned in both Tatler and The Lady as 'the up-and-coming Henley-on-Thames'; the fact that it is not actually on the Thames is a minor detail. The streets are leafy, the shops in its *bijou* centre are charming, and the houses boast enough plaques for an entire Wedgwood dinner service. The schools have an excellent reputation (though that's for the future!); in the meantime, there is a very grand, historic Tennis Club which I cannot wait to join.

Charles looked rather panic-stricken on our first visit to Upley Rising. I don't think he'd ever seen so much green space unless it was edging the runways at Heathrow. Apparently he'd been nursing an idea about renovating some rotting warehouse on the other side of Canary Wharf, not far from where he grew up. And of course it was a wrench leaving our London flat where we had such fun working and partying at the heart of city life. But now we have moved I can hardly believe we stayed there for so long, putting up with smelly tramps sleeping in doorways, the noisy traffic and nightmare parking. We really have the best of both worlds here, and Charles was very reassured when he realised that we are not far from the airport and only a 27-minute train journey into London. So he hasn't got to wait long until he can have a cigarette, as I have declared our new house a smoke-free zone.

We moved at the beginning of September, and I adore coming home from work to our rustic love nest. The estate agent's brochure sums it up better than I can: 'A snug period home that punches above its weight. With minimal improvements it will be ideal for the aspiring young family or for entertaining in style.' We have already started on the improvements.

In other news, we celebrated my 30$^{th}$ birthday in June this year. To mark the occasion Charles pushed the boat out and booked a table at Bibendum. I was expecting a romantic dinner for two, so imagine my surprise and delight to be greeted on arrival by 20 of our dearest friends! Ditch, Charles's rock star brother, couldn't join us as he was appearing at the Glastonbury Festival, but he sent a spectacular bouquet. Thanks so much again, to those of you who were invited, for making my new decade so memorable.

Our big move meant not much of a holiday this year – just a quick week's skiing in Verbier in a luxury chalet belonging to Charles's boss, who rents it out at a reasonable rate to staff, complete with chalet girl. Charles and his colleagues went off piste quite a lot while I and a couple of others took private lessons with an instructor called Jean-Paul, whose technique is 'one slope, one *vin chaud*' which worked very well.

Mother is coming to stay for Christmas this year. She thinks Upley Rising is a far superior location to Hammersmith and Fulham, which she always described as insalubrious, and is determined to see how we are getting on with the house. She lent us some money so I could get the improvements under way as quickly as possible. The previous owner, an elderly lady who died, had been living downstairs and using a revolting prefabricated plastic shower room, beyond description, slotted in next to the kitchen. I had to get the builders to board this up before I would move in. Luckily we aren't bothered by all the noise and dust from the builders during the day as we are both out working long hours. We are looking forward to meeting the neighbours.

For Christmas we will clear some space and camouflage the boarded-up shower room with an enormous tree covered with fairy lights, so our first house will look twinkly and festive. It will be magical.

Wishing you all a very Happy Christmas,

*Caroline and Charles Wright*

## December 1990

*18 Everspring Road*
*Upley Rising, Thameshire*

## Dear Everyone,

In case you missed the entry in The Times Social and Personal column, we are delighted to announce the birth of Maximilian Percival Shoreditch Charles Wright, on July 10th at 2.30pm. He weighed 8lbs 9ozs and was born exactly on his due date, which puts him in the top five per cent of babies. Maximilian is named after both his grandfathers, his famous rock star uncle and of course his father. As the enclosed photograph taken on the steps of the Portland Hospital shows, he has the Wright strong chin and the striking cornflower blue eyes from my side of the family. Charles and I are both immensely proud of our tiny miracle.

Motherhood has been a humbling experience. It has taught me that being an outstandingly successful Events Manager is not everything, and that being responsible for a tiny human seven days a week is one of the hardest jobs in the world.

On Mother's recommendation we employed a night nanny. This was a godsend. I don't know why every new parent doesn't have one. She arrives every evening at 8.30pm and takes complete charge of the nursery; she even sleeps there on a camp bed so that we are not disturbed when Max wakes in the night. Our original plan was to help me recover from my pre-planned Caesarean, but when the first nanny left after a fortnight, Charles and I were plunged into a nightmare world of having to wake up and feed Max every two or three hours.

Clearly this could not work for us as a family. I have always been very strict about getting my beauty sleep, and Charles was particularly stressed. Not only did he have his quarterly targets to meet, but as he is banned from smoking in the house, he had been making a real effort to give up again. Until one night, when I caught him pacing up and down the garden at 3am, baby Max in his arms, holding the feeding bottle in one hand and a smouldering filter tip in the other. I shudder to think what might have happened next. I forgave him just the once as he was still getting over England losing in the World Cup semi-finals. He had been so thrilled to get corporate tickets to take some new clients out to Turin, but football fans are notoriously superstitious, and soon afterwards the clients switched to a different agency. Charles blames the England team.

So our replacement night nurse will be with us until Christmas, by which time both Max and Charles should be more settled, and I will have put my maternity leave to good use to get more established here in Upley Rising.

I have already put our names down for the South Thameshire Lawn Tennis Club. You may have seen the feature on it in June's Sunday Times magazine: ('Thameshire's Wimbledon in Waiting?') Its main building looks more like an exclusive hotel than a clubhouse, though some of the grass courts look rather muddy and I intend to put forward a proposal that they are replaced with Astroturf. The club operates an old-fashioned waiting list system, and we are expected to find proposers to nominate us which seems a bit unfair as we have only just moved here. We have started by joining our nearby 13th-century church. No waiting list there: the vicar signed us up without even checking our religion, saying he could do with some more congregants as most people seem to be playing tennis on Sunday mornings. We are going to ask him to change services to a more convenient time.

Charles also persuaded the vicar to move the date of another couple's long-planned wedding so that we could hold Max's christening while Ditch Wright, the international rock star and Charles's brother, was in the country between world tour dates. The beautiful christening ceremony must have been the first in the church's history to witness the mobbing of a famous godparent. When Ditch arrived he was greeted by dozens of screaming teenage fans waving banners and leaping out from behind the gravestones as he walked in. Of course the vicar was within his rights to bolt the door to keep them out, though we did think he might have shown more appreciation for the new customers we had found for him.

We held a guest reception after the service in the nearby Rising Pheasant Country Hotel. Ditch made a very tender speech, and Mother managed not to be rude to Charles's parents. Charles and his brother did have a bit of a heated discussion after Ditch was kind enough to make some admiring comments about my slender post-baby figure, but on the whole Charles's family were quite well behaved and there were no fights, which I put down to my decision to offer just a single glass of champagne per person followed by a cash bar.

Our son was sensible enough to arrive after most of the building work on our house was finished. Our home is now a real pastoral idyll; Liberty floral swags and valances could have been invented for Upley Rising. And Max's bedroom is an authentic nursery with a rocking horse. I have had the walls papered with a ships and planes pattern to encourage him to think of a career in industry. You can't start too soon!

We have also brightened up our whole road now that we have taken down an unsightly ancient tree that was towering over the house. The old couple who live next door made a terrible fuss about it having some sort of historical significance, and if they hadn't barged into our front garden when they heard the chainsaws starting up then the tree surgeons' ladder would never have shattered their front windows and the husband wouldn't have had a minor heart attack. We stopped short of taking action against them for trespass, and they really should thank us for letting so much light into both our houses, especially as the husband can't go out much anymore.

Our next project will be the kitchen.

I plan to return to work at Imperative Events in the new year. I am proud to regard myself as a modern feminist and will be back at my desk in January looking like I have never given birth. I agree with Mrs Thatcher on the importance of impeccable appearance and good presentation. I sat in front of the television with Maximilian in my arms and a lump in my throat, watching the PM make her resignation speech from the steps of Number 10. I was full of admiration at how perfectly her hair was styled and her pearls matched her earrings even in that moment of high drama. Having a child is wonderful, but I am determined not to let myself go and become one of those leaky NCT mothers. As Mother says, parenthood is not an excuse to sit at home snacking when you could be out having a good time. Charles and I will be socialising and networking as much as ever, setting an example for Max.

We are spending Christmas this year with Mother. She has claimed priority as Maximilian is her first grandchild and so takes pride of place in our family. I can't wait to see his little face light up at the colourful sparkling tree and the huge pile of parcels underneath waiting for him.

Wishing you all a very Happy Christmas,

*Caroline and Charles Wright*

# PART TWO 1991-1992: ALI, CAROLINE

## Christmas 1991

**15 Paradise View**
**Upley Rising**
**Thameshire**

Dear Friends

Hoping you have all had a good year. Here's news of ours:

### Family Annual Report for 1991

Against all odds, Alison and Antonio have survived their first full year as parents. Now 19 months, Eleanor and Felipe have stormed though their developmental milestones. They can (1) knock over a full cup of coffee if it's left within two inches of the edge of the table; (2) climb out of their cot at 5.30am, undo the baby gate, toddle downstairs and empty a cereal box all over the floor 'for breakfast'; and (3) most outstanding of all, they can write: huge loops of Antonio's permanent black marker pens all over the hall wall. Ant compares this with the marvel of early cave painting.

## Statistics for the year

- Average hours parents slept per night: 3

- Dummies fished out of gutters, grubby corners, the toilet etc.: 27

- Nappies changed this year: 3,650

- Nights out together in cosy pub just at bottom of road: 0

- Times Ant has been asked: are they identical? 35

- Times parents stayed awake through Spitting Image: 1

## Conclusion

You get the drift. The twins may be making progress but it's a different story for Ant and me. Highly qualified, us? Where is the answer to night terrors in a Diploma on the History of Periodicals Cataloguing? And what's the point of a 40,000-word dissertation on Art Reinterpreting Displaced Heritage (available in English and Spanish) when it comes to potty training? Our collection of BAs, MAs and MScs would be more use in a tin of alphabetti spaghetti.

But as lower intermediate parents we are slowly getting the hang of things. So the installation artist has worked out how to squeeze our double buggy in and out of the boot of a 19-year-old Citroen 2CV, which is theoretically impossible. And who would have guessed, eight years of meticulously sticking coloured classification stickers onto book spines doubles as a warm-up course for labelling a month's batch of toddler meals for the freezer.*

When Ant and I are at home and awake at the same time we have been getting to know Upley Rising. One side of town – where Vanessa lives – has made it into the late 20th century, with a craft shop and even a deli which actually sells olives. But the north side, where we are, is full of people who look like they spent the War in the Home Guard and are still on the lookout for an enemy invasion. Every Saturday morning we venture out to the adventure playground in Upley Riverside Park. It's our weekly challenge to get out of the house in under an hour, which is how long it takes to collect twins, mittens, shoes, favourite cuddly toy, snacks, crowbar the double buggy out of the boot, then find the twins again. The moment we emerge from behind our privet hedge (note to self – must prune hedge) we get stares and comments. I get it that we are the only family in the area that doesn't own a polished chrome pram that costs more than our car did, but not why several people have asked Antonio what part of India he's from.

The first time we turned up at the playground all the parents were chatting to each other in tight little groups, and when we eventually broke into a conversation we found out we should have signed the twins up before they were born for the area playgroup that 'everyone joins'. But then someone found out that Ant was an artist; she'd read about him winning the Clapham Prize, got really excited and commissioned a portrait.

Ant was beyond chuffed. His first Upley Rising commission: the world or at least Thameshire was his oyster. But something got lost in translation, probably Ant not quite explaining what he means by contemporary sculpture, and she flatly refused to have the end result in her house ('devastated' was the word she used down the phone). Blind to the beauty of the abstract, said Ant – with a face like hers he'd thought a cubist approach was a kindness.

There's an unexpected flipside to Upley Rising. It has its very own annual festival, called the Wellspring. Pagan roots in the Home Counties! Every July the Upley Maiden and her maid attendants parade through the streets to the Market Square, where the maiden is ceremonially lowered down the old well and hauled up again by competing teams of local lads. It's something to do with watering the summer harvest, with witch-ducking overtones. Once the maiden has emerged safe and sound from the well she and her attendants get to throw buckets of water all over the losing team. We went along with the twins expecting some kind of country fair. Everyone, without exception, had dressed up in vaguely primeval costumes. The maiden's procession was led by a chief Druid wearing a silver wig and carrying a flaming torch, with long blue robes trailing along the ground. A woman in some sort of Wilma Flintstone outfit who I recognised from the dry cleaners had the cheek to ask me if I didn't find all this a bit refined after growing up in Yorkshire. I said did she mean the same Yorkshire that lowers people down mineshafts (or did when we had a mining industry) with proper attention to health and safety, as opposed to chucking a young girl down a well. Just then Eleanor had one of her tantrums, with perfect timing for once.

After all this excitement, going to work every day would be a relief if it weren't for the sleepless nights. My main objective at the library this year has been to look as if I am awake at all times. I am now tasked with organising the University's entire new CD-Rom collection. This happened because I heard my name through a waking doze in a team meeting and automatically sat upright and said, "Yes of course!" with my most enthusiastic face on. I detected a glint of satisfaction in the Head Librarian's eye as he passed me the four-inch-thick file. No pay rise for me until I've sorted this one out.

Meanwhile Ant has taken a part-time job teaching sixth form a few miles away at East Thameshire Senior High School. He's very popular with the kids, and the end of term exhibition was full of Che Guevara portraits – wrong country, right idea. These are kids who come from homes where Chile is how you feel before you turn the heating up, ha ha. Still, the teaching is going really well. The Head wanted him to go full time but he's spending every spare minute on the Tapworth Prize entry again. While he and I are slaving away, the twins lead a life of leisure at our expense at Sunny Seedlings day nursery – the 'other one' in playground parent jargon, but Eleanor and Felipe couldn't care less about playground snobbery, and neither could we.

We had a big family celebration for the twins' 1st birthday in April. Felipe woke up on the morning of the big day with an angry rash all down his face. We called the doctor, who eventually arrived after her morning calls, just as 13 of us were gathered round the table in our front room. My parents and sister Gill with her daughter had all made the trip. We were all singing Happy Birthday, which partly drowned out Felipe's crying. The doctor turned down the offer of cake, diagnosed teething temperature, and recommended less excitement and no sugary food. Still, I think everyone enjoyed themselves and Vanessa took lots of lovely photos.

So that's our year. It's not been too bad really. As I write, the twins are having a very rare nap, and Ant is in the studio putting the finishing touches to a piece which he is calling 'Tranquillity'. A shoe-in for the Tapworth entry if there's any justice in the world.

Wishing you all a tranquil Christmas and new year,

*Alison and Antonio*

*\* The Dewey decimal cataloguing system could have been invented for toddler vegetable/fruit mixes. For example:*

*100: vegetables; 110 root veg, 120 green veg, etc.*

*200: fruit, 210 citrus, 220 apples, pears, 230 berries, etc.*

*So e.g. 245.2.ALI 19.5.91 is raspberries, unsweetened, packed by Ali on 19th May. Simple!*

## Christmas 1992

**15 Paradise View**
**Upley Rising**
**Thameshire**

Dear Friends

Season's greetings, from the five of us. This family is now an odd number, but then you probably knew that already. Daniel Eduardo arrived on Sunday 30th August, weighing 7lb 9oz, and with a mystifying mop of bright red hair. Just when we thought we were glimpsing the light at the end of the tunnel. Now we're back to a 24-hour grind of changing nappies, washing babygrows, and stumbling across a dark bedroom on autopilot for yet another 3am night feed.

Daniel's birth coincided with our long-planned big

Bank Holiday outing to Thameshire Wildlife World: the grand finale to several months of cutting two-for-one tokens out of cereal packets. After half an hour driving round the car park in the heat, we had just beaten another car to the only free space when my waters broke. So off we went again down the motorway at the car's top speed of 63mph towards the nearest hospital. The twins kept asking at ten-second intervals when they were going to see the lions. Then a summer shower morphed into a violent thunderstorm, the car windscreen became a rain-lashed blank, and in minutes we were stuck in the motorway tailback from hell, crawling in a single lane alongside miles of orange cones mysteriously roping off half the road. By now the twins were crying their eyes out in the back, Antonio was gripping the wheel and swearing in Chilean dialect, and I was in danger of giving birth in the front of a very small, very old car on a flooded motorway.

We finally screeched to a halt outside the Royal Thameshire 'Marie Celeste' Hospital: gleaming, state-of-the-art machinery everywhere but not a staff member in sight. Who could possibly need emergency treatment on August Bank Holiday weekend? Antonio went rushing round looking for medics while I curled up on a bench holding the twins' hands. When the midwife arrived with Antonio, they found all three of us kneeling in front of the bench doing rhythmic breathing together. I suppose it was one way for the twins to learn to count to 20.

Antonio drove off to take the twins to Vanessa (thank you again Vanessa) and managed to get back for Daniel's birth at 2.40pm. He had found time to phone the Cones Hotline to complain about the traffic hold-up but forgot to bring the birth music cassette I had spent weeks recording. Luckily the tape doubles as a lullaby compilation* for

Daniel, who is a very peaceful baby by and large. Just as well, as three children under three was never our plan.

Ant is in charge of the mayhem we call home since I went back to work. His job teaching sixth form has come to an abrupt halt. It had all been going swimmingly; he inspired the students, coursework grades shot up, the Head at East Thameshire Senior High sounded him out about leading a class trip to Barcelona. Until Ant came up with the theme 'Love without Borders' for the big end of year show. Obviously he was thinking peace signs on flags, papier mâché doves, collages of Vietnamese boat people. But 17-year-olds round here have different things on their minds. By which I mean one thing. We were both gobsmacked at some of the interpretations they came up with; they weren't from any sex education books I ever read. Who could have guessed the well-brought up sixth formers of Thameshire had such devious imaginations?

The word 'censorship' is not in Antonio's vocabulary (Spanish or English), and the show went ahead. It elicited 47 furious complaints from parents, and three solicitors' letters. There was talk of a mass removal of children from school, and of a Section 28 prosecution. A special governors' meeting was called, for the first time in the school's history, and enraged parents stood outside heckling the governors as they went in. Ant wanted to go in and deliver an impassioned defence on behalf of his students, but the Head told him that he couldn't be responsible for his safety. The sinister underbelly of Thameshire society in action is not a pretty sight. The Head managed to smooth it all over, but Ant had to step down.

At first he thought the publicity would be good for the Tapworth Prize, which is meant to be for 'cutting-edge art that challenges our thinking', but someone on the prize entry committee threw a wobbly and decided Ant must be some sort of child molester. He got a phone call from the committee chair 'strongly discouraging' him from applying.

So much for artistic freedom in this country. Ant was more angry than I've ever seen him; I found Chilean passport application forms for the children half filled out in his studio, and he's making a point of talking to them in Spanish most of the time, even though they can't understand a word he's saying and we both know that a move is not going to happen. He's still nervous about repercussions from his past, though he won't give specifics.

Anyway, I got to get back at the sinister underbelly brigade while I was on maternity leave.

The battleground was the Rising Bean, a coffee shop overlooking Upley Rising's duck pond that's been there for yonks. It's really popular with local families – or was, until a large sign suddenly appeared on the noticeboard inside (ballet lessons, childminder vacancies, sponsored cycle rides for charity, etc.): 'Mothers are required to refrain from breastfeeding in front of customers, and instead to please use the ladies' facilities.' By which they meant that breastfeeding babies had to take place in/on the windswept toilet at the back with its grubby changing mat and dripping cold water tap.

This could not be stood for. Vanessa and I put our heads together and organised a Feed In. Twenty of us – plus babies – turned up at the café first thing one morning, bagged all the window seats, and ordered coffee, sandwiches and cake. At the signal (which was three babies crying at once) there was a mass taking off of jackets to reveal specially printed 'Upley Sucks' T-shirts in which we proceeded to feed our babies in full view of customers and passers-by.

We soon flushed out the source of the problem. An elderly couple who were sitting at the back of the café monopolising all the Sunday papers over a single cup of tea got up and marched over to the counter, where a conversation in hissing stage whispers ensued. The staff – two middle-aged waitresses who look like they've been there for centuries – couldn't bring themselves to ask us to stop; but leaning across multiple wobbling boobs to put our sandwiches on the table was a visible trauma involving avoidance of eye contact. When Vanessa asked one of them to bring a double milkshake, we thought the poor woman was going to explode. A phone call was made, then the manager appeared. He took one look at the quantities of food we had ordered and got the message. The sign came down and I never thought the visible impact of spending power could make me so smug.

That's about it for our year. I've started running again, Vanessa and I splash along the towpath together at weekends; sometimes I take Daniel in the backpack, which is my version of resistance training. I went back to work in October, where I've been mostly confined to the basement archives working on our rare books collection. This is meant to be some sort of privilege; I even get to wear white kid gloves. But you can imagine the effect of dim lighting and the background hum of a humidifier when you're lucky if you've had 15 minutes' uninterrupted sleep all night. No holiday for us this year, with Ant not working and the mortgage to pay. But my parents came down for two weeks when Daniel was born and did some proper babysitting. We finally got to the pub at the end of the road, and never has chicken in the basket tasted so good.

My new year's resolutions are:

- Stay awake at work
- Play guitar without Daniel/twins screaming at me to stop
- Learn Spanish (so I can understand what Ant is saying to our kids)
- Have a proper holiday.

Festive Greetings from us all,

*Alison and Antonio, Eleanor, Felipe and Daniel*

*\*Lullaby tape tracks:*

- *Mozart Serenade no 13: Eine Kleine Nachtmusik*
- *Roberta Flack: Killing Me Softly*
- *Brahms: Wiegenlied*
- *The Everly Brothers: All I Have to do is Dream*
- *Tim Rice: Any Dream Will Do*
- *Eurythmics: Sweet Dreams*
- *Satie: Gymnopédie No.1*
- *Chopin: Nocturne No 2*
- *Ditch Wright: Cotton On*
- *Sex Pistols: Anarchy in the UK*
  *(if none of the others have worked by now, this should).*

\* \* \* \* \*

# December 1991

*18 Everspring Road*
*Upley Rising, Thameshire*

## Dear Everyone,

Many people use annual Christmas letters to list the ups and downs of the past year, but I am delighted to report that 1991 for Charles and me has been all ups.

Returning to work was the best decision I could have made. It was a wrench to tear myself away from baby Max, but the moment I opened my wardrobe and saw my rows of designer suits and silk blouses just waiting to be slipped on with a pair of heels, I realised that my career must come first. What's more, I simply couldn't turn down the return-to-work assignment offered to me by Dominic, the Managing Director of Imperative Events.

'Second Time A Gown' was our auction of wedding dresses worn by famous divorcees. Held at the Dorchester Hotel, it was a star-studded benefit event for the Dress Africa! Foundation. Well-known celebrities, from supermodels to TV stars, who had made a tragic error of judgement in their choice of marriage partner, agreed to donate the beautiful wedding dress that now had no further meaning for them. These selfless women accepted no financial reward apart from the publicity they generated by taking part. Some of them (those who had not put on a few pounds) managed to overcome the associated bad memories and modelled their own gowns. I volunteered for the modelling shortlist but had to withdraw as I am too petite. Most of the stars are quite tall; some of their shoe sizes have to be seen to be believed.

We lifted the curtain on our star-studded event with a short film made by Dress Africa! all about the many young girls from that inspirational continent who would feel so much more confident if only they could make their own fashion choices. The audience was almost in tears by the end, but we soon lifted the mood with champagne and canapés all round, which also helped everyone forget that our country is supposed to be in the middle of a recession. This was followed by the glittering bridal collection parade.

As well as organising the scattering on the catwalk of 10,000 fresh blossoms imported just for the occasion, I arranged for a surprise guest appearance by Ditch Wright, Charles's famous rock star brother. His solo acoustic performance of Cotton On, a moving song specially written for the show, brought the house down. It has been released as a Christmas single so if you haven't already bought a copy, it's not too late to do your bit for Dress Africa!

Supervising the auction tested my professional skills to the limit. Not only was there a noisy unemployment protest going on outside the Dorchester, but several divorce lawyers tried to force their way in, claiming that ownership of some of the dresses was disputed. Then my PA, Jessica, kept raising her hand during the bidding for a dazzling Christian Lacroix creation encrusted with crystals. Afterwards she claimed that she was simply trying to get the catering staff to bring over more Veuve Cliquot. I have my doubts since Jessica has quite recently become engaged to be married and she does tend to get a bit carried away. She almost set Imperative Events back by several thousand pounds. Luckily for her she was outbid by a determined Countess from somewhere in Eastern

Europe, and the dress sold for far more than the expected price.

Although I am not allowed to talk about company profit, I can reveal that we sold every dress, and that my bonus this year is guaranteed. It feels so rewarding to have accomplished something meaningful for charity.

Maximilian is thriving with his nanny Emma. She's a very caring girl, if a bit on the slow side, who came with excellent references. She is happy to scrub the house clean while he takes his morning nap, then devote herself to our son in the afternoons. By the time we get home from work he is in his pyjamas ready for a story and a good night's sleep. Max passed all his first-year milestones well ahead of schedule. He was sitting up in his highchair at seven months, and he can say 'Emma, Dada and Mama'. Best of all, he chose the day he turned one to show off his very first steps.

I was determined to have his party at the South Thameshire Lawn Tennis Club, even though their outdated waiting list system means that our membership is taking a frustratingly long time. So I arranged an appointment in my professional capacity regarding a possible film location shoot at the club.

The club secretary couldn't have been more charming. He offered me coffee in his oak-panelled office, where I explained that the project was hush hush at this stage (Imperative Events doesn't actually organise film locations) but provisionally involved Alec Guinness and Diana Rigg. This was barely stretching the truth as it's not hard to imagine both of them looking very comfortable at the club. By the end of our chat he was delighted to arrange privileged access for us and 30 guests. Mother bought Maximilian a miniature Fred Perry sporty polo shirt and shorts for his big day, and just as we'd lit the candle on his Grand Slam cake he stood up and tottered across the floor waving his new toy tennis racquet. We think he definitely has star potential!

When we tried to contact the club secretary afterwards to query the bill, we were shocked to find he had been asked to step down from his post. Charles was very angry and wanted to write a letter of complaint, but we decided not to jeopardise our membership acceptance.

Charles has made the most of the recession by switching jobs. He has negotiated a new position at Strong Barker, one of the most up-and-coming agencies of the moment. He took his secretary and three of his most successful clients with him, and now has a much bigger office with its own leather three-piece suite.

We had our first family holiday this year, two weeks in a tennis resort nestled in 20 wooded acres of Sardinian coastline and recommended by Charles's new boss. Charles took lessons and prospected for clients, and I got in some long overdue sunbathing. I spotted Cilla Black who apparently spends a lot of time there. Poor Max got a tummy upset, probably from having too much fun playing with the resort's team of nannies all day in one of the hotel's three outdoor pools.

We are spending this Christmas with Charles's parents. As he is part of a big extended family they are used to small children running around and won't mind how much baby paraphernalia we bring for the day. Max gets very upset if he hasn't got his cosy car, his push-along walker and his toy trainset. Going to Charles's family means driving all the way over to Shoreditch, and Mother is refusing to come. I have been inventive with my presents. The tasteful products in Upley Rising's charming gift shops being unsuitable for Charles's relatives, I have chosen some clever ideas from the Innovations catalogue. Battery-operated spider catchers and slippers with headlights really are quite practical, and mail order is so much easier when you have a small child to manage.

We will all be singing Knees up Mother Brown round the piano, passing angelic baby Max from cousin to cousin, drinking Guinness, or in my case St Clements – so appropriate given we'll be within the sound of Bow Bells. It will be a proper cockney Christmas!

Wishing you all a very Happy Christmas,

*Caroline and Charles Wright*


*December 1992*

*18 Everspring Road*
*Upley Rising, Thameshire*

*Dear Everyone,*

As Charles and I toasted each other over our 5th anniversary (yes, really!) dinner at The Ivy, we agreed that life has indeed showered blessings upon us.

We live in a beautiful house in a sought-after area, we both have successful careers, and we possess two adorable children. Our exquisite daughter Clementine Charlotte was born on June 1st. Her birth was problem free, apart from Charles's flight back from a New York business trip being held up. He so wanted to be present, but you can't delay a baby's arrival: the consultant obstetrician I had selected for the Caesarean delivery had booked a holiday for the next day, so we had to go ahead. Charles burst through the door holding a huge bouquet of pink and white roses just a few hours after the big event.

'Monday's child is fair of face' goes the saying – and with her blonde curls and dark blue eyes, everyone says that Clementine resembles me at the same age. She shares her birthdate with Marilyn Monroe. She only cries occasionally and started sleeping through the night at four weeks. Charles and I have agreed that now we have 'the set' we can relax, pursue our ambitions and enjoy ourselves to the full.

On the work front, I could never have guessed that by the end of this year my new job title would be Chief Executive!

On my return from maternity leave, Dominic the Managing Director personally called me in for a chat. He was so happy with my progress at Imperative Events that he had created a special role, just for me. He wanted me to develop New Concept Conferencing, an important strategic exercise for the future of the company. Though this would take me away from working hands-on with clients, where I have always excelled, I agreed it was time to accept a new level of responsibility

I threw myself into my new role with my trademark enthusiasm, and spent several weeks in a closed room at head office brainstorming ideas with myself. I got through the company's entire yearly sticky note budget, but at least they won't have to redecorate the walls for a while.

At the next quarterly Directors' meeting I slipped New Concept Conferencing onto the agenda, then spent 35 minutes delivering my groundbreaking vision for the company to the Board. They sat in amazed silence, having never seen the like of my slide presentation before. I was so comprehensive that the only question I was asked at the end was whether the board lunch would still be warm.

In retrospect, perhaps I should not have been surprised that even in an organisation as dynamic as Imperative Events there are some very stuffy old Directors who fuss over outdated notions like the bottom line at the expense of creativity and imagination.

It is a credit to Dominic that he bore no grudge towards his colleagues for turning down my trailblazing proposals. He has always been a true mentor to me, and at our debrief he came up with a brainwave: that I should leave the company to start up my own business. He recognised that my skills were waiting to be given free rein without tedious corporate constraints. So with his full support, I decided the time was right to branch out alone, and I am now Chief Executive of Caroline Wright Events.

Becoming my own boss has been the best decision of my life so far. I can plan my own time to suit myself. I spend most mornings on the phone from my office at home, which I have had redecorated. Upley Rising is an ideal base for my new venture; there are lots of quietly well-connected future clients here, and I have already pitched for the events contract at the Tennis Club, which should guarantee us lifetime membership as well as access to its mailing list. As the newly elected chair of the committee which runs Max's playgroup, Little Networks, I am busy generating contacts as well as persuading the other mums that we must recast ourselves as a women's entrepreneurs group instead of obsessing over minutiae like playground safety and vaccinations.

My old job has gone to my former PA Jessica; I made a very gracious speech at my leaving do, and got a round of applause when I reassured her that stepping into my shoes was always going to be a hard act to follow, since my feet are a petite size five.

No year is entirely problem free. Not long before Clementine was born we had to sack our nanny Emma. Outwardly she was ideal for the job, but I began to have doubts when I picked up the vermouth bottle to create a dinner party dessert only to find it was almost empty. I was devastated as I always work to tight deadlines and there was no time to get more for the rum babas. I knew it couldn't be Charles, as he is a strict devotee of single malt unless he is really desperate.

My suspicions of Emma were right, but for a different reason. A few days later I happened to make sure I got home unexpectedly at Max's teatime, where I caught Emma red-handed in the act of handing Max a BEEF sandwich. My poor child was powerless, strapped in his highchair. I managed to snatch the sandwich away before it reached his mouth, but I could almost see the BSE germs floating in the air around it.

At Accident & Emergency the doctors shook their heads and said they can't test for mad cow disease, so we are in the horrendous position of having to wait and hope over the years ahead, which will be a constant underlying stress. Emma had the cheek to claim unfair dismissal, saying she had witnesses to some horrible untruths about her working conditions; I think she must have gossiped with our neighbours who have not been able to move on from the historic tree incident, and are secretly envious of our tastefully planted new garden. We instructed solicitors, and following a series of letters between them and the nanny agency we have been awarded an undisclosed sum in compensation.

Our new nanny trained at Norlands and I followed the same vetting process as MI5 before confirming her appointment. We took her with us on holiday to Ditch's luxury new villa in an unspoilt corner of Majorca. He bought it with the royalties from his latest LP, as a getaway from the stressful world of showbusiness. It was a perfect summer retreat for us, where I was able to spend time by the pool getting my body back into shape out of the limelight.

Charles is rising up the ladder at Strong Barker. He has been made Global Roving Client Activator, and his expense account is larger than our nanny's salary. This year he has visited New York, San Francisco, Singapore, Tokyo and Sydney. With so much travelling he tends to lose track of time, and if the phone rings in the middle of the night I always know it is him calling to say hello to the children, so now the nanny answers it.

Charles turned 35 this year, and I found the ideal gift for his birthday: a Give Up Smoking hypnosis course. I bought it after discovering him and Ditch smoking at the bottom of the garden of the Majorca villa one night. When they saw me they both acted very oddly, and dissolved into uncontrollable giggles like two schoolboys. I told my husband he needed to reform; that a cigarette between the well-defined lips of a rock idol might look sexy, but it didn't do Charles, as a father of two with family responsibilities, any favours.

I also told Ditch he should think about enhancing his earnings by discreetly endorsing a suitable branded cigarette, rather than the big roll-ups he seems to prefer.

We will be celebrating Christmas at home as a family. We used the settlement from the nanny agency to put in a new kitchen. I was getting flashbacks to the beef incident every time I went in to make a coffee between work calls, and the varnished yellow pine cupboards were giving me migraines. Mother is coming to stay; she had been planning to go on a cruise but had to change her plans after Black Wednesday. Although she dislikes cooking, she will be up to pouring gin and tonics and handing round appetisers, which will be useful as we are holding a select gathering for like-minded friends and contacts.

Wishing you all a wonderful Christmas,

*Caroline, Charles, Maximilian and Clementine Wright*

# A PERFECT YEAR?

# PART THREE 1993-1994:

# ROBERT, ALI, CHARLES, CAROLINE

### 14 Paradise View, Upley Rising, Thameshire

### Christmas 1993

I feel like the Ghost of Christmas Past. Back in my childhood bedroom, hunched over my old school desk by the window, I am writing my seasonal missive overlooking the once familiar neighbourhood, its church spire visible at the bottom of the street through the bare branches of the giant wisteria that covers our house and whose woody stems coil across my view.

Vague memories of struggles with mathematics homework stir in my subconscious. Downstairs I can hear the gentle clatter of pans in the kitchen and there is muffled chatter on the television in the study which could easily be Blue Peter. Like Dickens' fugacious spirit, I am both old and young. The overpowering sense of nostalgia would be completed by a powdering of snow over the streets of Upley Rising, but I cannot remember the last time I experienced a white Christmas, whatever impression the card manufacturers, mostly operating from China these days, try and create.

I moved back here in October. My mother is as bright and sharp mentally as she ever was; indeed she can still finish The Times crossword before me. But physically things have begun to take their toll. She has trouble getting up and down the stairs now, and though she continues to drive, I suspect that her eyesight is not what it was, there having been one or two incidents involving cavorting lampposts that she maintains careered into her car as she was parking. She has some sort of medical issue (female) for which she is taking medication and seeing the doctor. All in all, circumstances dictated that the logical course of action was for me to base myself back in Upley Rising and ensure that she is coping.

We did briefly contemplate moving. The road is still lovely but many of the old neighbours have gone, and some of the newer people are quite different; either less considerate or just busier. But my mother has been here far too long to move now, and the change would unsettle Colin enormously. After making various enquiries through long-standing acquaintances, I secured a partnership in a local firm whose property and private client work is expanding.

I parted company with Wilson Mountfield after more years than I care to think about. My colleagues gave me a pretty decent send-off, and I am glad to say have promoted one of the younger women to take over my role. Nothing can replace the ambience of Marylebone High Street and I can't pretend it wasn't a wrench to leave my flat; but I have kept my account at Daunts bookshop and intend to return regularly for visits to the NMMR Society, as well as for music rehearsals. In the meantime, it has been a question of settling in, organising more help for my mother, and considering what works to undertake on the house, which has needed updating for some time. The coming few months will see me spending weekends planning home improvements and having discussions with tradesmen.

Aside from the upheaval of moving home and changing jobs, it has been a pleasant year. I had two weeks away with the Montague Ensemble, our European summer tour. Singing Tallis in the open air on a sublime July evening with Lake Konstanz shimmering below us was a moment to treasure. The highlight of the year for my mother was our trip to see the Buckingham Palace apartments, newly opened to the public. Although she knew that her Majesty would be safely ensconced away from the masses at Sandringham, she nevertheless put on her best Jaeger suit and pearls, and chatted with animation to several of the staff; raising some eyebrows with anecdotes about the Sèvres porcelain collection that were not included on their laminated crib sheets. Colin was thrilled with the grand day out, though we had to explain to him repeatedly why everything was not made of gold.

We shall celebrate Christmas together as usual. Although I am here most years, being a permanent resident again has a wholly different feel. I have already found a box of old decorations in the loft that will be pressed back into use, and Christmas Eve will see me up the ladder in the living room with a painted Bakelite star in my hand, poised to give the top of the tree its finishing flourish, much as my father used to do.

With Christmas wishes,

**Robert**

## 14 Paradise View, Upley Rising, Thameshire

### Christmas 1994

This year has seen me gainfully employed, both at work and at home. Somehow word spread through the secret arteries that percolate the lifeblood of information through Upley Rising that a recent arrival (more colloquially known as 'fresh meat') could be put to good use. In the past month alone I have delivered 400 mince pies to two of Upley Rising's hospices; put up strings of Christmas lights in the day care centre; and given the annual address to the Women's Institute Christmas lunch on the subject: Could Fred West have reached Thameshire? Having consumed far more sweet sherry than anyone should, I feel quite literally soaked in seasonal spirit.

Contrary to my early expectations, returning to my childhood home has been surprisingly welcoming, rather like sinking into a beloved old armchair. When I am not at work I am enveloped in a gossamer network of my mother's silver-haired acquaintances, who have made unstinting efforts to get me painlessly reabsorbed into life in the place I grew up. Pleasant evenings drifting down Marylebone Lane to an early concert at the Wigmore Hall have become a distant, albeit sometimes wistful, memory.

I have settled into working life at Coburn Briggs. At the beginning some of my colleagues may have seen the arrival of a new partner as an opportunity to offload one or two less appealing cases, including a family trust issue knottier than Bleak House and the local council estate 'right to buy' conveyancing portfolio. However, 24 years of legal practice in London's West End have, if nothing else, finely tuned my skills in office politics. I took the opportunity to have a word with the senior partner's secretary about some client invoicing errors I unearthed in the files of one or two of the less meticulous partners, and there have been no further choreographed suggestions from them at the weekly management meetings. I generally find the working culture refreshingly civilised, in particular leaving every day at 5.30pm sharp, which enables me to devote time to duties at home.

My mother's health has continued to give recurrent cause for concern. She may be fine for a few days at a time, meeting a WI friend for a light lunch, or planting lettuce seeds in the garden with Colin; then an indefinable frailty sets in and I might arrive home to find her sitting vacantly on the sofa with unthreaded knitting on her lap or watching one of those brash quiz shows on afternoon television which have never been to her taste.

On one occasion I came back from work to find her poring over The Upley Herald, which had decided to rerun the notorious Paradise View murders story that propelled our road into the national news 30 years ago. Most of the time we never give those distant events a second thought, but the photographs were graphic, and the journalism left nothing to the imagination. My mother was heavily underscoring sections of the story and writing illegible comments in the margins. She seemed quite cheerful and I concluded that she was confusing the article with the cryptic crossword. But over the following few weeks it became obvious that it was unwise for her to soldier on with sole responsibility for Colin's care, so I set up a meeting with her general practitioner and we now have a rota of NHS support workers who come three days a week. They are reliable but rather strident, tending to talk to my mother and Colin as if they are both deaf, which is not the case. However, their presence gives my mother much needed respite time when she is able to see friends for more than a quick hour, or rest. On the whole she is in good form. She has taken to popping out in the car on Sunday afternoons, ostensibly for some fresh air, but returning with carrier bags from the town supermarket; she finds the new Sunday trading relaxation rather a novelty, which surprised me as I thought she would strongly disapprove. To accommodate her new timetable, our traditional Sunday lunch now happens at 6pm, which my father would never have tolerated.

This year's summer trip with the Montague Ensemble was to Northern Italy. In retrospect, performing Verdi's Requiem in Milan (not, alas, La Scala but an ornate church on the outskirts of the city) was all too easily construed as an audacious act of musical piracy. Our initial reception was warm, but after the already voluble native audience had consumed considerable quantities of Chianti Classico in the overlong interval, there were persistent interruptions throughout the Sanctus and Benedictus movements correcting our Latin pronunciation. Buoyed by the vigorous conducting of our choir leader, we sang on undeterred.

Evening trips into London have been less frequent than I would have liked but all the more gratifying. David Hare's Skylight was a richly rewarding excursion. I also managed to attend most of the North Marylebone Model Railway Society meetings, where we have embarked on an ambitious project to recreate the St Pancras layout alongside our treasured King's Cross configuration.

Much needed updating works on the house were completed by the son of the trusted decorator my father used to employ. This continuity paid off as he – the son

– even had a note of the exact shade of white which has always been used in the hall. The house this Christmas feels fresher and brighter than it has for many years. When I come in I can almost hear myself and Colin as small children running around the place on rainy days, playing soldiers or hide-and-seek.

With Christmas wishes,

**Robert**

\* \* \* \* \*

## Christmas 1993

**15 Paradise View**
**Upley Rising**
**Thameshire**

Dear Friends

Christmas already, and last year's wrapping paper still not thrown out. A lucky find when we were clearing out the loft – no one will know once I've ironed out the creases.

Here's our family news for 1993:

### Ali
If you're not sitting down you'd better: after ten years in thrall to London University I've got a new job! It's not that I didn't love cataloguing academic journals; anyone who doesn't must be bonkers. But someone at work – probably

an anonymous colleague wanting to get rid of me – left the Librarian's News open on my desk with a big red biro ring around an ad in the jobs section. In a mad moment during a rainy lunch hour in July I applied, and after two terrifying interviews and bribing everyone I've ever worked with to scrape together not two but six required professional references, I was offered the post of Deputy Head Librarian at a real Oxford University college. At last, career recognition at the age of 34! World domination follows. Best of all, Havisham Hall is postgrad only, so no more having to mother 18-year-olds who left home with a string of A levels but no clue how to send a fax or get change out of a coffee machine.

There was just one snag – the commute by train takes two hours each way. Could I hold down the job of my dreams and keep up any semblance of happy family life? Not without time travel or Mary Poppins. So we held a family meeting (me, Ant, two wailing toddlers and a teething Daniel) and decided that we will do this thing properly. We have put our house on the market and we are moving to Oxford. Now's the time to go while the children are small. Living in Upley Rising with its la-di-da shops, creepy clock tower and weird Wellspring Festival will become an affectionate memory to laugh about once the horror recedes. We are looking at houses near Banbury, and Ant has applied to two Foundations to fund his forthcoming radical Oxford Period.

In the meantime I am leaving the house in the dark at 6.45am and getting home around 7.30pm. I have been taken on to 'steer the college's move into digital librarianship'. All those hours spent wresting continuous green stationery out of the dot matrix printer and moving coffee cups away from keyboards was time well spent after all. And yes, I know I am moving to one of the most elitist institutions in the country, but I do have a hidden agenda to subvert the system and change values. Havisham Hall doesn't know what's coming to it.

Anyway there's no turning back now, not after my leaving do. All the library staff were gathered in the back office for farewell cake and smarmy speeches. For once there was no one on the library floor, in flagrant contravention of College Library By-Rule 262 (a) (1) or somesuch. But then who would want to be using the library at 5.10pm on a sunny Friday afternoon in freshers' week? The place was empty apart from a couple of first-year students snogging at the far end of the Sociology aisle.

This was the moment the Vice Chancellor decided to make a surprise visit with two VIPS from somewhere in the Far East. Chaperoned of course by the Head Librarian. They wandered past the deserted front desk, made a brief stop at Oriental Studies then on through Sociology, stepping over the trail of clothes the first-year students had cast off in the throes of passion. A short silence followed before they appeared at the back office. Here they were faced with eight librarians clutching glasses of bubbly and slabs of chocolate cake in multicoloured paper napkins. And me wearing my 'F*** Off To Your New Job' badge. The Head Librarian, who has never been seen to smile, had an icy rictus grin pinned to his face. On the few occasions I've met the VC over the past ten years I've never managed to come up with more than a pathetic stammer. But this time the Lambrusco must have done the trick, before he could speak I fulfilled a lifetime's ambition. "You can't fire me," I slurred. "cos I've already quit!"

So I've burnt my bridges now.

**Ant**

Ant has been carving out a role as the official New Man of Upley Rising. He gets two mornings a week studio time when the twins and Daniel go to nursery, otherwise his job description is Primary Carer. He won't answer to 'Stay at Home Dad' – he says it sounds more like an order than a description. As well as being a dab hand at grilling fish fingers (plated up with abstract designs in ketchup), he is the token father at coffee mornings. Even our various Home Guard neighbours have mostly stopped muttering about foreigners when they see him striding along pushing the double buggy, with Daniel strapped to his front in a batik baby sling he hand dyed at home.

He has sold several new works – honing his selling skills on coffee morning mothers with fat cheque books and no shortage of free time. Most of the sale proceeds went on a ginormous chunk of the Berlin Wall which had to be specially shipped over. It's earmarked for a future installation, but at the moment it's taking up most of our back garden, a giant tarpaulin-covered representation of the state of our finances. Moving it to Oxford will use up my minuscule relocation allowance.

**Children**

Eleanor and Felipe run this family very efficiently. They wake us at 5.25am every morning, and make the important decisions, like what time we should all go to bed or how many sweets they are allowed. They always work as a team; but we think that Eleanor is the primary decision maker while Felipe is the chief communicator with his cheeky smile.

They asked for a play dough party for their 3rd birthday. By the end the living room looked like the aftermath of a Clangers chainsaw massacre. We spent three hours clearing up before it dawned on us that Daniel had disappeared from his cot. After a frantic search, Ant found him at the very bottom of the washing basket, under a pile of dirty towels and clothes. Still sleeping peacefully. The twins had heard me complaining about filthy children and were trying to help.

**Outings and highlights**

We had a week in North Devon in August with my parents, who came down in their caravan for Daniel's 1st birthday. There was one sunny day, which was the day we left, but at least the cold weather kept the jellyfish away. My dad and Ant spent a whole afternoon working together in the mud to fix one of the caravan wheels. Not a cross word was exchanged; Dad forgot to ask Ant when he was going to get a proper job, and I even overhead Ant absent-mindedly calling my father 'Dad' – a big step given his family history.

The earth-shattering event in our house this year was the end of BBC's Eldorado. Ant started watching it as he thought it was going to be in Spanish and he and the twins got hooked. We all watched the last episode. Felipe cried when we said there weren't going to be any more so we've bought him the compilation video for Christmas.

**Looking ahead**

This will be our last Christmas in Upley Rising. I never thought I could go all soft on a Home Counties suburb. With the village centre draped in lights and a giant lit-up snowman (plastic but tasteful in a way only this place can manage) by the pond, it could almost melt your heart. Almost but not quite. We are going to make the most of it all before the big move to Oxford.

Festive Greetings to you all,

*Alison and Antonio, Eleanor, Felipe and Daniel*

## Christmas 1994

**15 Paradise View**
**Upley Rising**
**Thameshire**

Dear Friends

I know what you're thinking. Isn't that last year's address? Didn't she land some big job in Oxford? Weren't they going to move out of that pretentious suburb? So let's get things straight. Any previous Christmas newsletters from me giving the impression this family is in control of its own destiny were just seasonal wishful thinking. I should have known better.

We tried. I spent the first three months of this year slogging there and back to my new glittering career – leaving home in the cold, getting back in the dark. Tiptoeing upstairs to pick up sleeping tots and kiss them goodnight, then sitting down to cold pasta cooked by Antonio before he rushed down the garden for some evening studio time. But isn't that what busy executives do? We had found a house on the edge of Oxford which we could just about afford with my new salary and the awards Ant was going to win for campus art sponsored by American billionaires with legacy issues. He was already working on an idea for a giant acrylic dreaming spire.

Fast forward to April 1ˢᵗ – our lucky date, the twins' birthday. We were signing the house contracts straight after their party. We invited 36 other noisy four-year-olds who they'd never see again, splashed out on wine and cheese for the parents, stuffed the going home bags with overpriced rubbish, printed up new address cards designed by Ant. I remember looking round my kitchen filled with gobby people I'd never really got to know, all rabbiting on to each other while swilling my wine, and thinking how glad I was to be escaping to somewhere more authentic.

We arrived at the solicitor's office (March, Ferret and Gladdington, serving the residents of Upley Rising since 1882) just before they closed, slightly out of breath, me wiping icing out of Ant's beard. The skinny conveyancer assigned to us – one of the Ferrets – looked whey-faced and flustered behind an oak desk about three sizes too big for him. He'd been trying to call us. There was … erm … a small complication. Our buyer had pulled out. Not just a wobble. Had a complete change of heart and was looking at properties in Hampshire.

It was a sunny spring afternoon. Upley Rising was covered in cherry blossom. Half of London has been trying to move here, for the schools, the parks, even the effing tennis club. We stared at him, the effects of the party Prosecco draining away. The Ferret's fingers strayed towards the local paper lying open on his desk.

And there it was in black and white. A four-page anniversary issue full of purple prose and foggy snapshots from the archives of The Upley Herald. We lived – no, we live – in a Murderer's House. Our half-timbered home with its unpruneable privet hedge, hideous fireplace and avocado bathroom is also the sinister Heart of Darkness occupied by the notorious Pervert of Paradise View, who committed a series of sickening atrocities in the 1960s then disappeared, leaving an anonymous, blood-stained confession, just as the police were about to arrest him. Quiet Local Road Awash with Blood. The identity parade of victims stared out: a blurry woman with a beehive hairdo – former waitress – strangled with a washing line. A stable boy in sepia – buried trussed up in a horse harness in our own front garden. And so on. You couldn't make it up.

I had early meetings at work all the following week. My professional future hung on a thread twisted round the hands of a vanished sadistic killer. Faced with an impossible dilemma, we made the decision to slash the house price to bargain basement levels. But the bank stepped in, the manager shaking his head sadly down the phone. I always thought negative equity was something to do with particle physics. Now I know better. We were trapped.

On April 6th, the day after Kurt Kobain died, I gave in my notice at Havisham Hall. To be honest, it wasn't the end of the world. Oxford and I have about as much in common as Mary Whitehouse and Madonna. All those endless stone corridors with walls too thick to drill a computer power point. The antiquated library with its tiny windows and flickering lights, antediluvian professors looming up out of the shadows with obscure requests about medieval tomes. It was like working in Gormenghast. I was in charge of a massive budget but wasn't allowed to use it for anything written or invented after 1950. In meetings, fossilised old men leant forward across the table and cupped their ears to understand my accent (how far away is South Yorkshire from Oxford??) and someone made a snide comment about my denim skirt.

I took the summer off to be a full-time mother. I decided it was about time I had a go at this parenting thing since I'm obviously rubbish at climbing the librarianship career ladder (joke). The idea being to leave Ant free for creative work which will win us some serious prize money. He's spending long hours in the studio working with mixtures of bones that he gets free from the butchers.

The bottom line is that one of us needs to start earning soon. Daniel has never had any new clothes of his own, and child benefit barely covers a week's worth of pasta and sauce, let alone our terrifying new council tax bill. There's no exemption for living in a murderer's house. Not that it bothers me living here. But the children keep picking up aggressive answerphone messages from journalists, and though he won't admit it I'm sure all the disruption is giving Ant flashbacks to his childhood in Santiago and the police hammering on the door in the middle of the night to drag his father away. Too cash-strapped for a summer holiday, we tried 'fun' home projects like family gardening. But murder tourists (it's an official term) kept skulking round our front gate, and the back garden is still mostly Berlin Wall.

We haven't done much else this year. For my 35th birthday Ant treated me to a night out in the West End to see the Phantom of the Opera. I would love to have seen Bryan Adams at Wembley, but he'd got tickets months ahead, and even booked a babysitter. Given the subject matter, we tried to see the funny side.

We're having a back-to-basics Christmas. We spent the money put aside for the electricity bill on National Lottery tickets and haven't even won ten quid. Daniel keeps crying that Santa won't visit our 'bad house', so we are driving up to my sister Gill's place. She doesn't believe in heating their cottage unless the temperature drops below freezing, and she's experimenting with veganism. Eleanor and Felipe call Saffron, my niece, Cousin Shrub, and they have a point. She has rarely been seen to move, and sits biting her nails and reading all the time behind a mammoth fringe that has never been cut. She manages to spook our kids out without saying a word. But Hallowe'en here was bad enough – try picturing the Murderer's House with Christmas lights outside and a tree. It'll just be more fodder for The Upley Herald.

Festive Greetings to you all,

*Alison and Antonio, Eleanor, Felipe and Daniel*

*PS I've just reread this letter and decided I need to get a grip. What's more, the photocopy shop on the High Street reads everything they're given – they once suggested a series of corrections to my CV. So I'm not going to send it. You can all make do with just a card this year.*

\* \* \* \* \*

## December 1993

### 18 Everspring Road
### Upley Rising, Thameshire

## Wotcha, People!

Christmas is coming, the goose is getting fat, so is the

mother-in-law, and you've got four long days to get through with the old trouble and strife not to mention the rest of her family.

So here's a bit of light reading to lift the spirits when you're not all squashed together on the couch watching Morecombe and Wise on the box, your only hope of respite being to nip out for a breath of nicotine-perfumed fresh air when the ads come on. With the notable exception of one or two ads that yours truly had a hand in. Let's just say there'll be a certain brand of strong coffee featuring in the ITV breaks this year which you'll be needing when your delightful band of sprogettes surge in on Christmas morning swarming all over the bed like the SAS and shouting CAN I OPEN MY PRESENTS YET DAD DAD DAD just as you're dreaming of persuading the wife that this is her big chance to get the real Santa Special experience. Sorry and all that to the ladies who are reading this but you gotta admit, the old red coat and cotton wool beard is a bit of a novelty, a change is as good as a rest and all that.

But back to the task in question. As you've probably worked out by now, MBW, otherwise known far and wide as My Beautiful Wife, though she'll give me a right talking to if she finds me using the word 'wide' in a ten-mile radius of her lovely self – has done a nifty bit of delegation this year.

Two small children, a new business to run and the nanny from hell to manage have raised her self-confidence to superpower levels, such that when I'm not in the office or on a plane I am putty in her perfectly manicured hands. In this case just when I thought I'd earned a long lie-in after the office Christmas do – which in case you have other ideas is strictly business and means working overtime for no pay up to 3am. You gotta smile nicely to the boss when the waiter comes round with the dregs of a bottle of red at the very moment you've finally steered him onto the subject of bonuses, saying Oh You Have the last glass Sir as if you really mean it. Or be Mr Charming Global Roving Client Activator to the junior staff when it's funny how the stationery cupboard is all of a sudden the place everyone wants to party, you turf 'em out saying Get Back Out There and mingle with the clients you dumbos that's how you get your promotion and I'll have that bottle of Scotch it's company property if you don't mind.

So I wake up with this throbbing headache after about two hours sleep and in comes MBW wafting expensive perfume everywhere, it can't be later than 11am and she says I'm going shopping with Mother and don't forget you promised to write the Christmas letter this year to show off your famous creative skills. It's the last posting day today so you need to get it done by 5pm but there's nothing like a deadline for focus, it's the nanny's day off and there's broccoli salad in the fridge for the children see you later.

Saying no to MBW is not a thing a man contemplates lightly. Also I am given to understand that the Wright family news is eagerly awaited as it drops through letterboxes from London to Los Angeles, last year an extract even made it into the Nigel Dempster column. So here I am at the kitchen table with a giant mug of the aforementioned coffee to hand, Max parked in front of a video, my gorgeous daughter sleeping like an angel in her hand-carved Italian cot, and a couple of packets of fags within sight just in case I accidentally forget I've given up.

It's been quite a year mind you, just wait till you find out what we've been up to.

But yo! Saved by the bell. Can it be nearly 4.30 already? Gotta run ... So our news in the proverbial nutshell: we've had a great year. Maxie is a real trooper, getting straight As at playschool I'm told. Adorable daughter. I've been to Kuala Lumpur, Singapore, South Africa where I bumped into Mark Thatcher, and my fave place of all, New York. MBW is brilliant, her little business taking off like a rocket.

Have a Cool Yule y'all,

**Charles X**

\* \* \* \* \*

*December 1994*

*Paradise House, Paradise View,*
*Upley Rising, Thameshire*

*Paradise House Christmas News*

*Dear Everyone,*

This year has ended with us literally in Paradise.

Dream homes do not happen exclusively to celebrities. This year the Wrights became the proud owners of an enviable double-fronted Victorian villa in Paradise View, one of Upley Rising's most *recherché r*oads, and we owe it all to Charles's ingenuity.

I had seen the For Sale sign outside Paradise House while on one of my regular prospecting drives along Paradise View. I couldn't resist making enquiries and discovered that it was a bank repossession, standing bleak and empty because the previous occupants, two doctors, had carelessly overstretched themselves and got caught out by the recession. Charles and I reviewed our finances, and taking into account his expected bonus and my business income forecast, the price was only just out of our reach.

Then fate stepped in with a helping hand. Charles was having a rare Sunday afternoon at home. Although using Concorde has cut his trips to New York to just three and a half hours, the time he saves seems to go on longer working hours, or getting over jet lag. It's worth it though, as the inflight gifts are to die for. I don't know how I ever got a decent night's sleep without a cashmere eye mask, or started the day without white truffle toothpaste. What's more, Charles has taken advantage of Concorde's narrower seating to nab both David Frost and Luciano Pavarotti (separately) for a business chat over champagne and caramelized macadamia nuts.

So Charles was spending the quiet Sunday afternoon sorting out our garden shed (which he jokingly calls the Smoking Room) when he came across a box of yellowing old newspapers. He was about to throw them out, when he spotted on the top of the pile an ancient but legible copy of The Upley Herald from 1964. The headline caught his eye at once: 'Murder in Paradise!' Reading the article together, we discovered there had been a series of gruesome murders in this very road, which had terrified the residents and perplexed the police. All the killings occurred in the dead of night. The murderer was never brought to justice but a local man who disappeared was the prime suspect. Hideously disfigured bodies were found in various front gardens and in one case impaled on a lamppost.

Realising that The Herald would hate to miss the chance to mark the 30th anniversary of this gripping piece of Upley Rising's history, Charles dropped in to their offices on the High Street next to the post office, where he wasted no time in striking up a friendship with the owner. A full double-page spread duly appeared the following week, complete with photos of the victims and descriptions of their grisly injuries. And the good news is that all three prospective buyers who were bidding for Paradise House dropped out within days.

We went to see the estate agent. On his office wall was a large whiteboard headed Monthly Targets, covered in numbers which had been crossed out in red pen. He was furious about The Herald's article, but given the blight it cast on the road he had no choice but to accept the offer we made – which was very reasonable in the circumstances. But we reassured him that there would be plenty of other houses to sell. Indeed, we soon sold our old house in Everspring Road, its value had ballooned due to our clever improvements, and in a few short weeks Charles had carried me over our new threshold. It was the perfect present for my 35th birthday.

We feel as if we were destined to live here. Paradise House is one of just three detached houses in this beautiful road, with a large rear garden, and looks down imposingly over the town. It's a short distance from the Tennis Club, where we need just three more members to die before we rise to the top of the waiting list. They are taking their time about it, and two of them are not even playing anymore, which seems unfair on us.

While we are waiting, the world of work is keeping us as busy as ever.

Caroline Wright Events has blossomed this year. My clientele inhabit some of Thameshire's many minor stately homes. They may be hidden away behind high walls and in extensive wooded grounds, but just like ordinary people they want to make sure the sound system is loud enough to impress the neighbours at their son's 18th, or that security is tight for a delicate corporate takeover meeting. Professional confidentiality means I cannot reveal their names; they include two Premier League football players, a retired Cabinet minister, and a reclusive record producer who is a friend of Charles's rock star brother Ditch. They all appreciate my discreet efficiency. I ensure that everything runs like clockwork – apart from just one small helipad mix-up, though as I later told Air Traffic Control, one big 'H' on a lawn looks much like another.

I apply the same professional approach to both work and family. I can't understand why people go on about work-life balance: you simply do those three things in that order. After a short early morning run, a shower and a small cup of herbal tea, my working day starts at 8am. Running downstairs with my Valentino attaché case (a birthday gift from Charles) under my arm, I pass Clementine to the nanny, who presses half a croissant into my hand as I give Maximilian a swift hug, then step out of our very grand front door to my waiting car and whichever appointment my Filofax tells me is first. Easy!

Both our children are flourishing in their new home environment. Max loves having more space to run around being Darth Vader and attacking the postman with his toy lightsaber. He starts school in January. Upley Primary, though a state school, is rated Outstanding by Ofsted. Mixing with children from different social backgrounds will be good for him, though Mother says that Charles's family should be more than enough.

Clementine is full of energy like every two-year-old,

and nearly as busy as me. Three mornings a week the nanny takes her to Little Networks, where she is learning to socialise, then there is swimming, ballet, Drama Queens and French club. Her favourite game is pretend play, especially swapping roles with the nanny and telling her what to do. They have such fun.

We are looking forward to our first Christmas in Paradise House. Mother has some mysterious plans of her own, so we have invited Charles's family, who won't notice that we haven't started redecorating it yet and will be able to make as much mess as they like. I am hoping that Charles's rock idol brother Ditch may fly back from LA, where he is spending more time these days, to complete the gathering. The superstar who has just been voted number 25 in Cosmopolitan's Sexy Celebrity Top 50 still takes the trouble to call long distance, and to send me flowers on my birthday every year.

Most intriguing of all, Charles says he has a big surprise for me, which he is infuriatingly refusing to reveal until it is definite. Can it be Tennis Club membership at last? I can't wait to find out.

In the meantime, we are looking forward to our new year in Paradise!

Wishing you all a very Happy Christmas,

*Caroline, Charles, Maximilian and Clementine Wright*

# PART FOUR 1995-1997:

# ROBERT, CAROLINE, CHARLES, ALI

## 14 Paradise View, Upley Rising, Thameshire

### Christmas 1995

Scraping the frost off the car windscreen on this sharp December morning prompted a piercing reminder of the heatwave we experienced in the summer. Upley Rising always seems best suited to the colder months, when drifts of bronzed autumn leaves bring colour to the pavements or the church steeple is coated in icicles. Back in July and August the whole of Southern England felt as if it was struggling to breathe. Here in Thameshire our usually verdant parks became a uniform expanse of flat yellow, and the civic flower bed that proudly spells out Upley Rising in begonias every summer degenerated into indecipherable brown detritus.

The inevitable hosepipe bans threatened to incite riots, and at Coburn Briggs we even received a letter asking if it was possible to sue the Council for the hot weather. At home our own vegetable patch was painstakingly nursed by my mother, with the aid of kneeling pads for her stiff joints and Colin carrying jugs out from the kitchen tap to bring succour to our desperate tomato plants and sclerotic spinach. Even the hardy wisteria which has graced the front of our house for decades began to wilt dangerously. I was an unwilling witness to a number of flagrant breaches of the hosepipe ban by various neighbours, who clearly underestimated the angle of vision offered by our upstairs windows.

Of greater import was the dwindling of the Up, the town's eponymous spring. By early July the underground stream which gushes under the grates in the Market Square had dwindled to an alluvial trickle which threatened to dry up the Square's famous well altogether. This had not happened in living memory, indeed the last recorded instance was in the black year of 1657 when it was seen as a terrible omen and led to the burning of one Agnes Bartwell, aged 19, as a witch.

Little wonder then that this year's Wellspring, our own time-honoured festival, was a tense affair. I had not attended the procession through the town for years, and have always had mixed feelings about an event whose success revolves around a ceremony that simulates human sacrifice. But Colin was very keen to go and the firm effectively closed for the day (leaving Jones from accounts to pick up any calls) so along we went.

The temperature must have been well into the 80s. We managed to squeeze into a small patch of shade under the awning of the hardware store with a good view over the Square. We were soon hemmed in by a large group of teenagers communicating with each other through high-pitched shrieks, and lacking any awareness of personal space boundaries. I had forgotten how many onlookers turn out for the Wellspring. Looking at the people lining the streets it was not hard to identify modern Agnes

Bartwells among the faces; those with just a bit more intelligence and animation than their peers, whose strong personality can all too easily become a target. Progress is not a straightforward phenomenon; fortunately we no longer burn witches, but we do – in Upley Rising at least – still congregate to gape as a young woman is chosen to be publicly lowered down a well on a hot summer's day.

As the procession entered the Market Square and the ceremony began, the hubbub from the crowd subsided. Everyone from grandparents to small children stood through the heat in anxious silence, forgotten ice lollies melting down sticky hands, waiting for the Upley Maiden's annual reappearance from the depths. This year's cohort of boys recruited to pull her up had some sort of problem with the rope, which I later heard had been made much longer than usual as the well was so low and it was considered essential for the maiden to bring up evidence of water in her bucket. The process dragged on for a very long time, during which Colin punctuated the strained silence by asking in his most booming voice if the maiden had gone to Australia. This in turn led to some unpleasant jibes about my brother from the teenagers around us, which brought on one of Colin's hysterical attacks and I had to take him home, missing the raising up of the maiden and some melodrama involving her mother collapsing in the heat. I started to wonder if it might be time to recast the annual celebration into something more sensible, and sent a letter outlining possibilities to the organising committee. But once an institution is approaching 350 years old it attains a degree of permanence and inviolability that is hard to challenge. My proposal was given short shrift. The brief reply I received referred to the continued popularity of the Pamplona festival despite the inherent risk of tragedy there, as well as mentioning ongoing rivalry with the Burning Tar Barrel procession at Ottery St Mary. To tone down our own festival would clearly be seen as a sign of weakness.

Parched gardens and maidens aside, I was pleased to be approached by the Upley Society regarding the installation of a memorial plaque to my father, acknowledging his civic contribution over many years. Discussions are ongoing regarding the exact location and wording and will no doubt need various committee approvals.

I had two enjoyable trips away this year. Serendipity had a hand in the Montague Ensemble's choice of Suffolk for the summer tour, where we enjoyed record-breaking temperatures on the coast near Aldeburgh, and your Seasonal Epistolarian was spotted dipping a limb or two into the water. Were it not for the brooding presence of Sizewell B on the skyline, we could almost have been in the South of France. At Easter I represented the North Marylebone Miniature Railway Society at this year's four nations convention: a foray north of the border into Glasgow. Our English pastoral layout survived the journey remarkably well, with just minor damage to some of the miniature rose bushes constructed by one of our lady members.

My mother has had a good year healthwise, benefitting from the regular care service for Colin. There was just one incident when she parked her car on the wrong side of the road during a memory lapse caused by tiredness and tried to let herself into the house opposite ours. We were all taken aback to learn that her key worked perfectly well in their lock, which says something about the practices of locksmiths. The current occupants, who are temporary tenants, thought she was the agent's representative doing a surprise house inspection and gave her a comprehensive tour of the property. Rising to the occasion, my mother instructed them to tidy up the airing cupboard and to pull out the couch grass choking the lavender in the back garden, before they discovered the truth and delivered her home safely and in some embarrassment.

They are actors, and an unexpected outcome of the mix-up was my being presented with a complimentary ticket to see Blithe Spirit at the Thameshire Royal Theatre, in which one of them was appearing as Dr Bradman. Really quite a decent performance for repertory theatre.

As I put the finishing touches to this letter it is the eve of the office Christmas party. This year's theme is 'Cyberspace', which poses all kinds of challenges. The Oxford Dictionary defines the subject as 'an imaginary space without a physical location in which communication over computer networks takes place'. I am not sure how I am going to represent myself as an imaginary space, given I am experiencing enough difficulties operating this invisible new technology at work. One of the secretaries, trying to be helpful, suggested I draw inspiration from the television series Star Trek, but I have no intention of distinguishing myself, or otherwise, by making an appearance in some kind of silver-painted cardboard box. I shall have to make do with an ornamental sprig of tinsel on my bow tie.

With Christmas wishes,

**Robert**

## 14 Paradise View, Upley Rising, Thameshire

## Christmas 1996

My year began with an unanticipated drama. Its unlikely trigger was an obscure question of taxation law.

In January I was visited by some new clients, a brother and sister both in their 40s, who came to me in great distress. Following the death of their much loved, and incidentally prosperous, father they were receiving threatening letters from the Inland Revenue. Their deceased father had drawn up a labyrinthine family trust, intent on diverting as much of his accrued wealth as possible away from the government and in the direction of his children – a practice otherwise known as avoiding Inheritance Tax. To the dismay of my clients, the Revenue disputed the wording of the trust (65 pages, definitely not drawn up by my own firm Coburn Briggs) and was pursuing them for sums of money which they had already set aside for such essential items as school fees and trips abroad.

To sort out the finer details of the case I was obliged to seek advice from a taxation expert. While to some extent this work can be done by correspondence, when I was invited to meet with the specialist in person I was pleased to take the opportunity. My visits to London are fewer than they used to be and this particular practitioner was based at Canary Wharf, which afforded me a rare opportunity to travel, using the firm's expenses, on the Docklands Light Railway, a delightful light rapid transport system whose carriages are designed with forward-facing seats at their glass fronts, making it possible to imagine oneself as the driver.

I was anticipating a productive and enjoyable day, but you may guess what is coming, since it dominated the news earlier this year. Following the meeting, which went on later than planned, we emerged from the modernistic glass and steel tower in which the expert was based, to be confronted by a wall of flashing blue lights and a police cordon. We were instructed from a safe distance by megaphone to stay inside, and so returned to the office where, trying not to worry or look out at the police activity below, we spent a strained two hours drinking coffee and making small talk. In such quasi-social situations one soon discovers how little one has in common with fellow professionals outside of work. The expert described in prolix detail her three cats and her recent trip down the Nile. In return I began a summary of the history of the Docklands Light Railway. I was in the middle of explaining the line's formidably sharp angle of approach into South Quay station, when the massive IRA bomb of 9th February detonated just yards from us. We experienced this as an overwhelming implosion of the office's floor-to-ceiling window onto the area where we were sitting. I briefly lost consciousness and my recall is even now extremely fragmented. Suffice it to say I spent two nights in hospital and was lucky to get away with some deep cuts to my face from shards of glass, and severe burns to my arms which I threw up in defence as the office's very large, heavy and expensive coffee machine tipped onto me with all its steaming contents. The taxation adviser was fortunate to escape with only minor cuts and bruises and I am most grateful to her for calling the paramedics over to me in the chaotic aftermath of the explosion.

All this was a relative reprieve compared with the poor souls who lost their lives. It is sobering to suffer a close encounter with death, and to note how the repercussions of a bomb explosion travel way beyond the immediate area of the blast. Both my mother and Colin were distraught to receive a late-night call from Guy's Hospital with minimal information about my condition, and were thrown off course for some weeks. Colin still turns his head away when I come into the room, as the scars on my face will take some time to heal given that 27 stitches were necessary.

While recovering I was able to work from home. My heavily bandaged arms gave me every reason to refuse the firm's offer of a home computer, relying instead on my dictation machine along with visits from some of the office staff to drop off books and files. It was quite a novelty to be in the house during the working day and observe the various comings and goings in our road. I am not sure we made the right decision last year to turn down the installation of speed humps, as local mothers seem to treat the school run as if they are fleeing a war zone.

I was back at work by the summer, when we had a visit from my Aunt Celia who lives in Toronto when she is not on a cruise or a safari. She and my mother are very unalike both physically and in character, but she is my mother's only remaining family and we were pleased to accommodate her (in the best bedroom). Aunt Celia is a woman who holds an opinion on most matters, which she relished airing to our rota of carers. I repeatedly found them clustered round the kitchen table, cups of tea and plates of fig rolls staked out in battle lines, while they cut a swathe through the state of English politics, the National Health Service, royal divorces, Mr Bill Clinton and the Spice Girls. My mother wisely stayed on the edges of the fray; she has the intellectual advantage of thinking before she speaks and would have made a fine lawyer. Colin joined in, singing 'Wannabe' with gusto, and though pitch is not his strength he surprised us all with his perfect memorisation of the lyrics.

My mother was hoping that the memorial plaque to my father being prepared by the Upley Society would be ready to show her sister, but its progress has got bogged down, in no small part because she has been objecting to its proposed siting on the wall of the building that currently houses the Job Centre.

Regrettably I was unable to accompany the Montagu Ensemble on their summer tour to Finland, as rehearsing was too painful while my bomb injuries were healing. I participated in the choruses at our annual November Christmas concert at St Luke's in Bloomsbury, though my regular solos were taken by a new tenor, a cousin of the choir master, who joined earlier this year.

Colin and I made our annual visit to Hamleys at the beginning of December before it gets too busy. He talks of nothing else for weeks ahead. We always allow three full hours inside the store, starting on the top floor with the large items like Wendy houses and toy kitchens. Some of the older staff remember Colin from year to year and are quite happy to let him explore, as long as we are careful not to break anything. On the ground floor Colin chose his own surprise present, an Etch A Sketch which he was very taken with, his own from childhood having broken long ago. He spent the train journey home drawing what looked like Frankenstein's monster, which he said was me with my stitches. I have to confess that I also allowed myself a small treat at Hamleys, three 1952 coal wagons for my Welsh mining layout project.

I have wrapped all these up to be freshly opened on

Christmas morning. They will do as presents from my mother who has been increasingly forgetful. She bought me a set of Famous Five books for my birthday, and I anticipate her Christmas shopping will be just as erratic.

With Christmas wishes,

**Robert**

\* \* \* \* \*

*December 1995*

*12967 Oceanreach Drive South West*
*Santa Mojave*
*Los Angeles 91034*
*USA*

        *Christmas Letter from America*

*Dear Everyone,*

When Charles presented me with a gift-wrapped air ticket to Los Angeles for Christmas last year, how could I possibly refuse? Strong Barker had decided that he was their number one choice to get their new Californian office up and running. I can't pretend it wasn't a wrench to leave my new dream home in Upley Rising, but if life presents a golden opportunity on a platter you have to grasp it with both hands, and naturally I agreed to join him. After all, it wasn't as if he was asking me to go to Cardiff or Macclesfield.

The firm needed him there as soon as possible, so we rented Paradise House out to two lovely actors, old friends of Charles who wanted a quiet bolthole away from the West End. I leased my burgeoning Caroline Wright business to my old employer, Imperative Events, for the year. By the end of January we were 30,000 feet above the Atlantic in business class. Eleven heavenly months later find me writing this Christmas message from my poolside lounger, a margarita on the table beside me and one pedicured foot dangling in the water.

If you've seen *A Star is Born* you might begin to glimpse the glitz and glamour we live and breathe on a daily basis out here. The sun shines all the time, there are film stars everywhere acting just like normal people, every street from Sunset Boulevard to Mulholland Drive is straight out of a movie – and it's all next to some of the world's best beaches. It's heaven, as long as you avoid the downtown area which is apparently quite unwholesome and we've kept our distance. England feels a world away and Upley Rising like a miniscule model village from the 1950s that you'd trip over if it was in your sun-drenched LA backyard.

Charles has spent most of the year lunching new clients on lobster and Californian Sauvignon Blanc. They love his accent, one of them actually thought he was Michael Caine and cheeky Charles only put him right after contracts had been signed. And we've been invited to some amazing parties.

The Americans certainly love to entertain lavishly, and from a professional viewpoint as an events specialist I have to admit there are lessons to be learned. Some of the cultural differences are intriguing. The buffets are extravagant but you never see anyone eating anything, at least not the women. People have very short attention spans, in fact the most anyone has ever spoken to me at a party was for about 30 seconds before moving quickly on. And short memories too, as they never seem to recognise me in the street the next day. Everyone is beautifully turned out, but the dress code can be baffling; several times Charles and I arrived at events in our finery to find everyone else in polo shirts and jeans.

We have both had our teeth whitened.

As a pupil at Estrella Vista Elementary School, Maximilian has been a big hit, entertaining the staff with his 'quaint' English spelling. He made everyone laugh when he asked if Mr Clinton's wife was the Queen. In his spare time he has tennis lessons, as by starting now he could be worth a fortune in endorsements when he's older.

Charles's brother, rock star Ditch Wright, lives just a few miles down the freeway, cloistered in a gated villa in the hills with its own guitar-shaped swimming pool. He is based here most of the time, since both the recording studios and the tax regime suit him better. We haven't seen as much of Ditch as I was expecting, which is understandable given he has megastar status these days. Apart from a new manager, Jared, who keeps him on rather a tight leash, he spends a lot of time with his girlfriend Helena. She is a model, very stunning in that sun-bleached California girl way, all legs and suntan but rather lacking in intelligence. On the occasions I get together with Ditch, he loves to corner me for some genuine, in-depth conversation.

Mother flew out in July for a visit, bringing a stack of treats from England: Twinings tea, an everyday hamper from Fortnums, twiglets for the children and a pile of English Vogues and Hello! magazines for me so I could keep up to date with the royals. While she was here,

Charles arranged for us all to be present for a unique and privileged opportunity: watching Ditch record his new American album.

It was so funny when we arrived at the studio; the two enormous gun-carrying minders on the gates had missed the brief that special VIP guests were expected. They wouldn't let us in until they had searched us quite intrusively before radioing through to the main building. Once we finally got past all the checks and into the studio, Mother, who likes Ditch but whose musical tastes veer more towards Tony Bennett, started chattering to Jared about the Wright family's alleged links with London gangs. She didn't realise that the mike between the control room and the live studio was switched on. Ditch stormed out and shouted at her to keep her voice down, which was a bit of an overreaction as all that was years and years ago and most of it was rumour anyway. Then Hermesita (as Mother and I call Helena) drifted over and asked if Mother and I were sisters. I was not offended, as what can you expect from someone who thinks Italy is the capital of London? Mother, who was still a bit jet-lagged, started laughing hysterically, Clementine burst into tears and we had to leave.

I did get a big bouquet from Ditch afterwards with a very affectionate handwritten note of apology. The album hasn't sold as well as the last; I think Ditch is a bit distracted by Helena. It is overproduced and hasn't got the edgy quality of his earlier work.

The newest star in the Wright family is our daughter Clementine, who aged just three and a half, has taken the first steps on her own modelling career. One of Charles's colleagues put me in touch with a child acting agency, where they instantly fell in love with her blue eyes and

Shirley Temple curls. She has featured in several mail order catalogues for children's clothes, looking adorable if I say so myself, and even in a TV commercial for pizza-flavoured salad dressing, which is a clever idea to get children to eat fresh greens. Driving Clementine to her assignments can be an adventure in itself. Only last week we found ourselves gridlocked on the freeway alongside none other than O. J. Simpson, enjoying his newfound taste of freedom. He's very handsome. I leaned out of my window and asked for a quick autograph for Maximilian, and he was gracious enough to ask what an English Rose like me was doing in the Golden State, and was I by any chance related to Lady Diana. Life here is straight out of a film script!

But our beautiful American dream must come to an end, and we are soon jetsetting back to England at the end of a truly memorable year. Charles's boss has decided that he needs Charles closer to hand at Strong Barker's London office. Charles is looking forward to seeing Dolly Parton in concert before we go, but I am beginning to miss England. All those poolside parties with perplexing dress codes and where no one actually swims can be exhausting. I can't wait to see Paradise House again, and to take back the reins at Caroline Wright Events, though I'm sure Jessica has been doing a reasonable job in my absence.

Before we leave we will enjoy a sumptuous American Christmas with all the trimmings, and we are bringing the best of the USA back with us. When I board the plane with our five extra suitcases full of new clothes and toys, holding my Prada Pochette crammed with business cards, I will be seeing Upley Rising afresh through American eyes: its ancient church and picturesque clock tower waiting to welcome us, looking like our very own Tinseltown fairy tale in the snow.

Wishing you all a very Happy Christmas,

*Caroline, Charles, Maximilian and Clementine Wright*

\* \* \* \* \*

## December 1996

Paradise House, Paradise View
Upley Rising, Thameshire

### Paradise House Christmas News

## Hi guys 'n gals,

Another year bites the dust and the missus finds her lovely self too busy to put pen to paper this Christmas, given all the kerfuffle we've had with what she calls her own *annus horribilis*.

It's true our 1996 didn't get off to the best of starts. Not that I was complaining about leaving the US. I'd had enough of living across the pond. California's great for a while but not all that health lark, the pressure to look like you dine on lettuce leaves every night, and who really wants to go jogging for miles along Venice Beach in the smog when you've been working a ten-hour day with a two-hour commute along the so-called freeways? About as free as a night out in Vegas. Nah, Europe's got more class any day of the week I reminded myself as we were boarding our flight home at the end of December. I was raring to get back to the old sceptred isle.

So after 11 interminable hours on the plane it's getting on for midnight when our cab arrives back in Upley Rising from Heathrow. Having left the American nanny behind we're at our wits' end by now with two kids hyper on E numbers, in-flight movies and about 30 minutes' sleep between them. The plan is to leave the unpacking till the morning and grab some much-needed shut-eye, New Year's Eve or not. But the people carrier turns the corner into our road – and right in front of us, where our tranquil home should be waiting for us, we find ourselves staring at a Paradise House-shaped object lit up all over and pulsating like the Blackpool Tower. I shove a wad of notes into the driver's hand, slide out of the car, tiptoe up the drive and ease open the front door.

To be greeted by a scene that would give Caligula sore eyes. The whole place is oozing with moving bodies, there are people all over the shop and definitely not the carefully selected types the wife likes to invite. Everyone's dancing, knocking back the booze like it's going out of fashion, chucking balloons around under a massive glitter ball – the whole shebang. It's a proper New Year's Eve party in full swing. You can't see the floor for fag ends and party poppers, there's smoke and a smell like cremated pizza coming from the kitchen, and a riff from none other than my beloved big brother's custom-made Gibson Les Paul blasting out over the stereo. Judging by the outfits, or lack of them, ancient Rome with all her kinky excesses is the theme of the evening.

An exquisite thought creeps into my jet-lagged head: someone has set up a surprise welcome party for us, oh please let it be true – then everything goes quiet as the entire roomful turns as one and looks at the Wright family blinking in the doorway with our designer suitcases, our flight-flattened hair and long-haul complexions, the kids still wearing their wrinkled business class pyjamas. In the crowd I spot a familiar face, it's one of the actors we rented the house to, his paunch flopping out of the white fabric draped over it – one of our 600 thread count Egyptian cotton bedsheets I noted – and nothing else except a plastic laurel crown slipping down his balding head. He sees me seeing him and time freezes for an interminable moment while a nauseous mix of horror and realisation sinks in on both sides, and someone's horizontal wine glass drips Valpolicella drop by drop onto our antique Persian rug.

I glance sideways at My Beautiful Wife and just as I'm wondering how I'm going to get out of this one, there's a scream that would wake the dead, and it's Maxie who's run upstairs to his bedroom then running down again, saying there are two grown-ups trying to wrestle each other to death in his pirate bed, they're making weird noises and they've got no clothes on he can see their bottoms and everything it's DISGUSTING Daddy.

MBW turns her head without the rest of her moving a nano inch; she looks at me and says in a glacial rasp: I'll be waiting in the car. Then she executes a 180-degree heel spin on her brand-new Jimmy Choos and exits the house with her head held high and one of my children glued to each hand. Just as blue flashing lights appear and the cops pull up outside at the behest of one of our leafy street's Neighbourhood Watch brigade.

This is what happens my friends when you rent your beloved home sweet home out to second cousins of friends of friends who don't need references because 'they are just adorable people, both actors you know, you may have seen one of them, the better-looking one, getting marvellous reviews at the Tricycle Theatre, they just need a base near London because they'll be away in rep most of the time'. We let the place to two rising stars and come back to find the entire cast of Cats in residence.

So while the luvvies are being turfed out and the whole house fumigated, we get to spend six weeks residing at Upley Rising's finest hostelry, the Rising Pheasant – nice one I bet you're thinking, living above the shop, coming home to a swift pint before nipping upstairs to put the old plates of meat up in our luxurious family suite. No cooking or cleaning for Caroline to worry about, staff tiptoeing around doing everything for her, she hasn't got to lift a finger. The kids took a bit of sorting though, especially Maxie after his experience that no child of that age should never have to go through.

I made it all up to him when he started at primary school by dropping him off in the shiny new motor. We turned quite a few heads I can tell you as we rolled up at the gates, but now the lad says he's being bullied. I tell 'im there's nothing wrong with being called Maxie Millions, if you're gonna get a number as a nickname then a million is no bad place to start. I did have a little chat with the Head though, would you believe he's a West Ham fan too, he totally got my meaning and promised to look out for the boy.

Continuing with the *annus horribilis* theme, it's been a good year for our solicitors (when isn't you might well ask). First they get to sue the firm that put together the rental contract, Upley Rising's very own March, Ferret and Gladdington, founded in 1882 and still stuck there, or how else do you make a mistake like Jan 31$^{st}$ instead of

Jan 1st on a tenancy agreement end date?

Next we let the Tom Sawyers loose on Imperative Events, Caroline's erstwhile employer and so-called commercial partner who ran her business while we were in the States. Can you believe it, they've decided for reasons of their own that they like being Caroline Wright Events so much that they don't want to part with it, in fact they are flat out refusing to return it to Caroline – the first sex change corporation I've ever come across.

We issue a writ to get the business back from them but they won't play ball, and put in a sneaky counterclaim that they weren't forewarned about some of the clientele being dangerous to work with. They supply a lengthy list of so-called attempted sexual assaults on their staff who 'in the absence of prior knowledge found themselves alone with and unprotected from said threatening clients on the premises or in the grounds of their massive country piles'.

Though if you ask me that stunner Jessica looks like she'd quite enjoy being chased around the private maze of a certain retired government minister.

In the end we settle for a tidy stash of cash in exchange for them keeping the events business. MBW was not happy at all, she'd poured her heart and soul into setting up Caroline Wright Events, and it came on top of the Return to Paradise House episode.

I can't ever bear to see her lovely blue eyes full of tears, I had to sit her down on our leather Chesterfield, take her by the hands and do the whole Charming Charles bit, promising I'd do whatever it took to make things right. If you ask me, she's well shot of Imperial Mince as they are now known chez nous, as she's got something much bigger to get her teeth into. It's a real cracker of a franchise idea she brought back all the way from LA, which she's been busy working up when she's not choosing paint colours for the new kitchen.

After all that things settled down, well they did if we leave out Euro 96, England penalty shootouts and Gareth Southgate, who would be exiled to Siberia for eternity if I had any say in things. It's only been half an *annus horribilis* really. We spent most of the cash from Imperial Mince on the house, MBW said that cleaning it from top to bottom wasn't enough, we had to change the whole look and feel. She's moved on from florals and is on a mission to show the rest of Upley Rising the meaning of Mid Atlantic Elegance. She's certainly got the net curtains twitching in our street. As well as our very own home cinema room we've imported a fridge from the USA you could spend a winter holiday in, and she's got an architect drawing up plans to expand our downstairs to fit in the rest of the new furniture that's still in storage. In the meantime one of the neighbours had the cheek to complain that the basketball net in the front garden was in breach of conservation area rules, but they got short shrift from me. The whole road should be well pleased to have us back home after a year of luvvies' extravagances.

As for the March Ferret's, they paid for us to go on a very pleasant spa retreat in the Maldives to get over the nervous shock and distress caused to us and the children. We didn't push things too far there, as the Senior Partner turns out to be a big nob on the tennis club committee.

So with 1997 rolling towards us faster than the mother-in-law can down a gin and tonic, there are no complaints from me. My Darling Clementine started school in September, such a sweetheart, how many four-year-olds begin reception class with a modelling career already up and running, as she showed them by walking into class on day one balancing a book on her head. Yes, this Christmas life is pretty good. I can't wait to see MBW's face when she opens her Christmas present, a fancy pro racquet to go with her surprise brand-new South Thameshire Lawn Tennis Club membership.

Have a Cool Yule y'all,

## Charles X

\* \* \* \* \*

## Christmas 1995

**15 Paradise View**
**Upley Rising**
**Thameshire**

Dear Friends

All change again at home this year.

### Beware the Tall Dark Stranger

Picture this. A May morning round our family breakfast table. Eleanor and Felipe are taking it in turns to rummage through the Frosties box to find the free Power Rangers figure. I'm immersed in the Guardian, which when open completely obscures my view of Daniel in his booster seat. He is slowly pouring milk out of his cup onto his place mat and beyond; then he looks up and bursts into tears. He howls one of his new words: 'Merrrdewerr!'

A stranger is standing in the doorway, sinister in a dark suit and tie, holding a briefcase. Felipe shrieks and drops the cornflake box upside down onto the floor.

Eleanor says: 'Daddy? Why are you dressed like that? Are you going to prison?'

Antonio, Upley Rising's lone New Man, got a job. A real one. He is a Field Sales Associate, working for Thameshire Creative Design & Print Services Ltd. Thanks to Vanessa, who dropped round one day and found him and the children making papier-mâché monsters out of stacks of unpaid bills (he thought 'final demand' meant they weren't going to ask us again). She's a friend of the sales director and somehow convinced her that Ant is a natural salesman as well as a famous artist. It's quite a cushy job – he gets to drive around to businesses in the area, produce sheaves of glossy brochures, and use all his Latin American charm to point out how the company could treble its income by printing up more glossy brochures.

But the very best thing about it – apart from the fact that it comes with a salary that pays our mortgage – is that he has a company car! What a lifesaver, we had got stopped in the 2CV twice by the police for breaking just about every existing child seat regulation. So every morning Ant sets off in his suit, which none of us knew he owned, except for Fridays, when he puts on his cement-splashed jeans and writes his weekly report, which I punctuate and correct before he sends it off by electronic mail. Then he disappears into his studio and hammers things.

### The best days of their lives

The other big change is that the twins have started school. On the first day of the January term, two four-year-olds set off for Upley Primary looking like a washing powder ad, with scrubbed faces, shiny shoes and neatly combed hair. We had asked for them to be put in the same class as research shows that twins settle in at school better if they are together. We hugged them goodbye at the school gates and went back home, but the house still felt eerily quiet even with Daniel there. Neither of us could get anything done so we all went out for lunch and sat in the Rising Bean until pickup time.

Back at the school gates it took us 15 anxious minutes to realise that the two unclaimed waifs sitting on a bench in a corner of the playground were our twins. Both were covered in mud, with unbuttoned shirts; both were starving. Their lunchboxes were unopened. Eleanor had lost her scrunchy and Felipe had a black eye. When Ant asked him how he got it he would only say it was a present from another boy. Neither of them knew their teacher's name though they had both drawn a big picture of Mr Bean in their exercise books. Most mysteriously, they couldn't wait to get back to school the next day. Welcome to the world of education.

## Mother Earth in action

Ant out working now leaves me and Daniel at home all day. We get on well, probably because we both take the Quentin Crisp approach to housework*. I've spent most of this year working towards level one Earth Mother status. I took up baking bread, until I found one of my loaves being used as a doorstop in Ant's studio. I decided to plant vegetables in the garden, just as it stopped raining and 1995 became the driest summer in recorded history. Even so I managed to bring on my cabbages quite well until someone put a note through our door 'reminding' me about the hosepipe ban

I was on the verge of knocking at every house in our road to ask why their lawns were allowed to stay suspiciously green all summer but not my home produce patch, when I got a call from a woman called Astrantia who had somehow heard that I used to be involved with CND and wondered if I would be interested in helping with this year's Wellspring Festival, Upley Rising's answer to the Stonehenge summer solstice.

At last, a chance to meet real people, different from the school-gate mothers who convene every day at 3.20pm in designer jeans and full make-up, and look sideways at me rushing in late in my dungarees with Daniel falling out the buggy as if I'm something the dog brought in. I went to Astrantia's house for a Wellspring Committee meeting; everyone seemed quite normal, we sat drinking herb tea and going through an agenda that included items like 'Upley Maiden selection criteria' and 'hemp supplies' (for the well rope). There was a small bald man bustling in and out of the kitchen who turned out to be Astrantia's brother and the chief Druid who leads the annual procession in his long silver wig and robes. I offered to play my guitar but there was obviously some sort of hierarchy thing going on so I agreed to be a traffic steward. I got to spend the day of the festival in a florescent yellow tabard doing semaphore in the car park. I missed the dipping of the Upley Maiden down the well because I was trying to diffuse tempers after a minor collision, but with the weather so dry this year the water levels were really low and several people, including the maiden's mother, fainted in the heat waiting for her to be hauled up from the depths.

**Humping activities**

The other highlight of our year was the Paradise View Speed Hump Campaign. Every house in our road got sent a letter asking us to tick a box agreeing to humps being installed, in line with the council's new traffic calming policy. You would have thought we had been asked to consent to having our legs cut off. Indignation in the suburbs is a sight to behold: people who we didn't know existed emerged from their houses and actually started talking to each other, openly, in the street.

The upshot was a residents' meeting, which we held at our house. It was packed out; I think a lot of the neighbours came out of curiosity to see behind the privet wall, especially after the grisly anniversary revelations in The Upley Herald last year. It's amazing what common ground you can find over a couple of glasses of red wine. People with political views further apart than Arthur Scargill and the BNP found themselves agreeing with each other that the humps were a Bad Idea: bad for yuppie types with posh cars who were worried about parking them half on a hump; bad for old folk setting off in an ambulance after a heart attack; and bad for those without posh cars, like me cycling in a rush with Daniel clinging on behind. And everyone agreed they were bad for property prices.

So the No Humping in Paradise campaign was born. And eight letters, two petitions, one front-page piece in The Upley Herald ('Sleeping Policemen in Murder Road?') and three modest demonstrations outside the council offices later, hooray for democracy, the council has retreated. Paradise View remains hump free.

## Adding to the Family

For the year ahead Ant is starting to talk about (1) applying for promotion to Field Sales Assistant Manager and (2) planning a family trip to Chile, an idea he's always resisted, but I think would be good for him. Learning Spanish is back at the top of my new year's resolutions – or second from top after Start Running Again.

We've bought the children a hamster for Christmas. I am picking it up in secret from the pet shop, and Ant has designed and built it a cage with a run inspired by a combination of Thorpe Park's Thunder River ride and Mousetrap. Christmas morning should be a right laugh.

Festive greetings to you all,

*Alison and Antonio, Eleanor, Felipe and Daniel*

*\*Quentin Crisp: 'There is no need to do any housework at all. After the first four years the dirt doesn't get any worse.'*

## Christmas 1996

**15 Paradise View**
**Upley Rising**
**Thameshire**

## Greetings, Humans!

This Christmas letter is brought to you by the newest member of the family. I moved in here almost a year ago, and I can tell you it's been a real insight into how you lot live. So much noise and so much rushing around for so little end result. These people seem to spend most of their time either yelling at each other then hugging me (I wish they wouldn't) or yelling my name then hugging each other.

I wouldn't call myself a gossip, but having spent the past six months living under the floorboards of 15 Paradise View I hear everything this family gets up to, and you wouldn't believe the half of it.

Alison is in a much better mood since she went back to work. She's got a job at something called the College of Further Education. She wasn't sure about accepting it at first. Working with a mixture of sixth formers and adults who are belatedly trying to catch up on schooldays misspent flicking elastic bands round the classroom has never been her thing. But to her surprise she really likes the job, and realises that in the past she was a bit of an academic snob. She won't admit it to the rest of the family, but I heard her telling her mum on the phone that the sixth formers seem much more focused that the university students she used to work with, who if they weren't dozing at their desks, expected her to run around bringing them books and even coffee as if she was some kind of servant. Not that she's dissing servants, who should be getting a decent living wage at the very least. And the evening class adults have proper manners. They say please and thank you, they show proper respect for her expertise and they even sometimes bring books back on time. What's more, the college has something called a positive working culture; she really feels she can shape its future, though I'm not sure why that matters.

Antonio on the other hand is much happier being at home again. He can get back to constructing strange objects, which judging by the cage he made me is really where his heart is.

Everyone was really upset when Ant lost his job. Actually that's a whopping understatement: it was more like the start of World War Three. This was when the shouting really took off – according to Ali, the bank manager was threatening to come round in person and chuck them out of their cursed house with all their pathetic possessions on view to the rest of the road, they should never have come to this stuck-up suburb, and she was seriously considering taking the children and moving in with her sister Gill in Yorkshire, where folk just got on with life instead of whinging. Ant was beyond useless, he couldn't even hold a basic sales job down at the age of 36, he was never going to be Damien Hirst and he needed to stop dreaming and care as much about his family as about his so-called art. There was a lot of crying, Felipe was clinging onto Antonio wailing that he didn't want to leave Daddy behind, and Eleanor was sobbing that NO WAY was she EVER going to share a bedroom with Cousin Shrub.

Everyone was so distracted that they left my cage open and, not being one for bad atmospheres, I slipped through a crack in the skirting boards and made a new home between the two floors. Being naturally nocturnal and solitary, I like it down here in the dark. There's loads of space, I get water from the place where there's a leaky pipe (which they really need to do something about), and it's amazing what you can find to eat. Crisps, furry old wine gums, you name it. I call the section under Eleanor and Felipe's bedroom my kitchen. I can sit munching and listen to the twins chatting. They both missed me at first and I was just starting to feel guilty but then I heard Eleanor saying to Felipe that at least they didn't have to clean out my cage anymore. Felipe says he's being bullied at school but he won't tell his parents and he's sworn Eleanor to secrecy, though I think she might have said something. I like it when Ant comes in and reads the Biff and Chip books with them snuggled up either side of him. Or Beef and Cheeps as he says, which makes them both laugh.

If I get bored I like to scrabble around under Daniel's room and scare him; he wakes up shouting something about a murderer, I don't know why as I'm completely harmless.

One of the big problems when Ant lost his job was giving back the company car. But when Alison got her new job they bought something called an estate, which I always thought meant a big place in the country. Alison's dad insists on calling it a station wagon. It's their new car but it's also very old which is confusing. They all went on holiday in it to somewhere called Dorset and I had a very peaceful couple of weeks.

That's about all the interesting stuff. Alison is working overtime today to earn some extra cash for Christmas. I hope they don't buy another hamster. Ant is in the studio at the bottom of the garden, and has left the children alone in the house. They've been playing the Macarena at full volume for hours, they're practising some sort of routine with the children from the house next door, who seem a bit up themselves but are fine when they come over here to play. The thumping is unbelievable, I'm a bit worried that they'll come crashing through the floorboards. But Antonio is completely oblivious; he's working really hard on some top-secret project as he really wants to prove Alison wrong about his art. So I'm going to have to listen to the Macarena all over again. And again.

Hope you all have a very happy Christmas,

Humpfree the Hamster

*On behalf of Alison and Antonio, Eleanor, Felipe and Daniel*

\* \* \* \* \*

## 14 Paradise View, Upley Rising, Thameshire

## Christmas 1997

There is normal life and there is life according to the newspapers. This year the two converged: 1997 was agreed by all to be momentous, heartbreaking, gamechanging. We lost a people's princess; gave up British Hong Kong; learned that a sheep had been cloned. Some say we came perilously close to losing our monarchy. The national net curtains were drawn back, to reveal extraordinary public outpourings of joy and grief. In August people wept as they laid wreaths on the same streets where in May they had cheered the youngest prime minister in living memory.

It is somehow reassuring that here in Upley Rising national events never threaten to eclipse routine. Everyday business has rumbled on, at present with seasonal overtones.

The High Street is festooned with illuminated angels swooping from shop to shop and the postman is cheerier and more communicative than usual, in unsubtle anticipation of a Christmas gratuity. As I picked the milk up off the doorstep this morning the family who live opposite were off to the school nativity assembly, cramming their numerous children all dressed as what looked like withered birch trees into their estate car with much snapping of frosted twigs and tempers. Meanwhile their own neighbour was readjusting the rather ostentatious Christmas wreath adorning her glossy front door. Momentous is not a word often heard in these parts. That being said, there have been unpleasant tensions in our road that have disrupted much of the year.

For the moment, these seem to have died down in a tacit Christmas truce; all is quiet on the Paradise View front.

In my own annual review I feel content with the year's modest advances. Coburn Briggs has been doing well and the partners decided to take the adventurous step of appointing a practice manager. Her role is apparently to 'free us all up' to concentrate on our real work by introducing greater efficiencies. So far her most high-profile contribution has been the introduction of something called Dress Down Friday. I do my best to fall into line by putting on one of my less formal ties, though every week brings a fresh surprise from the wardrobes of my more daring colleagues. The wording on a T-shirt can tell you a great deal about the wearer's habits. Fortunately we do not have many client appointments on Fridays.

At the model railway society, where wearing a proper tie is a given at every meeting, we have held two public open days which were both well attended. The dangers of subsidence became a stark reality at the first, with insufficient securing of a mossy embankment resulting in the Caledonian Sleeper plunging down a spontaneous sinkhole in front of 30 paying visitors. The second was a Thomas the Tank Engine and Friends day, which some of our membership felt was inappropriate for a serious model railway club, but were outvoted by those in favour of marking the passing in March of the Rev. W. Awdry.

Colin enjoyed both events enormously. My mother did not come with us. She has continued to withdraw into her own world, in fact she has not spoken at all since the election of Mr Blair. We now have a stable home help situation, replacing the triumvirate of minders which was proving precarious, in particular when I was obliged to spend a couple of days in hospital having further facial surgery following last year's accident. Mrs Hill arrives at 8.15am without fail, is not given to spending unnecessary time chatting, and apart from one tricky incident when she put Colin's tin soldier collection back in the wrong order after dusting, she has settled in well and pretty much taken charge of the house when I am not there. She has offered to cook us all Christmas dinner this year, and I will probably accept; she lives alone so the benefit will be mutual.

So let us look forward to 1998 with the renewed feeling of optimism that is pervading the rest of the country, and may I wish you all a very happy Christmas.

**Robert**

\* \* \* \* \*

## Christmas 1997

**15 Paradise View**
**Upley Rising**
**Thameshire**

## Dear Friends

Christmas again already. Choral muzak in the supermarket, snow in tins, chocolate at rip-off prices. And the annual newsletter. Be warned: our 1997 review is not for anyone with a weak stomach. It includes a family holiday tragedy, a bloodsucking insect invasion, a dental extortion scandal – and the mysterious case of the missing Berlin Wall.

## The children and other animals

This family has reached a significant milestone. After seven long years of being on emergency call 24 hours a day, seven days a week, a chink of light glimmered at the end of the tunnel. Since Easter, all three children have been at school full time. At last! Five and a half precious hours in the middle of the day for the parent at home. A chance to earn some much-needed extra cash, to train for a marathon, or produce a creative masterpiece. So how did Ant and I make the most of this long-awaited moment? We got a dog.

**Hector** is part Old English sheepdog (huge), part terrier (loves running off), with a dash of poodle (matted coat). He was leading a miserable life at the Thameshire animal rescue centre, and now he's ruling our lives. Hector needs food by the bucketload and round the clock attention. He has issues in his past that make him prone to bad moods and depression. The only therapy for his darker moments is to take him for a very long walk in all weathers. He's supposed to be housetrained but has regular memory lapses. We nearly took him back after week one, but the children lined up at the front door in their coats and scarves with their sleepover wheelie cases and threatened to leave home with him. So we caved in and Hector is here to stay.

**Eleanor**: We laughed out loud when Eleanor's end of term report said she was top of her class in maths. How could two arts graduates have produced this prodigy? But the joke was on us when she lost three baby teeth in a month and decided to charge the tooth fairy double for molars and to add interest for forgetting. She also checked with friends and found that the starting rate per tooth has gone up to £2 which she wanted backdated, for both her and Felipe who has also been carelessly losing teeth. Result: cancellation of my birthday meal out to pay for the backlog.

**Felipe** has always had a soft spot for animals. This is just as well as he has spent most of the year hosting a colony of headlice. His dark curls turn out to be the perfect home environment for the discerning female louse: warm, sheltered and with good transport links to other nearby children. Combing his hair was not an option unless we wanted a nightly visit from the police to investigate the screams. So now I coat his locks in mayonnaise, which doesn't smell as bad or cost as much as the chemical shampoos. This seems to work when Hector doesn't lick it all off.

**Daniel**: The baby of the family is now a full-time pupil at Upley Rising Primary. He turned five on August 31st but we had to keep a lid on any noise or evidence of fun at his party. The whole street was in shocked mourning for Princess Diana. Pumping out music in the back garden felt weird, as did supervising his birthday water pistol competition. The road was deserted as everyone was inside glued to the TV – though someone crept out and anonymously took down the balloons from our front gate. Daniel's been very quiet since he started Year 1. We think he's enjoying it but he prefers to tell his Teletubby collection about his day than to share it with us. Eh-Oh.

### The parents

In our house, Ant and I pride ourselves on working

together. That's what responsible parents do. We share information: say, about a child coming out in a rash, or another letter from the bank about our overdraft. We make big decisions jointly – like agreeing to plough a year's savings into a proper family holiday abroad.

No worries then – until a cream envelope dropped onto the mat earlier this year. Antonio rushed to pick it up, disappeared upstairs, then reappeared after a muffled shout with the announcement that the Royal Academy had shortlisted his entry for their Summer Exhibition. He had 'forgotten' to mention submitting his latest masterpiece, and I had just emptied our bank account to pay for a whole sun-drenched month's beach holiday in Greece. Our first real summer getaway in years. We decided not to panic – after all, two tons of chunks of Berlin Wall remodelled with broken glass, varnished cigarette ends and embedded army boots would never make it through to the final selection, would it? Wrong. I forgave him as we were still celebrating the general election result. With Labour in power nothing could spoil my mood. The long awaited four-week holiday had to be swapped for ten days (five of them stormy) in late August – how could we leave the country while his masterwork was on public view in the heart of Piccadilly?

I managed to get some of the holiday money back. Most of it went on cheeseburgers and chips to keep the children happy on our daily trips into London to check if there was a tiny red 'sold' dot on his sculpture, The Wall Speaks.

The other parent has also had her brief moment in the spotlight this year. This letter is brought to you by a genuine Acting Head of Department! I reached this dizzying pinnacle because the real Head, my boss, is on extended sick leave with a stress condition. I have come to realise that the title Acting is because I spend most of the working day looking as if I know what to do. I have learned to fix my staff with a blistering stare over the top of my glasses, and to hold a spreadsheet the right way up in meetings. For the time being I'm trying not to let the power go to my head.

## Artistic merit

Antonio is milking his moment of artistic glory by standing for chair of the school Parent Teachers Association. The Head is over the moon at the idea of a celebrity (or at least a well-known artist) running the PTA. He also landed a commission from the posh tennis club down the road, who had heard about his Royal Academy entry though clearly no one had seen it. We've never been inside the club but judging by the look of the outside they think he's going to produce a dainty oil painting. They are in for a shock. But it's helped to make up for The Wall Speaks not quite selling.

## Local life

Troubleshooting has been my new weekend activity this year. Our neighbours have spent the best part of 1997 building an extension that must be visible from outer space. It's bigger than their house, with more glass than a pub on New Year's Eve. No one knows how they got planning permission. On a good day the noise and lorries queuing down our road made the M25 look like a country lane. I ended up leading a delegation to ask them to be more considerate. They are a bit of a power couple and looked completely blank when we used words like 'understanding', 'compromise', or 'not before 8am on

Saturdays'.

The final straw was when The Wall Speaks was returned at the end of the Summer Exhibition. It was deposited outside our house while I was at work and Ant was out walking Hector. The builders came back from lunch, took a look under the tarpaulin, saw part of a wall, so – using builders' logic – got on and cemented it into the extension. When we demanded it back, our neighbours refused point blank and even had the barefaced cheek to offer to buy it for a fraction of the listed price. We've tried everything, including a whole family visit spearheaded by Hector dripping mud all over their white carpet. But so far they won't budge. Ant is incandescent with rage. We are considering all our options – legal or otherwise. Watch this space.

## Christmas

Back to seasonal goodwill. Eleanor, Felipe and Daniel are appearing collectively as the Enchanted Forest in this year's school Christmas play. I will give my staff an unexpected half day off before we close for Christmas. Ant and I will look at holiday brochures together for next year, which – somehow – we will make peaceful and uneventful.

Festive Greetings to you all,

*Alison, Antonio, Eleanor, Felipe and Daniel,*
*and Hector*

* * * * *

## December 1997

*Paradise House, Paradise View*
*Upley Rising, Thameshire*

### Paradise House Christmas News

## Dear Everyone,

Can life get any better? I'm delighted to announce another outstandingly successful year for the Wright family.

Starting with me, I have devoted 1997 to my thrilling new business start-up. Back in January, mapping out revenue projections in my walnut-panelled home office while the nanny collected the children from horse riding and fencing, I must admit to the tiniest flicker of self-doubt. Chewing on my Mont Blanc pen, I asked myself how I was going to meet this daunting new challenge. But defeat is not in my vocabulary and I can report that my new venture is exceeding all expectations. It's an idea I came across in California and brought back to Upley Rising, recognising its potential here.

Running a luxury lifestyle franchise is not for the faint hearted. Being a mother, a wife and a blossoming entrepreneur is a constant juggling act. How do I fit it all in? My secret is discipline: I rigorously fit in two tennis lessons every week at the exclusive South Thameshire Lawn Tennis Club, and I never miss a manicure, as image is vital at all times.

Following the tragic and untimely death of Lady Diana Princess of Wales, which so devastated us all, I did fear there would be fewer customers at my invitation-only Autumn Preview Event. But how wrong I was: the

Event was oversubscribed, and I had to bring in rows of extra chairs as people came together and channelled their grief into LavishCoast She ('The brand that lavishes lashings of luxury into your life'). Our autumn sales were the highest of the year. I was humbled to be named the corporation's tier two British franchisee of the month twice this year (April and September) and I am well on the way to reaching tier three – Pearl Level – which will give me priority booking for next year's LavishCoast She International Convention in Chicago.

Of course no year is without its low points, as Charles experienced at work.

Expectations at his agency are high, the pressure is unrelenting and the burnout rate can be cruel for anyone without the stamina. Everyone was devastated when one of the senior managers jumped off the roof, having just missed his half-year targets. But Charles's quick thinking in the face of tragedy was recognised: he applied for the unexpected vacancy the same day, and was duly promoted to Head of Client Optimisation (Western Hemisphere). The job comes with the previous holder's top-floor corner office, where Charles has tactfully screened the opening to the balcony with exotic plants, and leased some soothing paintings for the walls to smooth over awkward memories.

Despite the demands of both our important jobs, our wonderful children always come first.

Maximilian simply loves school. His main asset, according to his end of term report, is self-confidence. He was elected Form Captain, in a unanimous vote. Afterwards he told us that he managed this by promising all his classmates positions as deputies and monitors if they voted for him, which is impressively Machiavellian. Mother wants us to put his name down for Eton as she thinks he may have a future in politics.

Our son also gave his first public performance this year, at the annual school concert attended by the Deputy Mayor of Upley Rising and other VIPs. He is the school orchestra's only tuba player; we encouraged him to take it up, knowing that most of the other parents couldn't afford an instrument in the same price bracket. His concert solo received rapturous applause, completely drowning out the last three minutes.

Clementine started Year 1 full time this year, but I am not quite an empty nester yet! I have to be available to help her fit her schoolwork around her modelling schedule. Charles jokes that her resemblance to my side of the family is the only reasonable explanation for her being on the books of not just one but four agencies. People think that getting picked out to be a child model must mean endless rounds of freebies and fun, and it's true that Clementine looks blissfully happy in those soft-focus catalogue shots, running carefree through a meadow in a floral frock and branded trainers. But as her manager I can confirm that it's hard work for both of us, crisscrossing the West End traffic by taxi and sipping fruit juice in endless stuffy studio waiting rooms.

Clementine hasn't really missed out on schoolwork; Year 1 is only looking at pictures and playing in the sandpit. And all her hard work and model training has stood her in good stead; we were thrilled, though hardly surprised, when she was selected to play the lead role of Mary in the school nativity play.

Between Charles's international trips, Clementine's assignments, Max's first team mini-cricket matches and my work and tennis schedules, we just about managed to fit in a Mark Warner skiing trip at half term, a half-term break at Longleat Center Parcs in October, a romantic weekend in Venice to celebrate Charles's 40th birthday, and three weeks in a villa just outside Cannes over the summer. So it's no wonder that when it came to our contribution to the school Harvest for the Homeless assembly the most practical item I had in the cupboard was a tin of *confit de canard*. I only hope that the lucky recipient knew how to serve it properly – it's nothing without a lightly chilled glass of Bordeaux.

At home, we have spent much of the year adding a beautiful extension to our house. It has caused quite a stir among our neighbours. Designed by an award-winning architect, as an extra inspired touch it features a unique wall artwork created by a well-known local artist.

The builders finished it just in time for our 10th wedding anniversary in October. We had considered holding a celebration at the prestigious South Thameshire Tennis Club where we have paid the equivalent of some people's salaries to become members, but then we thought, when you have your own 200 square feet of newly created contemporary orangerie attached to your home, fitted with a brand-new Tuscan marble kitchen and a six speaker surround sound home entertainment system, why look elsewhere?

We will be pushing the boat out for Christmas this year. Mother is joining us with her new friend Rupert, and Charles's rock star brother Ditch is flying over from Los Angeles to Cool Britannia as he calls it, and will bring Charles's parents and that side of the family for the day. Mother thinks Ditch is expecting to be recognised in Mr Blair's New Year's honours list, but Charles says it's far too soon and anyway a knighthood at this stage of his career would damage his public image. There should be some interesting conversations over the lobster-stuffed goose breast, though we will have to steer people away from politics. Ditch is bringing his own chauffeur which is a mixed blessing; no one will have to worry about drinking, but I will have to make sure Rupert and Charles's father sit at opposite ends of the table.

Christmas will be rewarding but hard work; I have persuaded the nanny to help with the messier side of the cooking, and after she has done all the clearing up I will give her a delicious leftovers package to enjoy.

We are looking forward to 1998 – and this time next year I expect to be writing to you as a LavishCoast She Pearl Level Vice-Principal!

Wishing you all a very Happy Christmas,

*Caroline, Charles, Maximilian and Clementine Wright*

# PART FIVE 1998-1999:

# ROBERT, CAROLINE, ALI

## 14 Paradise View, Upley Rising, Thameshire

### Christmas 1998

An elegant silver-framed photograph sits on the desk in front of me as I write this year's Christmas bulletin. A gift from the Upley Society Committee, it shows my mother, dressed in her smartest suit and pearls, her hair 'done' and her face lit up with an animated smile. Taken in May, she is standing in front of the memorial plaque to my father, which is firmly affixed to the wall of the historic Market Hall building. She is flanked by the Mayoress and the Upley Society Chairman, to whom she has just presented my father's collection of leatherbound minute books filled with his meticulous cursive hand, and his inscribed inkwell.

We are all grateful that she lived long enough to enjoy this small commemoration which meant so much to her. It was one of her last properly lucid days, though her death just a few weeks later was hardly expected quite so soon. She had not driven for months, and although her licence had not been withdrawn, none of us expected her to use her car again. The car keys remained at the back of the kitchen drawer, overlooked by everyone except for my mother herself, who for reasons we will never fully know, put on her raincoat and hat while Mrs Hill our carer was upstairs helping Colin with a challenging jigsaw (an aerial view of Stonehenge), stepped outside holding her handbag and the car keys, then got into her Austin 1100. According to witnesses she emerged from the drive looking both ways with her usual caution, then accelerated to some 65 miles per hour down Paradise View, pitched round the corner without stopping and plunged straight into the churchyard boundary wall. Her driving skills dated from an era when seat belts were an optional accessory, and death was mercifully instantaneous. She was 78 and, apart from that last day, lived a peaceful, mostly happy and thoroughly decent life.

Born in a different age she might well have become a successful professional with the same efficient focus I observe in some of the female staff at work. Instead she chose – if it was a choice – to dedicate herself to my father, and to her sons. Her own memorial plaque is our tranquil home and our lovely garden.

She is buried in the churchyard close to the wall which she destroyed, alongside my father. A small group of relatives convened for the funeral. Her only sister, my Aunt Celia, sent an apology from Toronto (she had pre-booked a trip to New Zealand) and a kaleidoscopic floral tribute commingling gladioli, orchids and carnations. Following the burial, we held a small reception at our home. In the dining room, my mother's Women's Institute friends formed an impenetrable circle round me, ensuring I was plied with fish paste sandwiches and sympathy. As I made conversation, my peripheral vision registered distant cousins drifting round the house as if they were whiling away a spare afternoon in an antiques shop, picking up and turning over the various pieces that my mother had enjoyed collecting.

Colin misses our mother with passion and without comprehension. He vented his grief at the funeral with outraged sobs that matched the organ in volume, and in the weeks afterwards he kept wandering round the garden looking for her. As soon as I could take some time away from the office I organised a very special trip for the two of us.

One of the diminishing perks of being a founder Channel Tunnel shareholder is its generous travel entitlement. This year it was put to good use. Colin and I arrived at Waterloo with plenty of time to spare. We began by climbing to the station's upper level from where, godlike, you can supervise the arrivals and departures on at least 12 platforms simultaneously. Colin could have spent an entire, blissful day watching the incoming Surbiton service on platform five passing the Portsmouth train pulling out. But these delights were quickly forgotten once we made our way down to the dedicated Eurostar departure terminal. Here, travel wallets at the ready, we spurned the offer of complimentary tea and biscuits in the First Class lounge in order to claim prime position to watch the sleek class 373 trainset, fronted by its distinctive yellow and grey engine, nosing into the buffers with consummate grace. Colin used an entire roll of film before we had even boarded.

The journey through the Kent countryside was rainy and punctuated by the odd unexplained stop but Colin remained ahead of schedule, eating all his sandwiches by the time blackness descended as we entered the tunnel itself. Gazing at his reflection in the dark windows he demanded to know where the Tunnel was: it was impossible for him to comprehend how, viewed from the inside, it appeared invisible, bearing no resemblance to the moss-covered mounds on our home layouts. The weather in Paris was glorious, and rather than risking the Louvre we enjoyed walking through the Tuileries and along the Rive Gauche, where I purchased a vintage duotone print of the Parc de Versailles. Dinner in a brasserie was followed by a night in a small *pension* off the Champs Elysées. The following morning we took several Metro trips, then made a windswept ascent up the Eiffel Tower, sent a postcard to Colin's Wednesday Group, and bought Mrs Hill some fancy pastries near the Galeries Lafayette before returning to the Gare du Nord for the return journey home, on which the guard was pleased to give Colin his autograph.

When we got home, Mrs Hill had embarked on a bout of belated spring cleaning, including an exhaustive clear-out of my mother's bedroom. The large mahogany dressing table with its winged mirrors stood shockingly bare, like a gothic Kim's game setting. My memory kept shouting 'lipstick!', 'pearls!' or 'cut crystal perfume bottle!' but when I opened my eyes none of them had reappeared. Mrs Hill had been unsuccessful in her attempts to remove the ingrained marks on the dressing table's glass top, which was left with fossil-like imprints of the sterling silver hairbrush set that had been a permanent fixture.

Mrs Hill had set out the contents of the wardrobe and cupboards on the carpet in a row in neat black dustbin bags labelled 'Second Best Charity Shop', 'Church Bazaar', 'Not Worth Keeping', and other unequivocal designations. She then gave me two weeks' notice, which I had not expected. I concluded that she must prefer to have female company around. Since September we have reverted to peripatetic care staff, now supplied by an agency on contract to the council's adult social services department – an arrangement requiring me to bone up on what is known at work as 'crisis management skills'. These energetic women who ensure that Colin is fed, entertained and kept safe, regularly have their own personal emergencies: a child with suspected meningitis, a dog with prostate problems, a boyfriend unexpectedly detained by the police. Situations that involve me rushing back from Coburn Briggs, my briefcase bulging with files, and an afternoon in front of a video for Colin. The other partners have been extremely supportive. At the behest of the practice manager the firm is undertaking a programme called Investors in People and I suspect I am being invested in, with the aim of the firm earning some sort of gold star.

In view of the disruption to the year I took an informal sabbatical from the Montague Ensemble. Handling the probate for my mother's estate required more time and mental capacity than it did for my father, and I had to deal with a series of bold requests from the aforementioned cousins for family 'mementos' – all of considerable value – which my parents had allegedly pledged (though never in writing) would be passed on to them.

I am not sure what arrangements we will make for the holidays. We have received several invitations to Christmas lunch but I may opt for a quiet day at home as the past year has been quite exhausting and Colin's behaviour can be unpredictable.

With Christmas Wishes,

**Robert**

\* \* \* \* \*

## December 1998

*Paradise House, Paradise View*
*Upley Rising, Thameshire*

*Paradise House Christmas News*

## Dear Everyone,

This year I thought you would enjoy a glimpse into our cuttings album for 1998: these snippets of joy say it all far better than I can!

From the front page of the LavishUs Corporation's Global World Review 1998

LavishCoast She's Carolyn wins Top Award

> *No wonder they are all smiles: LavishCoast She representatives are in the money, as they celebrate another record-breaking year. Once again LavishUs has notched up bumper profits, all down to every hard-working affiliate. Pictured left is Pearl Level member Carolyn Wright, receiving this year's Lavish Leading Light Award (UK) from Senior Vice President Jean-Pierre M. Baluchini, at our Aspiring Executives Conference in London, England. Thanking Jean-Pierre for this singular honour, Ms Wright enthralled a rapt audience as she described her own personal LavishCoast She journey.*
> *Recounting how she was inspired to turn her back on life at the top of the ladder as a Chief Executive in order to become a LavishCoast She UK founder member,*

*Carolyn drew applause from the 500 strong audience of would-be franchisees. She described the challenges she had to overcome as a working mother, whose husband was often absent, struggling to make sure her children were fed and clothed. Fighting back the tears she told how she'd worked tirelessly, staying out night after night to attend social events with networking potential, to generate new sales leads for the world's fastest growing luxury brand.*

*Loving your legendary story, Carolyn! Here's to your continuing success with the LavishUs Corporation.*

## From The Upley Herald, June 30th 1998

*Mr Charles Wright, father of Maximilian (Year 4) and Clementine (Year 2) has been elected Chair of the Parent Teachers Association of Upley Primary School, rated Outstanding by Ofsted. The election, which is usually a formality, had attracted attention this year as it was the first in the school's history to be contested. The other candidate was artist Antonio García Cortinez, the front runner who had been widely expected to win and who by a quirky coincidence happens to be Mr Wright's next-door neighbour. A senior executive with PR and advertising agency Strong Barker, Charles Wright commented that he was sure that Mr Cortinez's election chances had been unaffected by revelations in this newspaper, shortly before the election, about the controversial Chilean's past. The Herald exclusive disclosed how the modernist artist and sculptor had previously been sacked from a teaching post at East Thameshire Senior High School following a scandal in which he allegedly encouraged pupils to produce pornographic artworks.*

*One of the High School's parent governors, who asked not to be named, said, "I thought my daughter was learning pottery with Mr Cortinez. Until she brought home an utterly obscene object from the school kiln. I don't know how he found people to model for it – or how they got into those positions – but they should all have been prosecuted. Seeing my daughter pick it up by the handle made me feel sick, and it was just as well my husband accidentally broke it."*

*"It's a real honour to have been elected head of this prestigious PTA," said Mr Wright, adding, "My experience on the award-winning campaigns for Hoarse Throat Lager and Bound, the dog biscuits you'd have to be barking not to buy your dog, should come in really handy for parents and kids at the school." And as the brother of Ditch Wright, the well-known pop musician, Mr Wright modestly admitted that the musical gene in the family had bypassed him completely in favour of his son Max, who is the talented lead tuba player with the school orchestra. Though he also quipped that he might just have one or two contacts who could liven up the school's Year 6 disco.*

From Grazia magazine, July edition:

### *Has Ditch ditched his girlfriend?*

*Snake-hipped rock idol Ditch Wright is caught on camera leaving Chelsea's select Hurlingham Club last night. The East London born musician, who spends most of his time in Los Angeles these days, was making a rare trip home to play at a private event being held by the LavishUs Corporation, the company behind the glossy American must-have brand which has been attracting*

*attention this side of the Atlantic. A spokesman said: "We were proud to have one of Great Britain's foremost music stars accept our invitation to play exclusively at our Aspiring Executives Conference. Ditch Wright embodies the ethos that makes LavishCoast She products so sought after: glitzy, irresistible, expensive."*
*Singer and guitarist Ditch is rumoured to be in six-figure-sum talks to front a line-up of male talent promoting a new LavishCoast He product range for LavishUs. Someone on his team certainly knows how to pull the strings. The sexy star left the Hurlingham Club by limousine with his arm round a petite unnamed blonde woman in a strappy black dress. Ditch, in trademark sunglasses and leather jacket, refused to comment on rumours that his engagement to Californian model Helena has been called off, though the glamourous couple have not been seen together in public for some time.*

From the South Thameshire Lawn Tennis Club Autumn Newsletter

*Mrs Caroline Wright has been appointed to chair the Club's newly created Improvements Committee. This has been set up following suggestions coordinated by Mrs Wright to provide necessary cosmetic uplifts as we approach the new millennium. We are grateful to Mrs Wright, who has recently joined the Club, for taking on this important task.*

And finally ...

Not to be left out of this star line-up, Clementine

insisted on designing the family Christmas card this year, and we hope you will enjoy her charmingly innocent painting of the three wise men demanding an upgrade on their room at the Inn. The story doesn't end there: her teacher entered Clem's artwork for Upley Rising's Rotary Club's Cards for Good Causes competition, where it touched the hearts of the judges enough to win first prize. Not bad for a busy schoolgirl who already has a second career as a model!

Wishing you all a very Happy Christmas,

*Caroline, Charles, Maximilian and Clementine Wright*

* * * * *

## Christmas 1998

**15 Paradise View**
**Upley Rising**
**Thameshire**

Dear Friends

Hoping you've all had a good year. Ours began with a veneer of normality.

Eleanor and Felipe played to their strengths at school. Eleanor was the last person in her class to be allowed to switch from pencil to a real pen for the manic cardiogram squiggles she calls her handwriting. We celebrated by buying her a proper fountain pen, which disappeared then had to be fished out of Hector's stomach by the vet for the cost of at least 50 fountain pens. Felipe has been both fruit monitor and book bag monitor. Daniel rode his bike without stabilizers, all the way down the hill and into the river. At home I heard the twins speaking Latin to each other – take that, rip-off local private schools, I thought – but they were practising spells from the Harry Potter boy wizard books, which they both spend every minute reading instead of doing homework.

I made it my mission to lead by example and show them how honest hard graft gets you to the top. I spent three weekends putting together my application for the job of Head Librarian at South Thameshire College of Further Education. By the day of the interview I was a shoe-in for the job. I'd spent nearly nine months as Acting Head, ruling fairly and compassionately. My new Social Awareness scheme abolishing late book fines for students on benefits was a runaway success – literally – as was the free staff coffee club I set up. I offset my popularity by introducing computer systems that only I understand, on the principle that Information is Power. I arrived at the interview armed with an impeccable CV and hours of interview practice in front of the mirror at home. I smiled nicely at everyone on the panel, sat down and remembered to cross my legs but not as in the infamous film scene.

No surprise then that the governors gave the job to some foetus with a snooty accent, wearing a suit and tie (a novelty in our college). Showing they have a sense of humour, as a sop I've been asked to lead an 'Investors in People' programme. Maybe I'll learn how to invest in myself for once.

At least my skills are valued closer to home. This summer I was initiated into the Inner Circle that runs the annual Wellspring Festival. No more car park stewarding or checking the portaloos for me! I was promoted to Lost Children Coordinator – a role for which I am clearly seen as well qualified. I got to spend the festival sitting in a gazebo dishing out biscuits and mopping up orange squash and vomit, while others were enjoying the festival knocking back the Wellspring Special Brew. At least I had a captive audience while I entertained a succession of crying children with my guitar playing.

Ant's art commission for our swanky tennis club was a big hit. Which is exactly what it was called, being a giant knobbly arm wielding a stained-glass racquet. It's been given pride of place in the club's pavilion, with a plaque under it describing Ant as 'the distinguished Royal Academician' (not entirely true but we're not arguing). There was an unveiling ceremony, which I went along to despite my opinions about élite sports clubs, as I was curious to see inside its hallowed walls. To their credit, the statue inauguration committee did it all properly, serving canapés and real champagne, with a speech from the club's secretary followed by a ripple of applause for Ant. For a group of middle Englanders who looked like they'd find a Rodin bronze on the daring side, that's praise indeed. Ant looked the real deal in his black suit with a black shirt and red tie. He held court, an uneaten mushroom vol-au-vent in one hand, while club veterans who had once almost made it to the Wimbledon qualifiers, and were still flushed with vicarious elation after Tim Henman's semi-finals victory, asked him if he would recommend Chile as a holiday destination.

So all things considered it's been a normal-ish year – apart from being stuck with our nightmare neighbours. Not the kind beloved of TV programmes who have open air sex on the lawn or knock through bathroom walls in the middle of the night. It's much more insidious than that. First there was the Berlin Wall Heist, their shameless appropriation of Ant's Summer Exhibition piece. As I write it's still helplessly embedded in their extension: a monstrosity that sits curled round their house like a giant glass python, glinting in a post-prandial doze while it slowly digests Ant's artwork. The GDR army boots which were so integral to The Wall Speaks as a symbol of the horror of partition are being used as planters for bright red geraniums, staring us in the face every time I do some weeding or Ant goes down to the studio. We reported the incident to the police: they took lots of notes then referred us to a dispute mediation service.

Then there's their son who practises scales on the tuba at six in the morning and puts live spiders in Felipe's lunchbox at school, even though they play together at weekends. The wife is always rushing off somewhere, never knows who I am and once mistook me for her garden company, waving vaguely at some daffodils dying back and asking me to get them sorted as she got into her car.

The husband was the one exception, or so we thought. He's hardly ever there, we only glimpse him getting taxis to and from the airport, but he seemed nice enough. Until he sprang a bolt from the blue by coming from nowhere to get elected Chair of the school PTA when Antonio had virtually been promised the role and had already started on a programme of events for the year. No one could believe it; Ant was far and away the most popular candidate. Some nasty, distorted stories about Ant's past started circulating shortly before the election and despite letters of support from other parents and some of the governors, the Head said he couldn't change the democratic process, even though it stank of corruption.

We couldn't work out what they've got against us. Is it possible to be anti-Chilean? Could they be jealous? Of our 18-year-old car, our rainy cottage holidays, our kitchen so retro that it wouldn't even qualify as kitsch? We even started thinking about moving again, but we are stuck with the small problem of who out there would want to buy an authentic serial killer's lair.

### Deliverance!

Deliverance arrived – in the unlikely form of my sister Gill's daughter Cousin Shrub (aka Saffron), who stayed with us over the summer holidays because she's 14, 'challenging', and she and Gill are in danger of murdering each other on a daily basis. Things must have been bad as she agreed to share a bedroom with six-year-old Daniel; in fact they have a fair bit in common, both spending hours in complete silence cross-legged on their beds playing on their Gameboys.

I put up with Cousin Shrub's moodiness, late-night TV addiction, refusal to go outside, and sleeping in until midday. Thousands wouldn't, but then I know what it's like to be a teenager in a remote Yorkshire village. So you could have knocked me over with the proverbial feather when I was making tea at 7.30am one Saturday morning, looked out the window and saw what I thought was Swampy up a tree in our back garden. Seeing me gawping, Cousin Shrub climbed down and rushed into the kitchen emitting a squeaky stream of consciousness gabble, more words than she'd ever come out with in one go before.

I sat her down and managed to get her to put the words in the right order. She'd been looking out of the window at 2am (don't ask) when she'd seen a massive dark limo pull up outside the house next door. Who should emerge, with his arm draped around Caroline our snooty neighbour, but Ditch Wright. That's THE Ditch Wright, he whose posters are blue- tacked over every inch of her bedroom wall at home, he whose name is inked in smudgy black biro all up her arms, and who occupies her every waking thought. She'd been up the tree all night in the hope of another sighting. Now that it was morning she absolutely had to see him in person IMMEDIATELY or she'd die.

Off she went, with me close behind trying to tell her that she couldn't just knock on their door and anyway Ditch Wright must be about three times her age. Cousin Shrub doesn't do listening at the best of times, even when she hasn't got headphones on. She charged across our neighbours' immaculate front garden and rammed their gold lion knocker into their Farrow & Ball French Gray front door. After her second knock the door was opened by their daughter, who's the same age as Daniel, holding a piece of half-eaten toast while dressed up in the sort of fairy princess outfit only allowed off the hanger for Very Special Occasions in other families. Cousin Shrub pushed past her, with me in my oldest stained tracky bottoms and librarian-on-a-Saturday-morning hair close behind.

And there they were in the living room. Cosied up on the sofa together over coffee, each in one of those his and hers towelling dressing gowns you fantasise about stealing from posh hotel rooms. Ditch Wright, in person, sipping a breakfast espresso in nothing but a fluffy robe flopping dangerously open. In Upley Rising, in the house next door to ours. Larger than life and every bit as drop dead gorgeous as in all the magazine photos.

Cousin Shrub and I just stood there. It was all one hundred per cent innocent – except that the husband was nowhere to be seen, and Caroline went the same shade of sunset pink as the lipstick my mother slaps on indiscriminately for family weddings or funerals. Ditch himself was charm personified. He offered to sign Cousin Shrub's T-shirt ('To Saffron', she asked, flummoxing me), and the Manic Street Preachers album cover* I'd grabbed by mistake in the rush. Cousin Shrub/Saffron volunteered that I play guitar too, completing my humiliation. Then we backed out as if we were in the presence of royalty (not that you'd ever catch me toadying up to anyone in the royal family), with me looking everywhere except at that loosely draped robe.

This isn't the end of the story. Far be it from me to speculate about hush money or whatever, but the very next day a cheque arrived signed Caroline Wright (she's his sister-in-law!!) for a sum with more zeros on the end than our average credit card bill, with a little handwritten note: 'To acknowledge receipt with thanks of your beautiful artwork.'

So we have reached the end of the year with a ceasefire. I persuaded Antonio to accept the blood money (as he calls it) for The Wall Speaks on the basis that the cheque was a huge and genuine compliment. When you find out your neighbours are related to rock aristocracy, small oversights like stealing and despoiling with geraniums a genuine Royal Academy art installation cease to matter. Ant seems to have accepted the outcome, though I sometimes see him training a torch on The Wall Speaks from his studio in the evenings. He's been very moody again with the arrival in London this autumn of Margaret Thatcher's opposite number General Pinochet, the dictator responsible for his father's disappearance and for Antonio having to flee his own country.

We're going to spend the money on a proper holiday next year, somewhere sunny and peaceful. This summer was spent – well spent as it turned out – minding Cousin Shrub. We didn't get away unless you count a six-hour detour to Hartlepool when we took her home, as Ant wanted to see the Angel of the North.

In the meantime I'm paying the children to watch out for more surprise visits, and I've promised Cousin Shrub that she can come back for Christmas.

Festive Greetings to you all,

*Alison, Antonio, Eleanor, Felipe, Daniel*
*and Hector*

*\* Manic Street Preacher's Everything Must Go – with my favourite*
*track, A Design for Life: a song about libraries!*

\* \* \* \* \*

### 14 Paradise View, Upley Rising, Thameshire

### Christmas 1999

Against my better judgement I have been drawn into the euphoric counting down exercise that is gripping the world. The ineludible confluence of year, century and millennium means that none of us is excepted from some degree of reflection and reassessment.

I began 1999 by deciding to sell the house in the spring. Being built as a family home it felt over large for just Colin and myself after my mother's death. A valuation agent arrived, admired the wisteria which was in spectacular bloom, then breezed through wielding a large camera and a sheaf of glossy brochures, noting the dimensions of every room. Even taking into account the fact that all estate agents swing towards the extreme end of the optimism scale (I think they must be born with a gene that guarantees them confidence in any given situation) the sale price he named brought a modest rush of blood to the head. I spent several weeks leafing through new possibilities ranging from smart London flats (close to theatres, the Barbican, etc.) to renovated farmhouses in Bologna. But Colin did not fit into any of these alluring scenarios and thoughts of residential care would have scandalised my mother. I do still need and want to work, and my pension at Coburn Briggs is becoming visible on the horizon. In the end the agent's effulgent description of our home backfired against him and I decided to stay put.

Unexpected personal developments forced a change in some of my activities this year. Travelling to the Montague Ensemble spring rehearsals I noticed strange physical symptoms. These included piercing headaches on the train into London, as well as severe insomnia most nights before a rehearsal. On a separate occasion, a work meeting near Moorgate ended in near disaster. We had been engaged by a new client, a pensions trust with property interests in Thameshire. As we sat in their meeting room working through the agenda, I realised that somehow I had put a completely erroneous set of files in my briefcase before leaving the office. I had never done anything like this before. Levels of embarrassment, followed by irritation, increased around the table as I scrambled to answer even the most basic questions that I had so painstakingly researched. Having always prided myself on quiet efficiency in client meetings, I now found myself sweating and trembling. One of the clients muttered and looked at his watch, and I got to my feet, knocking over his water glass in my agitated state, and walked out of the room.

I leant against the wall outside in the street, watching the buildings along London Wall buckle and bend, listening to a roaring in my head and clutching my chest.

Extensive medical tests fortunately revealed nothing physically wrong, but the doctor suggested that I was experiencing 'flashback' trauma symptoms induced by my exposure to the Canary Wharf bombing.

I reacted with doubt that an incident from 1996 could cast a medical shadow as many as three years later, but according to the doctor the evidence is unequivocal. On reflection I admitted that every episode I had experienced was connected with a journey into London. She offered me antidepressants, which I refused, or access to 'counselling' which I also declined. I really can't visualise myself sitting on a sofa in a subdued room with a box of tissues in front of me, pouring my heart out to someone whom I barely know.

The upshot is that I have stepped down from the Montague Ensemble after 17 years as its senior bass singer. I will miss it, and had particularly been looking forward to a full return after two disrupted years, and participating in the summer trip to Salzburg. On the other hand, my zygomaticus major muscles have never fully functioned since the bomb-induced scarring, and I had been struggling to sing to the end of some of the longer phrases. It had become obvious that there was no question of any further solos.

I have also resigned from the North Marylebone Model

Railway Society. Membership numbers have dwindled in recent years, and our last open day, in August, clashed with the first total eclipse of the sun over our shores since 1927. Only four people, all qualifying for reduced 'senior' entry, came along.

These changes are all for the best as in any event it had become harder to take an evening trip into London; Colin has become rather fussy about who sits with him, and gets very anxious if I am home late.

My life in the new millennium will concentrate on work and home. A chat with the senior partner after my hapless Moorgate meeting clarified that there was no ill will, indeed he even intimated that I might be considered a candidate to step into his shoes in due course. Various pastimes closer to home have flowed in to fill the leisure vacuum. Immediately after my mother's death there was a period of several weeks in which some of her friends appeared at the door with various enticements: at first, warm casserole dishes covered with aluminium foil which they had thoughtfully prepared for our supper; and after a decent interval, delicate suggestions that I might like to join a small group for a whist drive, or a charity fundraiser, or more appallingly a trip to the local garden centre for coffee. Partly to fend these off (though we do miss the casseroles) I have taken up the role of Coordinator for our area Neighbourhood Watch. I also accepted an invitation to join the Upley Society and was duly nominated and seconded at the AGM in October. I had some nervousness about treading in my venerable father's footsteps, but I do find myself drawn to the Society's objectives as stated in its constitution: 'To preserve the unique values and heritage of one of England's most historic localities.'

So far these two roles have involved, respectively,

mollifying the police when one of my neighbours called them out in the middle of the night to arrest an intruder which turned out to be a fox, and attending a series of meetings considering whether the Society should refer to Upley Rising in our literature as a town, a suburb or a village.

I turned 50 this year. Pushing thoughts of advancing mortality firmly to one side, I went to the office as usual, intending to ignore the date.

My colleagues at Coburn Briggs thought differently and I was subjected to a mass staff visit to my office at 3pm while I was engrossed in composing a detailed client letter. It seems that the practice manager, who has access to the staff records, keeps a spreadsheet of everyone's date of birth. She was at the vanguard of the intrusion, bearing an iced cake on which my name was inscribed in blue icing.

I was obliged to listen to a discordant rendering of 'happy birthday to you', blow out all the candles, exclaim at every signature on an overlarge card, smile at the little jokes, and unwrap a communal gift, which was actually quite a well-chosen silk bow tie to add to my collection. This had been, I learnt, selected by one of the solicitors in my department, Meera, to whose home Colin and I were recently invited to celebrate Diwali, the Hindu festival of lights. She and her family made us both extremely welcome, and Colin was enraptured by the multifarious decorations, the candles set out and twinkling in every room, and in particular the dyed rice footprints scattered across the floors, which he insisted on following one by one throughout the house to everyone's delight. I wore my new bow tie.

I have for the first time, and without the benefit of

professional counselling, pencilled in some new year's resolutions – or targets as I believe they are now called. They include getting the garden back into bloom to a standard that my mother would have appreciated; spending more time with Colin progressing our model of Clapham Junction station in the spare bedroom; and ensuring that no more files are misplaced at the office.

On the eve of the new millennium I will be on Upley Society duty in the marketplace, with Colin as my official helper, collecting funds for the upkeep of the clock tower whose responsibility falls under our auspices. It will be a late night out, the firework display will be a challenge for us both, and Colin will be irascible the next day from lack of sleep. But since none of us will be here for the next millennium it would be churlish to miss it.

Wishing you all a very Happy Christmas

**Robert**

* * * * *

*December 1999*

*Paradise House, Paradise View*
*Upley Rising, Thameshire*

Paradise House Christmas News

*Dear Everyone,*

Significant dates are the theme for this year's Wright

family Christmas news. Not only are we all eagerly anticipating a new millennium, but I too have reached a personal landmark. Believe it or not, I turned 40 in June. This amusing entry from my diary written in 1979 when I was a carefree 20-year-old made me smile:

'I've just handed in the last piece of coursework for my degree, hooray! Fingers crossed that my BA in Fine Arts and Business Studies will be the gateway to making my future dreams come true. I can't wait to escape from tedious lectures and dreary university libraries, and enter the world of real work. I sit through tutorials dreaming of arriving at a smart office every morning on the dot of nine o'clock, the doorman greeting me by name, then finding myself by chance in the lift with the Managing Director who will be so impressed by my insightful comments about the company's performance that he offers me instant promotion before the doors slide open at my floor. Dear Diary, I can only admit this to you, as I know it's not fashionable to be ambitious. For the past three years I've been surrounded by scruffy students in jeans who spend every spare moment demonstrating about some smelly animal that's determined to become extinct no matter how many placards they wave. But I have my own plans. I will be 40 in the year 1999, how incredible to think I will live through not only a new century but a new millennium. By the time that momentous date arrives, I am determined to have made something extraordinary of myself. Despite growing up fatherless since I was small, and being sent away to a bleak boarding school, I will overcome the odds that life has thrown at me. I will embark on a glittering career, and a magical marriage to a wonderful man; I will give birth (with lots of pain relief) to beautiful, talented children, and own a dream house in a beautiful place.'

Now that I have reached that milestone age, I feel proud to be able to tick all those boxes – especially without having visibly aged, or so I am told. Who needs a bucket list!

We marked my big day with a celebration at our Tennis Club. It was a beautiful summer's afternoon, we served Pimm's on ice with strawberries and cream, and Clementine and I wore matching pastel silk frocks from Harrods. It was a pleasure to welcome as guests so many of the luminaries we have made friends with (apologies if the club's limit on numbers meant you did not receive an invitation). The pavilion looked simply stunning. I had to smile at the club President's face when he walked in and saw the changes I have made since becoming Improvements Committee Chair. He was so overwhelmed he could hardly speak. Moving the trophy cabinets to the back corridor was my inspiration, they had interrupted the room's natural flow, and the whole place felt much brighter too once I had got the dark mahogany honours board shifted into the kitchen out of the way. The Head of Upley Rising's Chamber of Commerce, which I have recently joined, told me I have a natural flair for making an impact.

My next project is to replace the old-fashioned veranda with striking contemporary decking.

I stood in the centre of the room in a shaft of sunlight, surrounded by loved ones, listening to Charles's touching birthday speech followed by Maximilian and Clementine reading out poems they and the nanny had secretly written for the occasion. I felt truly blessed.

Counting one's blessings has been particularly poignant for our family this year. Charles and I have been reeling from the unexpected news about his brother.

I hadn't really been expecting Ditch to make a surprise appearance at my 40th, but I did note at the time that the spectacular floral arrangement he sent contained lilies, which he knows I dislike, rather than my favourite roses. This made sense when he later let slip that his manager Jared had placed the order on his behalf.

Of course being HIV positive is not the shock or stigma it would have been in the 1980s, and even Ditch says wryly that he's always been late to the party. But AIDS is the last thing anyone would have associated with him; tragically, he is not even gay. Although some of the revelations about his younger life which came out in the wake of the press conference organised by Jared to make the news public were a bit of a surprise even to Charles. Their father has been refusing to take Ditch's calls, though Charles thinks he'll come round once he's got over the shock. Helena, Ditch's ex-girlfriend, is trying to sue him, selfishly adding to the stress.

It has been a very worrying time for us all. Poor Maximilian and Clementine were on the receiving end of some vile comments at school. And I, having always had such a close relationship with Ditch, was absolutely devastated and consumed with worry. Fortunately the doctor did some tests, said it was just stress and gave me some pills to calm me down. Charles, concerned that I was not looking my usual self, even suggested we ask Mother to come and stay, but tact has never been one of her strengths and there was no point in making things worse.

Just when I was at my lowest, Ditch himself called long distance, the line crackling and his voice grating with tiredness and emotion over the 5,000 miles between Los Angeles and Upley Rising – and I suddenly found inner strength. I pictured Lady Diana and how she would have risen to this challenge and set an inspiring example for others to follow, gaining even greater worldwide publicity in the process. I told Ditch I would do everything in my power to help him through the years ahead. Charles agreed; now he is working with his brother to set up a high-profile fundraiser, and is pulling strings to set up a TV cameo on next year's Red Nose Day. Ditch's new tour is on hold until he sorts out a treatment plan with his doctors but sales of his latest single tripled in the weeks following the announcement.

So optimism is my message for the year 2000 and beyond. For me personally this means my career taking an exciting new direction. All these years of penning Christmas newsletters have stood me in good stead – I am now an Editor-in-Chief!

I have to admit to becoming disenchanted with the LavishUs Corporation when their Chief Operating Officer asked Ditch to step down as International Mens' Ambassador and terminated his contract with instant effect. I had put so much work into brokering a valuable deal on both sides, but some Americans can be very straight-laced. My concerns mounted further when my application to progress to Diamond Level was delayed, then my two company sponsors dropped out.

I will always be a big fan of LavishCoast She products but the corporation has a blind spot about understanding customers in this country. Women here can be soft and sentimental at the expense of beauty and appearance. Lavish Us's PR department should have been much quicker to stifle some unfortunate publicity about laboratory testing on small animals, followed by unverified stories claiming that they pay miniscule wages to factory workers somewhere abroad, and refuse them rest breaks. Not only was I disappointed by the corporation turning its back on Ditch in his hour of need, but using my business acumen I saw problems ahead. By the time an 'Abolish Lavish' petition stand appeared under Upley Rising's lovely gothic clock tower (it was manned by the bohemian eccentric that leads the town's summer 'Wellspring' festival every year and some of his outlandish friends), I had already put LavishCoast She behind me for good and come up with my brilliant new idea.

Leafing through a copy of Tatler at the beauty salon, I was wondering how to use the wealth of talent and experience I have built up when I realised that the answer was literally staring up at me from the glossy pages on my lap.

A few phone calls and a bit of research later, I had reinvented myself as the founder of a completely original idea: Upley Rising's very own high-end monthly magazine.

*Upley Itself* is a full colour publication showcasing the very best that Upley Rising has to offer: chic fashion emporia, bustling cafés and cosmopolitan delicatessens, all lining our historic High Street.

We leave humdrum news stories about road accidents to The Upley Herald, and we definitely won't touch small ads for barely used walking frames, so there is no competition between us. The real beauty of my business model is that we can deliver a free copy to every household in the higher council tax bands. How, you may ask? Because local businesses from independent schools to luxury spas are desperate to advertise with us or to pay for one of our 'advertorial' articles.

It feels so rewarding to be giving something back to my own community. As I write, the first issue of *Upley Itself* is at the printers and will launch at the start of the new millennium featuring your very own Editor-in-Chief interviewing Peregrine Hartley, the MP for Thameshire South.

We may need to depend on Clementine's and my income for a little while, as I am not the only one embarking on a new venture. Charles has been headhunted from Strong Barker to take up the role of International Marketing Entrepreneur with a new 'Dot Com' company. I was concerned about him taking such a risky step when we have two school-aged children with a busy programme of private tutors and extracurricular music and drama, as well as a year ahead crammed with tennis lessons, entertaining and holidays to fund. But the company, *'www.dotcomblast.com'*, has tripled in value in just six months and the prospects for share dividends are eye-watering. Even though the Directors are still deciding what it will be selling, they have already created a really clever web-site which apparently is what matters more. Charles has been teaching Max and Clementine how the stock market works. He says it's more important than the old-fashioned maths they do at school, and he's bought them each their own starter share portfolio for Christmas.

We are visiting Mother and her friend Rupert for Christmas this year. Rupert has a small estate in Scotland (not far from Balmoral), and we are looking forward to taking a well-earned break enjoying its 200 acres of wooded grounds and meeting what Mother calls his County Set. Charles is investigating a Wright tartan, and I have made a concession to my usual wardrobe rules and bought a pair of flat heels.

Then it's back for New Year's Eve, and I have saved the best news till last. Charles and I are VIP guests at the big millennium party at the new Dome in Greenwich! The invitation was actually meant for Ditch who is not able to come over, but Charles has arranged to use his ID. I love the Dome. I have no time for those pessimists who think this outstanding achievement for British culture, architecture and industry will be a damp squib. Max and Clemmie will be allowed to stay up and watch out for us on TV when the nanny brings them back from the Upley Rising fireworks display. You may like to look out for us too.

I can't wait to see if I can shake the hands of both the Queen and Mr Blair!

Wishing you all a very Happy Christmas,

*Caroline, Charles, Maximilian and Clementine Wright*

* * * * *

## Christmas 1999: Last month of the millennium …

**15 Paradise View**
**Upley Rising**
**Thameshire**

Dear Friends

As Christmas newsletters go, this could be worth a bit one day. It may be the last one we ever send, from Upley Rising or anywhere else.

I'm writing it sitting on a packing crate in our bare, echoing living room. This time next week we'll be the new occupants of Craigh Fuar House, Caithness, Northern Scotland. Get out your map of the UK, go as far north as possible without falling into the North Sea – the bit even the weather presenters ignore. Look for a timeworn dwelling built to withstand everything life can throw at it, and that's where you'll find us.

We have decided that for once this family will be proactive and get ahead of the curve of destiny. Here, in reverse order, are our reasons:

Five: We need to lie low. After years of almost succeeding, Ant has finally landed a criminal record. He got arrested at the big anti-Pinochet protest in London in March. He was caught on camera hurling a police helmet through a shop window, then after supergluing himself to the statue of Abraham Lincoln (he meant to pick Winston Churchill – for a sculptor you'd think he'd know his statues by now) he spent a night in the cells and was charged with public order offences. He was put on probation, fined a hefty sum and given 200 hours community service. He says he would do it all over again.

**Four:** I 'celebrated' my 40th birthday in May, on the day Ant had to start his community service. I've had to bin my bucket list* (see below) in the face of world events (also see below, reason two) and go for a complete lifestyle makeover instead.

**Three**: I need to get Ant as far away as possible from the South Thameshire Lawn Tennis Club. He went to collect Daniel from a birthday party in the pavilion and discovered that The Big Hit, his biggest art commission in recent years, had been moved to a cupboard – apparently to make space for some social event. Incensed doesn't begin to describe his reaction. I'm seriously worried that he's going to turn his criminal tendencies into a full-time career and blow the place up.

**Two:** We are on the cusp of entering a dystopian future.

The millennium bug is almost upon us. Like lots of people I was sceptical about the scare stories, until I was trying to upgrade our state-of-the-art cataloguing system at work and found that planning anything beyond 31st December 1999 was impossible. The same was true of all our other systems: try asking the computers about anything beyond the end of this year and there was a complete blank. In the year 2000 it looks like there will be no books, no journals, no budgets, no students; nothing. Just rows of computerised noughts and ones all going nowhere.

I went to see my boss to tell him that our Investors in People project was pointless, we are investing in people with no future after the end of this year. The Head Librarian, whose idea of forward planning is to rip today's date off his desk calendar on his way out at 5pm sharp, just laughed then asked me to fetch him another cup of coffee. But the more I looked into it the more I have become convinced that I am right. Come midnight on New Year's Eve planes will fall out of the sky, bank accounts will freeze, shops will run out of everything from pasta to loo paper and civilisation as we know it will grind to a halt. And I can't face the apocalypse here in Upley Rising.

I can just picture it: first the church, besieged with pious repenters, will stage a major comeback. The History Society will take overall control with 'we've-been-there-before' smugness. Meanwhile the High Street wine bar will sell home-made moonshine under the counter to favoured customers; anyone trying to get in from outside Thameshire will have to show a passport; and the 7.58 to London Marylebone will slowly rust on the station tracks.

Not for me thank you; I want our family to be in a place where we can be independent, self-reliant, the pioneers of a new world future. And our kids can stop being stared at every time we go out because the Murder House is now also the Leftie Criminal Rioter house.

Ant was sceptical at first. Being at home all day, doing the school run and everything else, he had become inexplicably attached to Upley Rising, given his current Pariah of Paradise View status. And he's never bothered much with computers. Surely the corner shop would stay open? It never closes, not even on Christmas Day. And what about the latest appeal to get General Pinochet extradited? The apocalypse might come but the world-famous British justice system was rock solid and he needed to be around to make sure it didn't let him down again. But while I struggled with rational argument, I had forgotten how superstitious he is. In the end what convinced him was a miracle. On August 11th we were all outside with our cardboard safety glasses waiting for the clouds to clear for a glimpse of the eclipse. Just as the sky became ominously dark, our old cat Salvador, who we left behind in North London over eight years ago, appeared out of the blue at our gate. Looking ravenous and desperate. A cat that can find its way from N6 to the outer reaches of a Home Counties suburb years after it should have gone to cat heaven? Clearly this was some kind of Portent. Ant agreed we should leave.

**One**: I'm pregnant again. Aged 40. And surprise surprise, it's twins again.

Due in March. Just when I was starting to think about life beyond work, children, work and children. Because of my track record in giving birth early and quickly, and because I'm now classified as a 'geriatric mother', we've decided to relocate to a part of the UK where the nearest hospital is about 100 miles away. Not that it will be functioning in the millennium bug world. We are taking backup in the form of my sister Gill, who once did a module in emergency midwifery as part of her social work qualification, and Cousin Shrub, who is strangely excited and has moved on from her Ditch Wright infatuation. Together we are going to form a community of the new millennium, growing our own vegetables, trading with neighbours for other essentials, keeping warm with wood we've chopped ourselves and knitting clothes with wool from the sheep contentedly grazing the hillsides. While softie Southerners are floundering in post-apocalyptic pandemonium, trying to trade their invisible assets for looted food, we will be digging the foundations of the future society.

Not that I want to scare you – but it's not too late. Join us!

I've taken extended maternity leave, our house is up for rent (ideal for murder tourists) and we leave in just over a week. We've taken all our savings out of the bank in cash; they take up about a quarter of the briefcase Ant used when he had a job. We'll stop on the way for Christmas with my parents in Yorkshire. Mum and Dad are convinced our move was Ant's idea. They've been acting all sanctimonious since he got arrested, and keep making pointed comments that as we're not married I don't need to stay with him, adding that he's even become a bad influence on Gill now. They turned down flat our offer of renting another cottage nearby and say they'll be perfectly OK in God's Own County with their building society books, watching on TV as the opening of the London Dome kicks off Armageddon. But my dad's put a padlocked fence around his allotment ('just in case love, you never know') and my mum's been stashing away tins of baked beans, which she claims is just an old habit from the post-war years.

Eleanor and Felipe are outraged. First at the prospect of losing their special status as the family twins. Then Eleanor was elected to the school council for the year, and Felipe was aiming for judo orange belt. Incomprehensibly, they are most furious at missing the school choir's New Year's Eve performance in the Upley Rising town celebrations. They staged a hunger strike which ran from 4pm one Friday to 5.45pm the same evening, then opted for civil disobedience measures, like buying back their old books and toys which I'd given to the school Christmas fair in a pre-move clear-out.

On the other hand, Hector our daft dog is in hound heaven – he thinks we're staging an escape from Salvador the cat who's been making his life a misery. As is Daniel, who isn't very good at making friends and who says he's looking forward to everyone around him disappearing for ever. The Wellspring Festival Committee members have been our biggest cheerleaders. They put together an essential supplies box for us including incense sticks, fair trade herbal teas and bamboo knitting needles, and have offered to look in on the house. It's an eye opener that when push comes to shove none of them can tear themselves away from their bricks and mortar investments in leafy Thameshire.

When its listed gothic clock chimes midnight on 31st December 1999, Upley Rising with its massed school choirs and Rotary Club sponsored fireworks will applaud politely as catastrophic oblivion strikes. And we'll be safe and sound in our 15th-century bothy with walls thick enough to withstand an earthquake. Till then, Antonio pats my pregnancy bump on his way out to pick up community service dog poo from the park and calls me the Gaia of the new world. Let's hope.

Festive Greetings to you all,

*Alison, Antonio, Eleanor, Felipe, Daniel, and Hector*

*and Salvador*

*Ali's defunct and revised 40th birthday bucket list:*

| Pre-millennium world | New millennium world |
|---|---|
| Train for the London Marathon. | Dig for peat as fuel. |
| Learn Spanish. | Learn Gaelic to communicate with other survivors. |
| Get standing ovation for headline speech at Association of Head Librarians Annual Conference. | Call sheep off the hills with newly discovered sheep whisperer technique. |
| Have dinner out with Ant without children or being summoned back by babysitter. | Stewed sheep dinner in candlelit bothy cooked by Gill while Cousin Shrub babysits. |
| Be called up onstage at packed Ditch Wright concert for impromptu guitar solo. | Start new Von Trapp style singing group with Ant and our many children. |
| A beach holiday anywhere hot with white sand, palm trees and lapping waves. | Northern Scotland has beaches too. |
| A spa weekend involving something called Me Time, candles, aromatherapy and unlimited champagne. | Candles are a way of life in our new world: every day is a spa day. Still working on the champagne. |

# PART SIX 2000-2002:

# ROBERT, CAROLINE, ALI

### 14 Paradise View, Upley Rising, Thameshire

### Christmas 2000

The first year of the new century has coincided with a cornucopia of new personal experiences.

I entered a hamburger restaurant for the first time. I played a participating role in Upley Rising's Wellspring Festival. I wore a T-shirt with my name printed on it. I bought a personal computer for home use; and learned to swear (these last two were not, as one might expect, connected).

The country has continued its joyous celebration of new bridges and commemorative buildings, all presided over by our Prime Minister's iridescent countenance, reminiscent of the large Sun in the Teletubbies TV programme which is one of Colin's occasional indulgences. Meanwhile Upley Rising accommodates the zeitgeist in its own way.

There were near riots at the council's planning committee meeting when a well-known 'fast food' chain had the effrontery to apply for a franchise on the High Street between the fine arts gallery and the doll's house establishment. Whereas a new branch of the supermarket Waitrose was voted in unanimously, and over 500 enthusiastic new customers turned out for its grand opening. Separately, our famous gothic clock was defaced by a gang of bored teenagers who have taken to drinking cider on its steps on warm summer evenings. I attended a stormy meeting of the Upley Society to discuss diverting the clock redecoration funds, set aside for the Queen's Golden Jubilee next year, to install a spiked fence or even hidden cameras. I volunteered to spend the following Sunday afternoon cleaning up the graffiti, which is how I came to expand my hitherto limited vocabulary in obscenities; the exercise was a veritable education.

At Coburn Briggs we were faced with a very 21st-century crisis. Full-page advertisements started appearing in The Upley Herald asking: 'Need legal advice? Ask a Ferret First!' Or 'Being sued? March in our direction!' They were the work of March, Ferret and Gladdington, our competitors whom we consider brash upstarts compared with our own two centuries of diligent lawyering from unchanged offices above the High Street bank. We ignored these base attempts at publicity on our daily walks to lunch at the Royal Oak, until our practice manager, who I am beginning to admire, convened a partners' meeting. She produced some alarming graphs showing plummeting referral rates, and disclosed inside knowledge that three of our most treasured clients were about to be tempted away to our rivals. On the very expensive advice of a public relations consultant we took action. We produced a tasteful set of leaflets to grace the reception areas of funeral parlours, hairdressers and for display in the hamburger restaurant (after two appeals the council had capitulated and granted the required planning permission); we also set up a promotional stand at the summer Wellspring Festival. Here, wearing the abovementioned T-shirt, I found myself fielding queries about injuries caused by children on scooters, as well as advising the anxious parents of this year's Upley Maiden about the validity of the agreement they had signed not to sue the organisers in the event of a tragedy.

There was a scare with Colin in September. A young newspaper reporter appeared at our house asking questions about the murders that took place in Paradise View back in the 1960s. Everyone in the road has got used to people turning up at intervals, either from the papers or just those with a morbid interest in tragedy. At Neighbourhood Watch meetings we have regular discussions about how to handle them; the usual consensus is to be polite and do nothing to upset property prices.

This reporter must have been particularly green as she didn't even knock at the right address. And she chose the moment when Sharon, Colin's Tuesday carer, was out of earshot sunning herself on the rear veranda while simultaneously drying the varnish on her toenails and chatting on her portable telephone to her sister, as she explained to me at length later. Thus the door was opened, against all the rules, by Colin himself.

The sense of importance this must have given him, to be in sole charge of the doorstep with a personable young woman before him, is impossible to exaggerate. He was in the process of saying an emphatic 'Yes!' to all the reporter's questions when disaster struck. The unkempt, giant mongrel belonging to the people opposite bounded across the road, through our front gate left open by the reporter, up the steps and straight into our front hall. In hot pursuit was a bullet-shaped grey blur which was the cat from the same house. An antique ormolu mounted vase which had been one of my mother's favourites was flung off its stand and shattered into unrecoverable splinters all over the mosaic floor tiles. Colin, whose balance is not good, went flying backwards with a scream that finally got Sharon off the phone, then had the good sense to bolt himself into the living room until order had been restored. The reporter ended up returning the pets to their rightful owners which also got her to the house she should have called at in the first place.

I took Colin for a full check-up by the GP. Given his conditions he was lucky to be unharmed, and Sharon is equally lucky to have kept her post. But the doctor took the opportunity to point out what I had been ignoring, that Colin has become rather overweight. I was given a set of diet sheets and sample menus to follow, all in very large print and with brightly coloured illustrations showing me what a radish looks like. Lasagne and oven chips are now off the menu, which annoys the carers. But Colin and I have been spending time cooking together at weekends, which we both rather enjoy.

I was mortified when I had to break a promise to Colin to take him to the Dome. Trying to address on my own terms the PTSD symptoms which crop up with irritating regularity, I had done an advance trial run into London the week before the date which had been ringed on the calendar for weeks. But as I walked through Trafalgar Square a flock of pigeons surrounded me, flapping their wings and screaming for food. The all too familiar sensation of terrifying giddiness and shaking came over me, and I had to stumble down to the Embankment and sit on a bench for two hours, allowing the gentle rhythm of boat traffic on the river to calm me down enough to return home. I was determined to make it up to Colin and am pleased to report that at the beginning of December we finally had a grand day out, visiting not only the Dome (we both agreed that the best part was North Greenwich Station) but also a trip on the London Eye.

Our strict diet will be suspended on December 25th, when we are attempting a complete Christmas dinner with all the trimmings. We have invited my colleague Meera for the day, together with her widowed mother, two brothers and a sister-in-law, and an aunt. I hope we are not being too ambitious. Preparations are in full swing, a large goose has been ordered from the butchers (fortunately they are not strictly vegetarian) and I have bought some new Christmas decorations. Sharon the carer pointed out with her usual percipience that our old ones were looking 'so last century'. Colin and I have even baked a home-made Christmas pudding with an old sixpence inside. I have marked the spot with a toothpick to try and make sure that this portion goes to the right person. I will have to remember to remove the toothpick before it is served; we don't want any more accidents at home this year.

With Christmas wishes,

**Robert**


### 14 Paradise View, Upley Rising, Thameshire

### Christmas 2001

Is it possible to sum up a year in a snapshot? A single moment can be both deceptive and misleading. If I show you a photograph of a kestrel hovering against a clear blue sky, how will you know that moments earlier this beautiful creature was gorging itself in the long grass on a hapless vole?

Filling out this year's national census questionnaire was a similar extra-contextual exercise. I found myself forced to squeeze the truth, distorting it in the process, into lines of tickable boxes. It was a brutal example of bureaucracy excelling in the art of reducing our complex, changing lives to the lowest common denominator.

In these annual Christmas letters I could take the same tack, and state that I spent most of the past year living in a house containing two people; eight rooms; gas central heating; and its own indoor bathroom – two, in fact. That we had no overnight visitors on the official census night of 29th April – or indeed any other. That I have one car, though I usually walk to work, and a professional qualification. That Colin is male, single, has no qualifications and is not actively looking for work or on any government-sponsored training scheme.

You would have no way of knowing that my hair has turned almost completely grey; that Colin lost half a stone in weight, then gained 12 lbs before losing another 4lbs; that my daily walk to work is enriched beyond measure in the spring by the blossom of the cherry trees lining our road, and in the autumn by the crunching underfoot of blazing foliage.

So I continue with my regular Christmastime endeavour to flesh out the past year with something in the way of diverting detail.

Work has been extremely busy this year, such that its pressures on my time led to unanticipated and far-reaching consequences at home.

The appetite of certain inhabitants of Thameshire for minimising their tax bills continues unabated. (Their determination seems to increase in inverse proportion to the altruism of the government of the moment, to whom a number of our clients incidentally provide consultancy services.) My skills in finding inventive solutions have been in great demand. Such was the pressure approaching the end of the tax year that I found myself holding a rare Saturday morning meeting with my colleague Meera in a local coffee shop.

We needed to go over some urgent paperwork and I try to make it a rule to avoid going into the office at weekends. The atmosphere in the café was very pleasant, and the meeting stretched to a second cup of coffee, with biscotti, which I had almost finished before realising that Colin was no longer sitting at the next table leafing through his Beano collection. A frantic search ensued, with me rushing home to see if he could possibly have found his way back alone, while Meera scoured the streets around the pond. He was eventually tracked down, by us both, at a charity shop located in a narrow road down the hill from the High Street. The shop has one of those life-sized fundraiser statues outside, in the form of a melancholy boy holding a donations box. Colin, facing the statue, was trying to wipe away a ceramic tear from its face. The staff had been unable to extricate him.

This Saturday morning drama lasted no more than 75 minutes but the aftermath went on for months. Word got back to Colin's care network and I was summoned to a meeting with South Thameshire Adult Social Services to discuss Colin's future.

As a lawyer I am used to there being at least two sides to every story. I sat at the table opposite no fewer than five highly qualified professionals (four of whom had never met me or Colin) and listened as a picture of our home life was painted in elaborate detail – except that it was no home life that I recognised. Apparently Colin was never allowed to change his clothes, or to use our home computer. Having his own friends was banned, and I was starving him. I can only conjecture that one of the carers had developed a grudge, and encouraged Colin to give certain answers when he was interviewed prior to the meeting. When my turn came to speak, I explained at length that Colin has tantrums if he wears anything other than his favourite red pullover; that spending time on the computer on his own had led to him deleting all my work files; that the no friends at home rule is to deal with his eruptions if his things are rearranged; and that the doctor had warned of dire consequences for his heart if he did not lose some weight.

The five multi-agency professionals listened closely, made lengthy notes, went away and had another meeting, then pronounced that Colin would be better off in residential care. A conversation with a brick wall would have been more empathetic. Letters and phone calls were exchanged, during which time Colin's carers and I kept our daily communications brief, with glacial civility. Eventually, to avoid further impact on Colin, who knowing something was up was becoming reclusive and taciturn, we compromised on a trial fortnight in a nearby care facility. Colin, who had received glowing reports of daily life at The Grey Willows, was ecstatic at the prospect.

Thus came about my summer holiday this year. I decided to make the best of things and took up the suggestion that I enjoy what is referred to in the office as downtime. I didn't want to leave the country in case of problems with Colin, and set off for Hay-on-Wye. The countryside was beautiful and I planned to do some healthy walking. Most of the paths were closed due to the foot and mouth outbreak, and after various futile excursions into the hills, and destroying my walking boots dunking them in ubiquitous disinfectant baths, I abandoned the walking. However I enjoyed browsing the many second-hand bookshops, as well as taking two trips on the Brecon Mountain Railway including the lately finished line extension to Dol-y-Gaer.

The powers that be had decreed I should not telephone or communicate with Colin while I was away. I did send him an unsigned postcard showing the mountain railway's number 2 Baldwin locomotive in full steam. On my return I unpacked then went to pick him up, arriving at The Grey Willows an hour and a half earlier than the agreed time.

It was not difficult to slip past the unmanned reception desk. I found Colin sitting in the day room in egg-stained pyjamas at four in the afternoon. He was clutching a bag of crisps which another resident was trying to grab from him. Colin was making distracted attempts to fend off the other inmate, without taking his eyes from the blank television screen in front of him. He looked up, pretended not to see me, then howled and ran off when an attendant came in. I later found bruise-like markings on his arms.

Further letters were exchanged with the social services team, and Colin came home for good.

I have redecorated his bedroom, in the face of his objections, but it does look fresher, and bought a new glass-fronted, lockable cabinet for his models. As well as his Wednesday group, he has started attending a basic reading class. By far the biggest change is the replacement of our trinity of carers.

We now have Tomasz who comes from Lublin and lives in with us full time. A change in arrangements which has meant me moving to my mother's old room so that Tomasz can occupy what was my bedroom. On non-diet days he treats us to stew with dumplings and cheesecake, prepared with ingredients which he buys from the new Polish shop in the town centre which has replaced the doll's house and miniatures shop. Tomasz has left his wife and family at home, and when he takes three weeks off twice a year to visit them, the care trio stand in for him and we are all on our best behaviour. So far the arrangement has been a great success.

Having a live-in carer means less privacy in exchange for more freedom. I have joined the town choir, the Rising Voices. It is not up to the standard of the Montague Ensemble, and like many such groups they are always short of men. The audition was perfunctory: having spent a couple of weeks rehearsing warm-up exercises in front of the mirror at home, I was simply asked if my bass range could stretch to a baritone, and if I was happy to help out with the tea-making rota. However they are a pleasant group of people and our choir leader managed to tease quite a decent performance of the Hallelujah Chorus out of us at the autumn concert. It feels good to be singing again, and my residual facial scarring has not so far been an impediment.

Membership of the Upley Society, by contrast, has been somewhat clouded. Our AGM took place at the beginning of December and was combined with a talk on Winter Trees of South Thameshire, followed by a Christmas Social. I invited my colleague Meera as a guest, knowing she has an interest in dendrology. The talk, illustrated by a slideshow, was informative and Meera made some knowledgeable contributions to the question-and-answer session. Afterwards, while we were grouped chatting over sherry and mince pies, our treasurer, without warning, turned to her and asked in a loud and slow voice how she enjoyed living in England. Before she could reply, the membership secretary standing next to him added that she must be feeling dreadfully ashamed about the September 11th attacks, and was she looking forward to going home soon.

Never has a mince pie tasted more like cardboard. Wishing one could drop through the floor is an expression I had always found puzzling until that moment. I was beyond mortified.

My great-grandfather was a founder member of the Society in 1894, and my father instilled in me an enduring respect for the many minor institutions that underpin our country's democratic values. But looking round the Upley Society's Churchill Room with its faded Axminster carpet and the reproduction portrait of the Queen frozen in time at the age of 35, I was drained of any desire to spend a moment longer there. I offered to take Meera home, but she had already called a taxi and excused herself. When I got home Colin was in bed but Tomasz was sitting up enjoying BBC Sports Personality of the Year, which had just been awarded to David Beckham.

The next day I wrote a long note to Meera, expressing my embarrassment and apologising. We went to lunch together and had a very open conversation. She had told her family that she came home early by taxi because she was feeling unwell. But one of her brothers, who in his professional life in the medical field had been involved with the Society's fundraising efforts for a new hospital scanner, guessed what might have happened. I told her

I planned to step down but she thinks it's better for me to fight from within, and joked that her house might yet win Upley Rising's Best Front Door Wreath competition, which is organised by the Upley Society.

The situation is further complicated because I have been asked to take charge of the Upley Society's Golden Jubilee celebration for next year, which involves a royal visit at a senior level. This is an honour by any measure, one which my father would have felt it his duty to fulfil. After careful consideration I plan to stay on and make the day an unqualified success.

To make amends I have once again invited Meera and her family to our house this year, for an early Christmas meal. Before he goes home for the holidays Tomasz has offered to prepare traditional Polish Christmas fare of borsht and trout. Colin and I will supply brandy snaps with whipped orange cream; and the Gupta clan are bringing a selection of home-made appetisers and some traditional confectionery. We will enjoy a banquet on culturally neutral territory, though there will not be a mince pie in sight.

With Christmas wishes,

**Robert**

\* \* \* \* \*


*December 2000*

*Paradise House, Paradise View,*
*Upley Rising, Thameshire*

*Paradise House Christmas News*

# Dear Everyone,

**From your Editor-in-Chief**

Welcome to the popular seasonal glimpse into the life and times of the Wright family. Our first year in the new millennium has been as busy and fun packed as you've come to expect, so sit back and enjoy the read. We start with a surprise guest contributor:

**From our Education Correspondent**

This is your roving schools reporter speaking, Maximilian P.S.C. Wright. I am ten years old and I go to Upley Primary School. This year I have been playing the tuba and Grand Theft Auto on my new PlayStation 2. I am a year 6 prefect and I am allowed to give detentions when I'm on dinner duty. I give detentions for everything, like looking happy in the lunch queue which is ridiculous as the lunches are disgusting, or not calling me Sir Prefect. I can confiscate Pokemon cards too which is the best, as I make the year 4s buy them back. My Dad is top cheese at my school's Parents Association so I never get into trouble. My Mum and Dad have bought a house in France so that I can speak French better. For my 10th birthday I had a paintball party and I killed all my friends. I got a video camera from Grandma and I took lots of secret videos of our nanny and when she found out she left, but I didn't like her much anyway. My sister Clemmie cried because the nanny took her two favourite Sylvanians with her, so now Dad is going to send her a solicitor's letter.

Happy Christmas everyone from Max.

## Local News

It's Happy First Birthday to *Upley Itself*, my publishing enterprise. I have realised I was always destined to run an exclusive magazine. Armed with my Moleskine reporter's notebook, I have spent the year fearlessly plumbing the hidden depths in Upley Rising, this jewel of Thameshire villages, which not many people know has won the influential Best Kept Outer London Suburb award not once but four times. *Upley Itself* has been so successful that I have had to take on two part-time staff. I even received a request to place an advertisement in this Christmas newsletter.

Groundbreaking news stories we have published this year include the opening of Upley Rising's very own Waitrose; a Health and Beauty in Thameshire special; and most thrilling of all: *Upley Itself's* first big scoop. I personally uncovered a secret member of the Royal Family living undiscovered in our midst! The full exposé is in my August edition in-depth interview: 'The Baffling Baron'.

The elusive aristocrat is, as I revealed, the charmingly eccentric character who is the force behind our town's quaint annual Wellspring Festival. With his greying ponytail, tie-dye trousers and sandals, I had often seen him handing out Greenpeace leaflets, or ambling out of the health food shop holding a bag of mung beans, and I had assumed he was just another ageing hippy who by some twist of fate found himself on Upley Rising's property ladder. But then he got in touch to ask about publicising the Wellspring Festival in *Upley Itself,* and turned out to be a fascinating raconteur with a real royal pedigree. Not only does he modestly conceal his roots as a true peer of the realm, but he is also a close relative (a third cousin twice removed) to the Queen Mother. He is a fount of marvellous stories, including some intriguing gossip which unfortunately I was advised to edit out of the article proofs.

A genuine Baron in our midst in Upley Rising: no wonder he looks so regal in his royal purple robes striding at the head of the festival procession every year.

**Business and Foreign Affairs**
Charles says I should headline this section: How we Escaped the Dotcom Bubble. He spent a fascinating ten months at ***www.dotcomblast.com***, and even began using mysterious words like 'server' and 'cyberspace' over dinner. But Charles really is a people person, and he grew increasingly frustrated with his colleagues, who were more at home with computer codes than conversation. They would reply to his friendly greetings with one-word answers, never stopped to chat at the water cooler, and conducted team meetings in silence by e-mail. Charles couldn't see the point in wearing jeans to the office when he's got several Savile Row suits, and his team couldn't understand why an International Marketing Entrepreneur needed an expense account for foreign travel. The Finance Director overheard him on the phone buying an air ticket to Madrid and objected, saying the meeting could be done from London using the firm's own software. But Charles knows that to land a deal you have to be face to face in the same room. He told the Director that wobbly video conferencing on a computer screen will never work: you have to be able to 'smell the whites of their eyes' as he puts it.

So when he was asked to join STEAL – a new spin-off from his old company – he jumped at the chance, cashing in his shares in ***www.dotcomblast.com*** at their peak and just three weeks before the company imploded, leaving the founders bankrupt and penniless. He has always had an impeccable sense of timing. We decided to invest the proceeds in good old-fashioned bricks and mortar. As a result we are now French property owners! Our *gite* is a *bijou* villa tucked away in the countryside not far from Provence. We bought it from a friend at the Tennis Club who had already put in a small court. We spent our first holiday there in the autumn half term to organise putting in a bigger pool. Three other club members own houses nearby, so we feel really at home and can spend time socialising with them instead of the natives, who can be a bit offhand. It will be marvellous for the children's French.

Joining STEAL means Charles is travelling to the States again. His rock star brother Ditch has moved from Los Angeles to New York where he is working on a radical music project exploring his own HIV journey. He is collaborating with the Manhattan Chamber Orchestra, so watch out for a mature new focus. A preview track was even played on Radio 3 recently.

We have been respecting Ditch's wishes for personal space, not bothering him too much as he enters this new phase of his life development. Thanks to all those of you who responded to Max and Clementine's 'HIV, it's You and Me!' fundraiser.

**The Women's Page**
Clementine's modelling career is temporarily on hold while her adult teeth come through, but she used her newfound spare time to get selected as one of the six maids of honour to accompany the Upley Maiden on the town procession at this year's Wellspring Festival.

Our daughter is full of initiative. She knew she was banned from applying for what we had seen as a dangerous and unsuitable custom, on a par with the Lewes Bonfire or Gloucester's cheese rolling contest. Both are a former events manager's ultimate nightmare. So she meticulously copied my signature onto the application form, presenting her parents with a *fait accompli* as they say in France.

Charles was set on visiting the organiser to warn him off luring young girls into treacherous practices, but I had just discovered that the festival was run by a respected member of the aristocracy and realised we could relax and stop worrying about health and safety matters.

It was a delight to see Clementine leading the other maid attendants through the town in her flowing costume, representing summer. She was quite the star of the day, and stole the show with her secretly rehearsed surprise song and dance routine while the Upley Maiden was stuck down the well.

**Crime and Mystery Section**

The big shock of the year was my being contacted out of the blue by my father. I am not sure how he tracked me down, though it is quite possible that a copy of *Upley Itself*, which is attracting a lot of attention, found its way to Brisbane. He telephoned from a London hotel in April just as I was on my way out. I was alone in the house; the children were at school and Charles had taken the day off as he felt obliged to go to Charlie Kray's funeral. I told my father that after 32 years of silence I was not about to cancel my tennis lesson for an unscheduled chat. Mother has also given him short shrift; she believes he has finally run out of money and had heard about Rupert coming into her life. She threatened to give his details to the Child Support Agency so they could bill him retrospectively and he immediately put the phone down. We think he has gone back to Australia as neither of us has heard from him again. His brief reappearance remains a mystery; at least

I have been able to show him that I have made a success of myself in spite of all the years of his not showing up for school prize days, and never remembering my birthday.

**And finally**

We are heading to Lapland for Christmas this year, for a totally authentic Yule experience. We will be dog sledding at midnight, enjoying reindeer steak in ice hotels and watching the Northern Lights from the comfort of our electrically heated fur-lined igloo. Max says he wants to meet the official Father Christmas before he gets too old to believe in him!

Wishing you all a very Happy Christmas,

*Caroline, Charles, Maximilian and Clementine Wright*

# December 2001

*Paradise House, Paradise View*
*Upley Rising, Thameshire*

*Paradise House Christmas News*

## Dear Everyone,

### A Family Tragedy

I had planned to begin this year's Christmas news with Max smashing his way to the finals of our Tennis Club's Junior Challenge, and Clementine's triumphant Tallulah, which is the starring role, in her drama group's Bugsy Malone. Instead I am reporting from the ruins of a shattered family. The pain of the past few weeks is only just beginning to recede but the grief is still raw.

We returned from holidaying in France at the end of August with no clue as to what the future held. We had spent a glorious month in our *maison de vacances,* swimming, playing tennis and enjoying ourselves in the sun away from the UK where Mother said it was either raining or reeking of burning cattle from the foot and mouth outbreak. Charles had to leave for New York on business a few days later. I was at home reviewing photos of Clem's drama performance for the front cover of *Upley Itself* when I got an unexpected call from Jared, Ditch's manager. He said that Charles's rock star brother had been taken into hospital; he knew that Charles was in New York but couldn't find him. I wasn't too worried as Ditch had recently started a new drug regime which seemed to be working well.

But I knew Charles would want to know and I managed

to get him to pick up his mobile telephone (his ringtone for calls from me is Bootylicious) during a business lunch with STEAL's financial backers in Lower Manhattan. He rushed off to the hospital – just in time to find Ditch's former girlfriend Helena at the bedside. She was waving a document she said was a retrospective prenuptial agreement and trying to press a pen into Ditch's trembling hand. She had bluffed her way in, claiming to be his next of kin.

Charles called me later that day sounding grim. Ditch had suffered a setback and had been put on oxygen, and Helena was still skulking around the reception area although he had got an attorney to call her and warn her to keep away. He was prepared to spend the night there if necessary and had stocked up on coffee and sandwiches, but there wasn't a cigarette machine in sight so I needn't worry on that score.

When I had heard nothing from Charles by the following morning, which was the 11th of September, I tried to call both him and Jared but all the lines were jammed. By then news of the attacks on the US was starting to come through. The two desperate days that followed were the worst of my entire existence. The reception desk at Ditch's private clinic was unobtainable, and I called Charles over and over again, only to hear the same voicemail message: 'You've reached Charles Wright, that's right! I'm either in a meeting or at the bar. Leave me a message and I'll get back in a jiff …'

Every time I turned on the television I saw New York in flames, the horrifying images of the twin towers and the other strikes. Despite using my press credentials as Editor-in-Chief of Upley Rising's premier monthly magazine, neither the BBC nor Reuters would share any information with me and I have since protested to the Press Complaints Commission.

Ditch Wright, Charles's larger than life big brother and my beloved brother-in-law, passed away in Manhattan's select Upper West Side Clinic as dawn broke on 11th September 2001, just a few weeks short of his 45th birthday. His last, noble act was to save his own brother's life. Charles had been due in meetings at the World Trade Centre, but instead he was at Ditch's side, holding his hand through the final hours and reminiscing to him about their carefree childhood days on the streets of London's East End: playing hopscotch, picking up pennies dropped in gutters, two lovable scamps running all kinds of errands for their grandfather's colourful gangland acquaintances. Ditch's last words were: "Love to Caroline, she's a real gem that one, look after her bruv."

The passing of one of the most innovative musicians this country has ever seen went uncelebrated while world news was distracted. The performer extraordinaire who won the Smash Hits Broken String award in both 1984 and 1986, who was voted Woman's Realm Smouldering Superstar of 1980, and whose album Shark's Tooth on Toast was described as 'pure untamed sound' by John Peel, died in near obscurity.

Someone had to give Ditch his due, and I gladly shouldered the burden. I prepared a full colour commemorative supplement to Upley Itself for distribution throughout Thameshire and beyond. It is a tribute to Ditch that the advertising space was completely oversubscribed, even at triple the usual price. I am enclosing a copy with this year's Christmas News, together with a reissued CD featuring Ditch's famous surprise cameo with Oasis at Knebworth.

We hope you will take a few moments over the Christmas break to treasure these special memories of our cherished celebrity relative.

* * * * *

**Max saves the day**
It is shocking that nothing in Charles's collection of executive membership cards could get him on a flight back to England for nearly two weeks following the attacks in the US.

So he missed the single ray of hope that shone through that dark time: seeing our son Maximilian set off for his first day at grammar school, looking every inch the future business mogul as he elbowed his way upstairs on the bus in his new blue uniform.

We are immensely proud that Max has won a place at one of the country's most prestigious schools, in such a difficult year for our family. Places at Queen's Grammar are hugely competitive and only children with parents intelligent enough to navigate its impenetrable admissions system can get in.

One of the reasons we moved to our lovely road, Paradise View, was its location in the Queen's Grammar's catchment area, giving automatic preference to children living here. But just as we had finished redecorating the ground-floor extension that is the envy of our neighbourhood, the local education authority, which is dominated by fanatical idealists, decided to shift the boundary line. We were devastated to be told that our dream home, in which we have invested so much, fell just on the wrong side of the boundary; meaning that children living in the ex-council houses at the bottom of the hill would benefit from grammar school places over and above our own hard-working son.

Complaining to the council met with a wall of undemocratic intransigence; our letters went unanswered and officious staff put the phone down every time I gave my name. We decided to change tack and Charles, always a genius at blue sky thinking, visited our next-door neighbours with a very generous offer to rent their garage. Not only is it in the Queen's catchment area, we probably already have some sort of legal claim to it when you take into account the tangled jungle of ivy invading our garden from its sagging roof. But they refused to accept the money, which we put down to the inordinate amount of child benefit they must be receiving.

So Max had no option but to take the school's entrance exam, and after weeks of gruelling special tuition which we'd had the foresight to organise in advance, I drove our brave son to a cold draughty hall to sit the papers. When the results letter arrived, he had come so close to the pass mark that it was obvious there must have been a terrible mix-up. We immediately pressed for justice.

Our legal team, represented by a top barrister, gave an impassioned address to the Education Appeals Panel. After five hours of listening to his impressively detailed arguments they had to concede the truth: poor Max was the victim of nervous stress brought on by his favourite Uncle Ditch's illness. (Ditch was experimenting with alternative therapies in a Hawaii clinic at the time Max was doing his preparation.) We won the appeal and what a relief it was to see Max take up his well-deserved place at one of the country's top three state grammars.

Not only will he be guaranteed a place at a good university, but we can use the money that would have gone on private school fees on other essentials, like adding a hot tub to our French home.

* * * * *

## The final goodbye

I am putting the final touches to our Christmas News just three weeks after Ditch's funeral, which was delayed while Charles's family battled with the US government for permission to bring the body back to this country. Heightened terrorism concerns led to the coffin being loaded then unloaded from four different flights; overzealous security staff kept classing it as a high-risk object and sending it back to the chapel of rest. Then Helena claimed that Ditch had wanted his ashes scattered in California, and in the meantime the US tax authorities decided to try and impound him.

In the end, Charles had to get someone he knew at the Foreign Office to intervene.

When it finally took place, the funeral was a proper East End affair, with the hearse on a carriage pulled by white horses bearing black plumes. The guitar-shaped coffin was barely visible under a mountain of floral tributes. Ditch's father insisted on walking the whole way behind it, head bowed, and Charles walked with him, gripping his arm. I travelled with Charles's mother, Maximilian and Clementine in the first of 15 funeral cars. The cortege held up the traffic in the Whitechapel Road for nearly an hour.

The church was packed. At the request of Ditch's parents the mourners were restricted to close friends and extended family; they wanted to avoid the service looking like a celebrity event, though Ditch's many contacts in the industry were welcome to make a donation to the good causes he had been supporting. Most of the black-clad mourners were concealed behind oversized dark glasses, as were the burly guards on the door.

Jared, Ditch's manager, was there, oozing New York style in a long fur coat and a black fedora hat. Then Helena made a surprise appearance in the November drizzle. She picked her way across the churchyard on spindly heels, wearing a tiny white dress. She came up to us to pay her respects and for a moment I thought Charles was going to punch her. He went pale with rage then controlled himself and walked away. The thought of a fight at Ditch's final farewell was more than I could bear so I made polite conversation.

She was actually very charming, and as one career woman to another I found myself respecting her, both of us bonding over both the memory of Ditch and the importance of attention to appearance in public. She explained that her outfit was inspired by Buddhist mourning rituals. She had obviously not given up on her prenuptial contract claim, and attending Ditch's funeral service, with the associated publicity, was a clear part of her strategy. But looking at the rows of grim-faced mourners in their Ray-Ban Predators, she must have begun to wonder whether her slick Californian lawyers were capable of taking on the Wright clan of Whitechapel.

Helena sat in isolation at the back of the church while we took our seats in the front row pew. The service was charged with emotion. Clementine gave the reading, the heartbreaking lyrics from Ditch's 1999 song Blood Ties Never Die. She stood on tiptoe on a step behind the pulpit; a brave figurine all in black, crowned by her halo of platinum curls. I heard stifled sobs from the congregation around me, and even Mother, in the row behind me with

Rupert, had a lace handkerchief pressed to her cheek. Then Max played the Last Post on his tuba, and the Bishop later complimented him that Ditch must have heard it from wherever he is now.

Charles delivered a moving eulogy blending poignant memories with lighter moments, putting the congregation at ease with an opening quip about the occasion reminding him of Ditch's 1992 Union Chapel gig. He finished by joking that even in his final stop and search at customs, as ever Ditch managed to elude the authorities. This rather cryptic remark brought on a ripple of relieved laughter from the congregation.

**Looking ahead: a golden year?**
Seeing our son start at one of the best schools in the country has buoyed me through the past few weeks. As for the year ahead, just as I was wondering how to rekindle motivation in my own life, fate stepped in. Grief had distracted me from remembering that 2002 marks the Golden Jubilee of Her Majesty the Queen, when the whole country will be celebrating her 50 years on the throne. Then I received a call from none other than the Mayor of Upley Rising, with a request that lifted my flagging spirits and filled me with new confidence.

Our own Upley Rising has been chosen for a truly historic visit during the nationwide celebrations. The details are still strictly under wraps and I can reveal nothing – other than that word has somehow spread about my expertise in organising memorable occasions. I will just say that I am deeply honoured and privileged to have been asked to play a humble but vital part in the festivities ahead in the coming jubilee year. I will keep you all posted!

## A wistful Christmas

Christmas in our house will be very quiet this year. Charles cheered up a bit when David Beckham's goal got England through to the World Cup finals, but he has lapsed into long silences again, and I am giving him room to grieve without commenting on the occasional whiff of tobacco, as long as it's kept to the garden. Max and Clementine have been very grown up about understanding that there won't be any big expensive presents from their Uncle Ditch this year. But it's so hard to accept that he won't appear at our house on Christmas Eve, a reprobate but irresistible Santa Claus in his trademark red leather jacket and black jeans, his craggy face breaking into a lazy smile as he stands by our ten-foot illuminated tree, his long fingers curling round his guitar, and his rich voice filling our capacious extension with his inimitable rendition of Silent Night.

Wishing you all a very Happy Christmas,

*Caroline, Charles, Maximilian and Clementine Wright*

# In Memoriam Ronald Percival Shoreditch Wright

## 1st November 1956–11th September 2001

\* \* \* \* \*

# Christmas 2000

**15 Paradise View**
**Upley Rising**
**Thameshire**

Dear Friends

~~What a fantastic start to the new millennium we've had.~~
~~With our heroes' welcome home by the mayor of Upley Rising~~
~~and grammar school scholarships for both the twins I've not~~
~~had a minute to enjoy my promotion to Head......~~

Mum started writing our Christmas letter then she fell
asleep so we are helping. Felipe and I do a lot of helping
now, we are in year 6 so we are responsible, and sometimes
Daniel helps when I tell him he's got to. We've got a new
baby brother and sister, they are twins too so Mum says
she's got double double trouble. We were in Scotland when
they arrived, the house was miles from anywhere, on a
windswept moor just like Hogwarts. It was really cold all
the time and we ate lots of vegetables, Auntie Gill said they
are good for us but they tasted manky. The TV didn't work
so we couldn't watch the new millennium. Mum and Dad
turned on the radio in the year 2000 and Dad said "Eet ees
just the same as before, nothing has changed, nada*!" and
Mum said "Rubbish, that's not possible!" and Auntie Gill
said words that I am not allowed to repeat, then we climbed
out of the bunker that Dad had dug, it was dark and raining
and we ran with our torches to the cottage and they all
drank cava and whisky and kissed each other and us and
couldn't stop laughing for ages. Mum played her guitar and
gave us home schooling and it got even colder for weeks
and weeks and it rained a lot and it was always dark so we

had to stay inside. One day Cousin Shrub put on a video called the Blair Witch Project because she said it was about the Prime Minister, it was really scary and we were all mega terrified and Daniel hid under the sofa. Then Mum started having the babies and the helicopter couldn't come because there was a storm so Auntie Gill lit candles and Dad put on music and we all helped and Mum screamed a lot even though we had turned off the scary film, then she said it was the most beautiful thing that had ever happened and she hugged us all and we all held the babies and Cousin Shrub cried a lot and Dad went out into the storm and no one could find him for ages.

Our new twins are called Fraser and Mackenzie, Mum and Dad found their names on the tartan tablemats in the house. They haven't got middle names as our parents had run out of ideas and anyway everyone only calls them the twinnies. They cry sometimes but it's not too bad.

When we came home we left Dad behind in Scotland, we haven't seen him for ages, and Mum goes to work on Mondays Tuesdays and Thursdays with the twinnies, they go to the crèche and Mum's got a job share. Felipe and I go to school and we take Daniel then we come home and later Mum comes home and she falls asleep and we help. Mum worries a lot about money so I have set up a business. Before she gets home from work I do Murder Visits Inc. for £1.50 each and they are a big success. Daniel hides in the wardrobe, we put ketchup on him and he pretends he's the body, then he runs down to the garden shed when no one's looking and hides again. Everyone in my class has been and they are telling all their friends. I write letters to Dad in Scotland every week and I hope he comes home soon for Christmas.

## Happy Christmas from Eleanor

*\* 'nada!' is Spanish for 'nothing!'*

Happy Christmas everyone,

I liked Scotland, it was massive, there was loads of space and we could see the sea from our house! But we had to come back for Easter as Mum said we needed our school places back or we wouldn't get into grammar school and if she had to eat another old potato she'd go bonkers and her milk would dry up and she had to go back to work because the government was not enlitened and wasn't going to keep paying her maternity pay because it was short sighted and didn't value the next generation. I was sad as I wanted to see the new vegetables come out of the ground and I liked chopping wood for the fire. There were real deer in our back garden in Scotland! I miss my Dad, he was in the front doorway waving to us when we got in the car and Mum said he needed Time for Himself so that's what she got him for his 40th birthday present and it least it didn't cost her an arm and a leg. Salvador stayed behind with Dad but Hector came back with us. I love Hector and one day he went with Mum and the twinnies to the crèche and everyone said it was very funny but Mum had to bring him home again.

Ellie and I fight a lot and Mum says there are too many of us in this house and she feels like the old woman who lived in a shoe. Mum said I should share Daniel's room but I don't want to share with Daniel as his lego is all over the place. Mum asked the Council if she can build another room and they said no because the other people in our road Paradise View objected, they didn't want any more bigger houses and Mum said that's typical tory council hippocracy so I have asked Santa for another room for Christmas. Auntie Vanessa comes and helps Mum sometimes and she brings us cakes and chips and calls us poor dears.

I am in year 6 now and I am Art supplies monitor. Eleanor does murder house visits and I help and I have also got a job. I am a delivery boy. I deliver the magazines that Max's mum next door makes, most houses in Upley Rising have to get one put through the letter box. Max is supposed to take them but he gives me 50p instead, they are very heavy and it's really hard work. Max's house has got lots of rooms, I can't see why we can't have some. My favourite subjects are art and science and I am working very hard to get my level 5 Sats.

Happy Christmas from Felipe


I am Daniel I don't like potatoes. I like Christmas I hope Santa will bring me some new batteries for my Gameboy. I have to change nappies for Fraser and Mackenzie it's stinky yuk but Ellie and Felipe say we've all got to have a helping job and that one is mine. I made a Scottish farm with my lego and Dad is the farmer. I don't like hiding in the wardrobe. For my birthday we went to the Dome because it was free and we had to wait for ages and ages to get in and it was raining but when we got in we could walk through a huge body it was amazing but Mum says it's got to go. I hope Cousin Shrub comes for Christmas.

Love from Daniel

PS Happy Christmas

## Christmas 2001

**15 Paradise View**
**Upley Rising**
**Thameshire**

Dear Friends

Welcome to the Christmas newsletter from the family that turns domestic chaos into an art form. For ease of reading I've organised this year's news into (1) Bog Standard Chaos and (2) Total Dysfunctionality.

**Bog Standard Chaos**
Three cheers for Eleanor and Felipe, who defied all expectations and landed a place – two places to be exact – at grammar school. Before you rip up this newsletter in disgust, Queen's Grammar charges NO FEES, being 100 per cent state school. It's also Thameshire's secret education powerhouse. Founded in 1349 to provide poor children with a proper schooling, rumour has it that two of the bastard progenies of one of the Plantagenets attended before ascending to dizzy heights in the church. Although they were later both murdered, their earlier successes emboldened the rich and ruthless to find weasely ways to procure Queen's Grammar places for their offspring – a practice that has been going on ever since.

These days the school is a rebuilt Victorian monstrosity

in real grounds with trees and its own swimming pool, perpetually covered in dead insects according to Eleanor. It's ranked the best school in Thameshire, and is number three in the country in the Sunday Times best state schools guide. People have been moving out here by the coachload, as anyone living in the school catchment gets first preference for a place. With the result that the catchment area has been shrivelling on an annual basis faster than the Incredible Shrinking Man.

Parents of local children shuttle in and out of Upley Rising's limited stock of rented flats to try and stay in it. One of Vanessa's friends spent six months separated from her husband, crammed with her two children into a sublet stockroom above the internet café. So this year we waited with bated breath for the annual map-drawing exercise from the education authority – and lo, 15 Paradise View fell exactly four feet the right side of the line. All the twins had to do to guarantee their place was get a level 5 in their SATs and attend an 'informal interview'.

This should have been a breeze given they'd had months of one-to-one home schooling in Scotland with no distractions, not even a working TV. They both scraped through by the skin of their teeth. Felipe wowed the interview panel with a story about his father braving the storms in a remote Scottish croft to defend his family against the wolves – they recommended he starts writing fiction. Eleanor produced one of her spreadsheets of family income and outgoings (including her murder house visitor attraction which she thinks I don't know about), designed to provoke horror and pity.

So they started at Queen's in September, and have gone all grown up on me. I don't get to rummage through their schoolbags anymore or to hear what went on in their day.

They are in separate classes for the first time, which seems to make them fight less at home.

At work I am now a year into my first ever job share: I am officially half Deputy Head Librarian – as well as being half full-time parent. (Not even Eleanor can make the maths work on that one.) Angie, my co-Deputy, divides the rest of her week between working for a birdwatching charity, entering line dancing competitions and training for triathlons.

I think the job share is going really well. When I ask Angie what she thinks she smiles politely and slides my gummy coffee cups and screwed up post-it notes off her half of our desk. We've both learned to give short shrift to students who swear to one of us that 'the other librarian' said it was OK to (1) take a precious reference book out of the building and return it with missing pages; (2) order in a beef vindaloo; (3) draw pornographic doodles in the margins of academic journals. The same approach applies to the Head Librarian who has a habit of asking us alternately to cover for him while he's at his grandfather's funeral – he's gone through four grandfathers in the past year.

Officially I work two and a half days a week, but unofficially I work at least 14 days a week if you include everything else I do. It's called work-life balance.

## Total Dysfunctionality

Antonio came back from his Scottish sabbatical. A week before Fraser and Mackenzie's first birthday in March, Daniel shouted out from the hall that there was a ghastly intruder on the doorstep and he had shut the door in his face in line with the family rulebook.

When I went to the door we just stared at each other. I

had to look for a long time before I was sure the stranger facing me was Ant. He'd lost tons of weight and his beard had white streaks for the first time. I had finally used the makeover voucher Vanessa bought me for my 40th birthday: goodbye shapeless jeans and my own greying hair, hello dangly earrings and copper highlights – Upley Rising's answer to David Bowie the hairdresser told me, though Daniel said I look like one of those antique shop copper kettles.

The nice solicitor who lives opposite happened to be walking past and made a point of stopping. He called out, "Is everything alright there Alison, is this man bothering you?" and pointed the umbrella he always carries at Ant, in the manner of a future James Bond on day release from the old people's home. In moments of crisis you can always rely on the Paradise View Neighbourhood Watch to break the ice. Ant and I both creased up and I shouted back that I always invite intruders in for a coffee. Ant hadn't given us advance warning as he had bought a mobile phone but didn't realise you had to put credit on it. He had lost the front door key to the house, and met a woman on the train who might be offering him a commission. The cat had travelled back with him in his backpack.

For the twinnies' first birthday we put together a video evening of everything Ant had missed: Fraser knocking out Mackenzie's first front tooth with a pint mug; Mackenzie falling off the kitchen counter; Daniel's nappy changing routine demonstration, putting the dirty nappies in Hector's mouth to take to the bin while he taped up the new ones. And all of us with ice creams at the Wellspring Festival, the twinnies screaming with delight in the double buggy as this year's maiden leapt into the well before the rope had been properly tied on.

Ant sat on the sofa watching with an arm round each sleeping twinnie (he's done this before, remember). He's been really quiet since he got back. There's been no mention of Pinochet, who with the collusion of the powers that be is now back in Chile pretending to be too ill to escape trial. It's all got so complicated I think Ant's given up. Art has been conspicuous by its absence although we did hear that our Scottish bothy, Craigh Fuar House, featuring the bunker he'd dug behind it, has been turned into a permanent millennium exhibit by its owners and is attracting visitors. Ant's been down to the studio a few times but not for long so it's mainly sat there all year dark and empty. I offered to go along to the tennis club to ask about his Big Hit piece that was mysteriously taken down, but Ant says he's moved on. I'm not so sure.

Our nasty neighbours, who are always on the lookout for new ways to spend their money, suddenly asked if they could rent the studio. The husband came round all smarmy smiles and carrying gifts – as if two bottles of Pinot Grigio could make up for ambushing the school PTA election (he's only ever made it to one meeting) and blocking anything we ever want to do to make our lives bearable. I was intrigued and sorely tempted to take the money. Pouring the wine, he admired my new hair and I started to wonder what he was after, as Ant was still in Caithness.

Then he casually asked whether the studio had the same address as our house, and it hit me that what they really wanted was our postcode. So their son Max, who bullies Felipe, could get a place at the Queen's Grammar without having to pass the exam for kids that are outside the catchment area – which their house is, by about six inches. So I said no.

We spent the summer holidays going up in the world – but not in the way you think. Desperate doesn't begin to describe how much we needed extra space at home, after my planning application for a miniscule extension was rejected by the council. So instead of going on holiday we decided to convert our loft. It would be a more positive experience than renting a damp country cottage with a panoramic view of foot and mouth corpses going up in smoke. After heated discussions about who would sleep where, Ant carved out two small attic bedrooms with a shared bathroom, and Eleanor and Felipe moved up there, which has given them an elevated sense of status and the privacy to get up to who knows what with their friends.

We were just starting to feel like some kind of normal family again. When the terrible attacks happened on September 11th we reassured ourselves that all in all, life crammed together with five children, a giant mudball of a dog, a senile incontinent cat and half a job, was something we should be thankful for. Two days later I had to make an emergency stop-off at Waitrose for pasta family packs. Both twinnies had a howling meltdown in the trolley all the way through the Two Minutes Silence, which was announced while we were in aisle five. The other customers stood frozen, holding their avocados and tubs of hummus and looking daggers at us, though the staff were very understanding.

When I got home Cousin Shrub was sobbing down the phone, asking if I'd heard about the death of Ditch Wright. I was flabbergasted – I knew he'd been ill with AIDS but assumed he led the charmed life of the rich rock star with endless cash for medical bills.

I had flickers of guilt about not renting our studio out to our neighbours – perhaps it was going to be somewhere for Ditch to recuperate, or a temporary recording bolthole while he was looked after in privacy by his family? Had I missed the chance to save his life? I decided to do The Right Thing and went to see Caroline and Charles to offer commiserations. She opened the door.

I'd never seen her without make-up or high heels. She looked much younger, with her hair in a ponytail, vulnerable and human with pallid skin and dark rings under her eyes. I actually felt sorry for her. I stammered out my condolences and proffered a bunch of garage forecourt chrysanthemums. She stared at me in her usual distracted way as if her mind was on something much further up her internal agenda.

Then she said, "You can't have that you know." She pointed at our new third-floor dormer windows reflecting the autumn sunshine. "Your ugly loft thing. This is a conservation area and it's against all the bye-laws. And those plastic windows are a monstrosity. I've written to the Council. It'll ruin our road for the Royal visit next year."

That was a new one on me. "Royal visit?"

"Yes, and I'm in charge." She waved up at Eleanor and Felipe's bedroom windows again – Eleanor had already plastered hers with Greenpeace stickers. "We're holding a street party to celebrate the Queen's Golden Jubilee. Not only that, we are going to be honoured with a visit from a very special top secret royal guest – and I'm going to make sure that no one in Paradise View lets us down."

Wishing you all a less chaotic Christmas than ours,

*Alison, Antonio, Eleanor, Felipe, Daniel, Fraser,*

*Mackenzie, and Hector and Salvador*

# Christmas 2002

**15 Paradise View**
**Upley Rising**
**Thameshire**

Dear Friends

## Annual Christmas Family Newsletter

### From Eleanor

I am in year 8 now and we all have to join a club at school so I joined the Public Speaking Society, where I delivered an oration about The Eurovision Song Contest's role in World Peace and I came second. My friend Lauren gave a speech called Mobile children Means Mobile Phones and she came first. I have joined Friends of the Earth. We didn't go on holiday this year but we all agreed that the best bit of the summer was our Big Protest.

Happy Christmas everyone.

### From Felipe

I am in a different class from Ellie, I am in 8F. I have joined the Pottery Club at school. There's a real kiln and Dad gave me some of his models to take in to fire for him and I won a prize. But then I said they were Dad's and I had to do a detention and sit outside the headmistress's office for two hours and take a letter home for Dad. Dad opened the letter and tore it up. The best thing this year was the Street Party even though Mum says we are outlaws in our own street now. I helped Dad make our banner.

Happy Christmas.

**From Daniel**

I am in year 6 now and I have to do my SATS, and there's a school trip to France. I like staying at home playing Super Mario. Our Big Protest was really scary and I had to go to the Doctor afterwards but he says there doesn't seem to be any damage.

Merry Christmas.

**From Ali and Ant**

Mary and Joseph had more room at Christmas than us this year. Three weeks to go, and we are spending our days crammed into Ant's studio at the bottom of the garden. Why? Because as well as an illegal loft, we've got a pile of rubble where most of our downstairs used to be.

But on the whole it's been a good year – and this may sound bonkers, but we owe it to the Queen.

We spent the first half of 2002 dodging any involvement in Golden Jubilee celebrations. Everyone around us had got themselves into a right royal ferment. While children in Mozambique were starving, the worthy folk of Upley Rising were regilding our gothic clock tower or running red, white and blue hanging basket competitions. Daniel's class spent their days sending haiku poems* to Buckingham Palace instead of studying for their SATs. Even our Wellspring Festival committee voted to have an Elf King and Queen theme. I was the lone objector and accused them of being secret royalist sympathiser hypocrites behind all their enthusiasm for drumming workshops and transcendental dance sessions.

On the Golden Jubilee front, this family decided on a policy of dignified silence. I got stuck into work – a satisfying analysis of our journals usage statistics. Ant looked after the twinnies on non-crèche days and worked on the commission he received from the woman he met on the train back from Scotland. She's been very good about it running over a year late. All the children spent their time obsessing over Pop Idol and trebled our phone bill voting for Gareth Gates.

But in March everyone in our road received the same letter, on thick cream paper, word-processed in an Italian gothic font. Because of the 'tireless energy' and 'special connections' of the Committee Chair, Paradise View's very own Golden Jubilee Street Party had been chosen by the town council for a visit by a member of the Royal Family at the highest possible level. This was an honour and a privilege and everyone in the road was expected to step up and do their bit, blah blah blah. We were given three months to whip our houses, front gardens and curtsey techniques into shape. This was to be the royal street party to put all other street parties in the shade. Expert advice was available from the Committee (an unelected group of residents who all just happened to be tennis club members) on paint colours – we should draw on a vintage pastoral palate – and choices of herbaceous border planting for our front gardens. Informal inspections (in a jokey tone) would be made.

The letter was signed Caroline Wright, Chair, Paradise View Jubilee Street Party Royal Visit Committee. A handwritten note on the bottom of our copy, in witchy lilac ink, 'reminded' us that our loft conversion was against the law and violated the Conservation Area regulations. Also that our privet front hedge (by now a towering 12 feet, quite a landmark) was an ongoing health hazard.

Think red rags and bulls. You won't catch a Pickthwaite kowtowing to anything walking a corgi or wearing a glorified pastry cutter on her or his head. Ant felt the same after the General Pinochet episode. He couldn't understand why the Queen as head of state hadn't intervened in person to bring him to justice. And for a while we were led to believe that Paradise View was in line for a visit by Ma'am herself, she who thinks the world smells of fresh paint. Why else were heritage paint colour cards shoved through our letterbox, along with weekly bulletins containing recipes for scones and embellished with photocopied coats of arms? By the time we found out that our visitation was actually to be from the Duchess of Thameshire (a minor royal who only ever gets into the back pages of Hello! according to Eleanor) our plans for the Pickthwaite-Cortinez royal street party Big Protest were already in place.

As my gran used to say, you can't make an omelette without breaking eggs.

The day of the visit dawned clear and sunny. Ant was up early with a borrowed chainsaw, pruning our giant hedge as instructed. The result was better than we'd expected. For the first time we could see all the way down the road, which was flapping in a suburban frenzy of fluttering bunting. By early afternoon a long line of trestle tables had appeared, covered in gingham cloths and laden with enough sugar to bankroll every dentist in Thameshire for years.

We were all in place outside our homes when the Duchess drew up in a swanky limo with a giant crest stuck on the top. I was surprised to see her accompanied by Robert, our solicitor neighbour who's usually very reserved, looking awkward with an elaborate gold chain over the dark suit he always wears even for gardening. Robert handed Her Royalness out of the car as if she were some sort of fragile flower, and was about to escort her along the road, but before they got any further our neighbour Caroline materialised out of a cloud of Poison by Dior so dense you could almost see it. She was done up to the nines in a sky-blue suit, poised on teetering heels with gold tips. A giant scarf – later christened a power pashmina by my friend Vanessa – swirled from her shoulders to her knees.

In less than three seconds she had shoehorned herself between Robert and her Duchessness and taken control of the afternoon.

They progressed down the road in our direction as if they were inspecting the troops. Accompanied by a silver-rinsed woman in a hat who was Caroline's mother, and a man in a hacking jacket who looked like he'd wandered away from a country pheasant shoot and got lost. Charles, the husband, was sloping along on the edge of the group with his hands in his pockets, looking smug and embarrassed at the same time. The retinue was completed by their son brandishing the video camera he takes everywhere and wearing a big badge reading 'Appointed Street Party Photographer'.

The residents of Paradise View stood by the buckling tables of food, to varying degrees of attention when they weren't hissing at their kids to keep their fingers off the French Fancies. The entourage stopped every few yards for Caroline to introduce the Duchess to pre-picked friends. At one point a little lad ran up to proffer an unscripted bunch of flowers and was swiftly despatched by Caroline's metallic stiletto. This was important as her daughter Clementine, yellow curls flowing from a glittery tiara, was stationed outside their own house (freshly painted, with a re-landscaped front garden) waiting to present the Official Posy.

The royal party slowed to an accidental halt in front of Clem. I heard Caroline saying, "… and we would be beyond honoured should your Grace consent to bestow your presence at our son's forthcoming tuba concert …" then as she saw her daughter her expression adjusted itself into Delighted Surprise mode.

Clem, in her diadem and new frilly frock, plunged earthwards into a low curtsey – just as I, yards away outside our own house, moved the double buggy aside and pulled away a faded Union Jack duvet cover. Thus revealing Eleanor and Felipe at their newly created Murder House Visits tickets kiosk, an MDF triumph painted black, dripping with fake blood and draped in skeleton bunting. Simultaneously Ant, in position upstairs, unfurled all 12 feet of his Abolish the Monarchy banner from the loft windows.

It was all meant to end there, our family demo: modestly exercising our democratic right to point out that there are more important things in the world than tea parties and unelected aristocracy swanning around on taxpayers' money. Even at that level it would have been the biggest upset in Upley Rising since the witch-ducking riots of 1659 that led to the Wellspring Festival.

But the law of unintended consequences takes no prisoners.

The Duchess looked across the top of Clem's prostrated head – her curtsey was so deep that all you could see was a mop of yellow curls spread out on the pavement like a flattened poodle. Her eyes fell on Felipe and Eleanor standing at their stall. "Twins!" she exclaimed, striding up to them. "I'm a twin too; my brother and I are the best of friends, though we used to fight like dogs when we were little. Who's the eldest, and by how many minutes?"

Our children are nothing if not well brought up. If Felipe hadn't felt duty bound to invite the Duchess for a Murder Visit things might have ended there. But she produced a £20 note (20 pounds!) from her purse, commenting about a refreshing change from the usual run of tea parties, and they disappeared down our path into our house.

Who could have foreseen that Daniel, who was sitting downstairs playing on his Gameboy, not expecting any actual murder customers, would be thrown into a panic? And instead of hiding in his usual upstairs wardrobe, would cram himself into the living room fireplace, forcing aside the ugly electric heater we'd been planning to replace ever since we moved in?

Who knew that said electric heater was the only thing holding up the fireplace, as the chimney above it had been crumbling away inside for years?

And who knew – only the Pervert of Paradise View – that as the chimney started disintegrating around our son, the decomposing body wedged above him in the flue would be pushed out of its 40-year-old hiding place like toothpaste out of a tube and come flying out, taking Daniel with it, and spattering grisly debris everywhere?

I didn't witness any of this. As I tried to follow the Duchess into our house, the twinnies' double buggy got jammed in the garden gateway – nightmare things, double buggies. I was trapped outside along with Caroline, who was desperately trying to follow the Duchess, and the rest of the royal entourage. We heard the screams from the living room, felt the ground rumble like an earthquake (said Ant later, recalling tremors from his Chilean childhood). A horrified hush fell over the entire street party, as we all watched the chimney stack implode and acrid smoke billow out of our front door. We held our breath as Felipe and Eleanor stumbled out, covered in grey dust. Followed, after an agonising pause during which Caroline sank every one of her fingernails into my arm, by two silhouettes, coated in soot and streaked with rivulets of blood. The Duchess was staring ahead in shock and holding Daniel by the hand in a scene straight out of every post-apocalyptic horror film. The little pillbox hat she had been wearing looked oddly distorted, until I realised that lodged on her head was a human skull, complete with hollow eye sockets and a few sparse hairs.

Ant came running down. He got the Duchess away from the house and sat her down on a folding chair by one of the party tables. I was seeing to Daniel, who was streaming with a mix of fake and real blood. Caroline pushed bits of cucumber sandwich into the Duchess's mouth while her mother mopped at her face with screwed-up jubilee napkins dipped in lemonade. Her Ladyship was covered in soot, plaster and bits of body. She smelt of rancid corpse. People were dialling 999 and rushing around with bandages and pieces of advice. You got the feeling the Home Guard elements in the road had been primed for this moment for years.

It could still have ended there: an overenthusiastic protest leading to a macabre building disaster, stopping short of full-scale war. But demons had been unleashed. Charles, presented with an opportunity to become the hero of the day, chose the scumbag option. He strolled over to the Duchess, lifted the skull off her head like an archbishop at a satanic coronation, then turned to face Ant. He stood lobbing the skull from one hand to the other, a crass grin on his face.

You have to wonder how much venom a snake can store up. Waving the skull, he looked Ant up and down.

"I suppose this is your latest bit of so-called Art!" he shouted, before throwing it onto the ground, where it cracked down the middle.

Ant just stood there, so Charles tried again. "No one wants this trash. And your bit of junk that ended up in my extension, it's more use holding up a wall than hanging on one." Ant still didn't move.

Charles went on, "You've royally screwed up a day that was meant to be special for our Queen – and for my wife. You know what, I'm really glad I got your pathetic excuse for a statue thrown out of my tennis club, you loser."

At this Ant finally cracked. And so there was a fight: a proper ruckus of the kind that happened outside the Cat & Fiddle most Friday nights where I grew up, but never seen before in genteel Upley Rising. Fists flew, noses leaked snot and blood, shirts were ripped. Two sweating grown men circled and panted and did their best to beat the living daylights out of each other. All in front of an audience who oohed and aahed, forgetting all about the tea going cold in the pots and the cucumber sandwiches curling at the edges. Until the two men lurched backwards together straight into a loaded trestle table. It tipped over with a crash, scattering cakes and jam and shattering the bone china tea service loaned by Mrs Brown from number 31.

A second hush fell across the crowd, stunned first by the devastation at the Murder House and now by the wanton destruction of three plates of scones and an entire Wedgwood heirloom. The silence was broken by the brother of our neighbour Robert; a lovely big child of a man who has some medical condition and who we don't often see out. He burst into loud giggles then started clapping his hands and shouting "More, more!" At which scumbag Charles got to his feet, walked up and slapped him hard round the face.

Step forward Robert, Mr respectable suburban solicitor. One minute an invisible fixture in a pinstriped suit, the next a berserk warrior. Ripping off his chain of office, he grabbed Charles by the lapels with one hand and began clouting him with the gold chain. He was shouting at Charles, who was hunched over trying to protect himself, to leave his brother out of things. Ant managed to pull him off, but not before Robert landed Charles a huge slug on the jaw. Charles careered backwards, straight into Caroline behind him. She tottered on her high heels, tried to find her balance, but tripped over her power pashmina and fell onto the Duchess, who tipped off the folding chair where Ant had sat her down (flimsy bits of engineering, folding chairs) and onto the pavement, where her fall was broken by the remains of a black forest gateau.

Poor Robert. He stood peering at the wreckage through misted-up spectacles, then crumpled to the ground in a dead faint.

Thus ended the Paradise View Royal Jubilee tea party – with the Pickthwaite-Cortinez family qualified to start a revolution. The Duchess of Thameshire (DT as her friends call her) was miraculously unscathed. She was unbelievably gracious about the whole episode, and probably saved us all from being arrested for treason. I found out later that she's not actually a blood royal. She married into the family but was born in Accrington, the daughter of a factory worker, which explains quite lot.

\* \* \* \* \*

This may be the longest Christmas news since the story of

Jesus, but there's more.

The next day Caroline appeared at our house, the first and only time she's ever been in. Ant's banner was still hanging in tatters from the loft windows. We were trying to clear a path through the rubble downstairs, while waiting for calls from the police (the Pervert of Paradise View file had never been closed) and the insurance company. She was looking as immaculate as ever, though I spotted a small bruise on her forehead only partly disguised by concealer. I started to tell her that she'd got her wish – the most memorable royal street party ever – but Felipe gave me a Look. I waved an arm towards an armchair that we'd covered in a dustsheet. She fixed her gaze slightly to the right of my head and said:

"I'm not stopping. I'm just here to let you know that you're going to regret you ever moved here. You are nothing but trouble. Your children are a disgrace, you've got far too many of them, your house is an eyesore and you should be prosecuted for what you've done to your front hedge. You are bringing down property values in this sought-after area. My husband was already experiencing depression after his tragic loss last year. Worst of all my business reputation is suffering. I'm getting up a petition to have you removed. You'll be hearing from my solicitors. We're going to sue you for every penny you've got."

I wished her luck. She's never seen our bank account – though I've seen hers. Once they put out their rubbish on the wrong day and went off for a long weekend in their French house or somewhere. Their credit card statement fluttered out of the bin and into our garden. I had to count the number of zeros twice and I still couldn't work out how they spend so much. £4,000 from a well-known Swiss make-up brand? Who can smear that amount of money on their face? Wearing that much foundation she must live in constant fear of subsidence.

To be honest we didn't have much time to quake in our boots about Caroline's threats. We were too busy dealing with the police, and the building inspectors who were trying to get us to move out of what they classed an unsafe building. With no downstairs living space apart from a kitchen coated in toxic brick dust they had a point. But waiting for the insurance money we had nowhere else to go.

In the end we compromised and set up home in Ant's studio, from where we sneak down the garden to cook in our illicit kitchen or get up to the bedrooms. At least we are out of sight of the murder tourists who soon started reappearing again – though one reporter lay in wait for Daniel and tried to interview him on his way to school.

The summer holidays arrived, things began to calm down a bit as the Pervert of Paradise View story died down again and our house was hidden behind scaffolding and giant tarpaulins. Other people in Upley Rising played tennis at their snooty club, or went on holiday to Tuscany. Our July and August were spent working, making endless cups of tea for gloomy detectives, getting Daniel checked out by a psychotherapist after his experience, and watching the privet hedge grow back.

Every week or so we got a letter from Messrs Urquhart and Lumley, Solicitors of Mayfair, demanding that we pay jaw-dropping sums of money forthwith for the distress and anguish caused to their clients, Mr and Mrs Wright. Ant took each letter and embedded it at a different angle onto a huge metal spike and we all watched a manila envelope tower take shape.

Then a few weeks ago Vanessa appeared at the studio door, squeezing in just as we were all sitting down to supper. She was carrying a copy of the News of the World and grinning. She spread it open over the table (aka Ant's workbench), ignoring our suppers.

I wondered why she had come over to show us a photo of an undernourished blonde in the bottom half of a miniscule bikini, and was trying to cover all the kids' eyes at once, until I saw next to it another snap of none other than Charles Wright. Below a headline all in capitals: 'DEATHBED DITCH BITCH'S WRIGHT ROMP.' We took it in turns to read out a sentence each. I would have included a copy of the cutting but Mackenzie ate it with her fish fingers. So just in case you don't buy my mother's favourite tabloid, here's a summary.

The blonde, a model from Idaho called Helena, had been the ex-fiancée of deceased rock musician Ditch Wright who passed away from AIDS last year (and whose signed album cover was immortalised in a gold frame on our living room wall, when we had a living room wall). Helena's attempts to claim her rightful share of Ditch's estate from his English family had been met first with hostile silence then with veiled threats. Sinister men with London accents had turned up at her Santa Monica apartment, waved a bottle of bleach in her face and warned her that her modelling days could be over for good if she carried on her legal battle. In despair Helena had gone public. Revealing how she had spent the night Ditch died 'consoling' his brother Charles. "It just kinda happened," according to the story. "We were two sad souls about to lose the one we both adored, finding comfort the only way we could. It was a crazy moment, our bodies exploring ways to articulate the grief that our minds couldn't accept."

There was a photo of the smart American hospital room where the two of them had grieved in tandem. Complete with motorised bed, it was just down the corridor from the suite where one of our great rock musicians languished alone in his final hours. Helena could never forgive herself for not being with Ditch as he departed this world – nor forgive his family for denying her proper share of his inheritance.

Apparently the crazy moment had lasted longer than that one night, as there were more pictures of the pair, holding hands in Central Park and nuzzling each other in a dark corner of a Manhattan bar. But now Helena had decided things could not go on any longer like this – neither taking comfort in Charles nor waiting for the chunk of Ditch's wealth she claimed was hers by right.

Charles Wright had not been available for comment. This last line alongside a final pic of their house in Paradise View – with ours, shrouded in plastic sheeting, next to it.

Vanessa left the ketchupy copy of the paper with us. She had thoughtfully purchased another six, which she went off to dot around the tennis club's public areas.

A couple of nights later, after we had all crept up the garden path to our illegal bedrooms, we were woken up by noises coming from the twinnies' room. This was nothing unusual, and usually just means Fraser is taking apart Mackenzie's cot, or Mackenzie is eating the cot screws then throwing up. But for once they were both sound asleep, and the noise was coming from the wall behind them.

Don't ask me why our neighbours, with their perfect pre-teen children, still have a baby monitor plugged in. Perhaps it's so they can check on their superfluous nanny. Or on us. Whatever, it was still in full working order and operating on the same frequency as ours. One by one by one we all crept in to listen in to the civil war that was playing out in the house next door. Eventually I sent Felipe, Eleanor and Daniel out of the room rather than expose them to any more of the language that was coming from Caroline. For someone who had never been heard using vocabulary more exotic than 'Versace' or 'Swarovski' she was quite impressive. I, a librarian, had never come across some of the words she used to describe Helena. The exchange between her and Charles was interrupted by shrieks and what sounded like French cast-iron casseroles being thrown at the walls.

Within 24 hours she was gone – in a taxi, loaded up with more suitcases than a team of footballers' wives take on tour. She hasn't been back. He's hardly ever there either. There's just a new nanny, who minds her own business and looks quite relaxed. I've even seen pizzas being delivered.

Normal life has resumed in our house, or will do as soon as the insurance money comes through. The weekly manila envelopes from Urquhart and Lumley have stopped arriving. The yellow crime scene tape around our gaping chimney has come down, though the police are still in touch and Eleanor has decided she wants to be a forensic scientist. The identity of the body in our chimney remains a mystery and it looks as though the case will never be resolved. The police are almost certain it was the murderer himself, but the dental records for the years he lived here have disappeared so we'll never know for sure.

We're just glad it's gone. As the seven of us and the dog celebrate a squashed Christmas under the fairy lights in Ant's studio we all feel strangely relaxed for the first time in years.

Festive Greetings to you all,

*Alison, Antonio, Eleanor, Felipe, Daniel, Fraser, Mackenzie, and Hector and Salvador*

*\* Daniel's school haiku sent to Buckingham Palace:*

*The Queen's on her throne*
*We all have to obey her.*
*But our dog runs free.*

\* \* \* \* \*

## 14 Paradise View, Upley Rising, Thameshire

### Christmas 2002

This has been a year for appreciating the ordinary pleasures in life. I took Colin to see Chitty Chitty Bang Bang at the London Palladium in May; grew a passable summer display of delphiniums and gave our wisteria a long overdue prune; sang Da Pacem Domine to a reasonably full Methodist church hall in October.

By contrast, it is more grandiose schemes which have brought unwanted and unnecessary disruption.

More of the year than I intended was taken up with preparations for Her Majesty the Queen's 50th anniversary celebrations in June. Upley Rising's rather optimistic petition for a royal title was turned down; in consolation we were granted the honour of a visit from a member of the Royal Family. Not only was the Duchess of Thameshire to be our guest, but her day would begin with an unanticipated privilege, a visit to the Upley Society.

The Duchess was due to arrive at the Society's Victorian Hall at 11.30am for early luncheon prior to an afternoon tour. As chair of the royal jubilee luncheon sub-committee I dedicated long spring evenings to scrutinising every detail, from the fine wine selection to the order in which

Society members would be presented to her Grace. (On this latter point, I was subjected to some shameless lobbying and even offered various financial inducements which I hardly need to say were peremptorily refused.) The day of the royal visit found me at the Victorian Hall before 8am to oversee the final cleaning and preparations. On her arrival, the Duchess proved to be a charming and personable guest, professional in her role and with a kind word for everyone present. I am pleased to report that the lunch went off without a hitch: the duckling was cooked to perfection, the speeches were short and free from the smutty references to which some members are prone, and the Nuits-Saint-Georges was served at the perfect temperature.

The Duchess's afternoon schedule featured two highlights: a visit to a traditional street party, to be followed by a more contemporary offering at the community centre on the council estate at Lower Rising. I was accorded the great privilege of accompanying her at the end of luncheon, as the street party designated for her visit was by coincidence in Paradise View, my own road. She was relaxed and conversational on the car journey, which included a stop at our beautifully renovated gothic clock tower, and a short detour to view the plaque commemorating my father, in which she took a most gratifying interest.

I wish I could report that the remainder of the visit went equally smoothly, but it would be dishonest of me to pretend otherwise.

On arrival at Paradise View, we were greeted by a fine sight: a proper community picnic reminiscent of my childhood, complete with chequered tablecloths and patriotic bunting, all thanks to the hard work of the organising committee. The atmosphere was cheery, with everyone turned out in their finest. The single exception was the multitudinous family who live opposite my own home. These people had taken the decision that the celebration of Her Majesty's Golden Jubilee was a suitable occasion to divert attention to their own republican viewpoint. In so doing they opened a Pandora's Box.

As the royal tour made its way along Paradise View towards my own house, I was taken aback to observe that during the morning the family in question had butchered their front hedge into a priapic motif, an obscene variation of the Victory sign. The husband, who is a modern artist and not, I understand, a husband in the legal sense, lay in wait for the Duchess's arrival to unfurl a grotesque banner from their rooftop. It depicted a distasteful, cartoonish version of Her Majesty in the unseemly grip of some military dictator. The artist amplified his protest with a megaphone; no one could understand what he was shouting, but God Save the Queen it definitely was not.

The children of the family then escalated things further, leading to a dreadful accident. They had set up a macabre kiosk on the street, a tawdry reminder of the murders that took place in our road many years ago which most of us would rather forget. The Duchess, with her impeccable manners, was too polite to refuse the invitation to inspect their ghoulish set-up, and was lured into their house, which has never looked very well maintained. By some miracle they all avoided being badly hurt when they were caught there at the very moment their chimney collapsed, revealing a corpse which had lain trapped and dormant since the gruesome events of the past.

It was an appalling incident which the whole road witnessed with horror. Just when we should all have been grateful that everyone, including Her Grace, escaped relatively unscathed, a fracas broke out. The artist and his next-door neighbour, who have some history of rivalry, began exchanging insults, then hitting out at each other. Losing all sense of self control, they went crashing into the tea party itself, with all too foreseeable consequences.

One of Colin's favourite ways of spending an afternoon is watching old Laurel and Hardy films. It was no surprise that seeing punches fly and tables tipping over sending their sticky contents flying in all directions, he thought the fight was part of the entertainment. He began laughing and applauding what he thought was a comic interlude. The neighbour, failing to appreciate Colin's limitations (though he must have seen him getting on and off the charity outings bus outside our house), then had the cowardly temerity to turn on my brother.

I am afraid I had no option but to defend Colin, which I was later told I did to the best of my ability. The disgraceful turn the afternoon had taken brought on one of my PTSD attacks and I cannot remember much beyond seeing the neighbour approaching Colin with fury in his eyes and several feet of Union flag bunting wound round his fists. But I later found out, to my eternal chagrin, that the Duchess was caught in the crossfire and I am utterly ashamed at my part in the final indignity which ended her visit to our road.

The best that can be salvaged from the day is that in the event there were no serious injuries to the Duchess or anyone else. But someone had to fall upon their sword. The Chairman of the Upley Society accepted with alacrity my offer to resign, thus bringing to an end four generations of dedicated service from my family. The Society has been part of our lives for as long as I can remember. Paintings of both my great-grandfather and my grandfather in their gold chains of office have always hung in our hall. Dedicating a plaque honouring my father's good works was one of my mother's proudest moments.

But oddly enough I have no regrets. I am not sure whether it is the institution or myself that has changed. Earlier this year one of our members stood as a British National Party councillor in the local elections, coming a narrow fifth behind the three main parties and the Equalise Education in Thameshire Party.

My other offer of resignation, from Coburn Briggs, was refused, so I soldier on there. The practice manager has recently surprised us all by defecting to our competitors, March, Ferret and Gladdington, leaving us halfway through a five-year strategy plan and with a series of Radio Thameshire advertisement slots booked that we have no clue how to fill

Colin recovered physically from the events of the summer, but has remained unsettled, especially as there have been successive police visits to the artist's house opposite following the discovery of the body in the chimney. Every time another chequered car pulls up he becomes difficult to manage, though Tomasz and I do our best to distract him.

We plan a quiet Christmas this year. Returning to my theme, there is greater comfort in the reliably mundane than in extraordinary events, with the disequilibrium they bring. The Gupta family have been kind enough to invite us for lunch, but as Tomasz will be in Lublin with his wife for the holidays, Colin and I plan to spend Christmas day in the spare room. With turkey sandwiches and slabs of Christmas cake to hand, we will enjoy a calm day working through the signalling intricacies of our

Clapham Junction station layout.

With Christmas wishes,

**Robert**

\* \* \* \* \*

*December 2002*

*Paradise House, Paradise View*
*Upley Rising, Thameshire*

The Wright family send everyone best wishes for Christmas and the New Year.

\* \* \* \* \*

# A PERFECT YEAR?

# PART SEVEN 2003-2004:

# ROBERT, ALI, CHARLES, CAROLINE

### 14 Paradise View, Upley Rising, Thameshire

### Christmas 2003

The year started with a freezing wind and torrential rains. The town's new year's firework display was snuffed out before it started and we were thankful to stay indoors out of the deluge.

The morning after the storms, New Year's Day, I awoke to a startling view from my bedroom window: an expanse of glittering silver water, supine in the near distance. Under the wintry sky it would have been a beautiful sight, but for the objects I could make out emerging from it. Telegraph pole tops; a supermarket sign; several floating cars, half submerged. And some figures clinging to a rooftop surrounded by water, waiting for rescue. Thameshire had not been spared the flooding which struck much of Southern England.

As I gazed out at the improvised lake, I received a telephone call from one of my mother's old friends, a fearsome woman in her late 80s who still chairs a school governors' board and runs Upley Rising's annual flower and produce show with a rod of iron. She was collecting anyone who could help families affected by the storm at the recently completed housing estate at Lower Rising. The River Up, having broken its banks, and further engorged with overflow from the sewage works, had surged through the roads of the low-lying estate causing devastation.

My details must have been in her address book along the lines of 'solicitor – professional, reliable, possibly useful'. I could not refuse, and armed with my raincoat, umbrella and a clipboard I reported for duty at a church hall which had been requisitioned as a temporary shelter.

I was shocked by the sight that met my eyes. A crowded church hall is associated in my mind with warmth, brightness and animated groups gossiping over refreshments. Here, where there was limited shelter but no electric power, about 60 people were standing silent and dispirited in the gloomy light, some gripping blankets round their shoulders. A woman was kneeling to change a baby's nappy on a coat on the floor. Other small children were wailing on different sides of the hall. A cold draught blew in from the door to the lavatories at the back every time anyone came through.

I had pictured myself seated at a reception desk, methodically noting down details of food and clothing requirements from a patient line of flood refugees. Instead I was assigned to emergency salvage duty and spent the day accompanying a building contractor from the estate on forays into the estate in his pickup van. It was utterly miserable work, wading knee deep through foul effluent to help retrieve bin bags of belongings from waterlogged and stinking homes. I helped one teenage boy in a frantic search for his GCSE coursework, but when we found it the pages were sopping and the ink had dissipated. In another house an elderly lady insisted on handing me a frozen chicken and other rock-hard contents from her freezer, to carry back to the hall on my lap as we all squeezed into the front of the builder's lorry.

When I got home in the evening, our dry warm house with the Christmas decorations still up seemed excessive. I spent the rest of the week helping the emergency effort; Colin joined me and was very useful moving large items and dragging mattresses out in rows on the hall floor. He enjoyed the sludgy mud and never noticed the smell, which continued to turn my stomach.

When word got round that I am a lawyer I found myself besieged with enquires from the hapless residents: about insurance claims, or whether they had to pay their mortgages/rent, or could they sue the developers who had assured them that building 80 houses on a flood plain was perfectly safe. I explained that my field was strictly probate and complex trusts and referred everyone to the area Citizens Advice Bureau. Only to discover, to my embarrassment, that it had closed down 18 months earlier.

Thus began my new parallel career as a pro bono lawyer. Since March I have spent two evenings every week dispensing free legal advice from a spare room above a bookmaker's establishment on the Lower Rising shopping parade.

My new clients, and the scenarios in which they find themselves, are infinitely more variegated than those we look after at Coburn Briggs. My very first advisee was a man whose son had been remanded in custody on charges of knife possession. I successfully applied for bail, which led to the loan of our unassuming premises by the grateful father, who is the manager of the bookmakers below. I advised a single mother who was juggling credit cards to try and keep up with her household bills and had sunk into horrific debt. I steered a riven family through their divorce process. I draw up wills, and counsel angry souped-up Ford Escort owners that it makes more sense to pay speeding fines than try and argue with the magistrates. My remit has expanded way beyond the original flood problems; I have had to revisit areas of law that I had not studied since my degree over 30 years ago.

Word spread and we began to attract visitors from further afield, including some of my own neighbours, who, without breaching client confidentiality, turned out to be quite different from my assumptions. The old adage about not judging a book by its cover is certainly true.

Most people are appreciative, though some are indifferent and assume that I am part of the government. I am not paid for my work though I have received some interesting small gifts. The old scars on my face from the IRA bomb in 1996, studiously ignored at Coburn Briggs, are a source of fascination. I have received admiring comments, an offer of free tattoos to enhance them, and even an invitation to join what sounds like a local vigilante set-up.

Coburn Briggs, after a lengthy partners' discussion from which I recused myself, endorsed my effort. I am seen as 'rounding out' the firm according to our new marketing manager, though some of the partners still worry that wealthier clients may be put off. Nevertheless my project was mentioned in our local radio campaign: ('Coburn Briggs, Thameshire's Caring Solicitors …' etc.). My colleague Meera began helping out regularly and had the idea to expand the venture. So since September we have become a small team comprising Meera, her brother Rajiv who is a manager at the hospital, a friend of Tomasz called Miroslav who speaks several languages and can organise interpreters in several more, and Emma, a disability benefits specialist who has helped Colin and me in the past. We even have a name: Thameshire Advice.

In July I took a long weekend to go to a small early music festival near Stratford, and explore some rarely heard medieval pieces in a delightful setting. I left Colin in Tomasz's care.

I returned to find that Colin has a girlfriend. They met on an outing with his Wednesday group and have been inseparable ever since. She lives in supported accommodation; her own family will not have much to do with her. Emerald has become a regular visitor to our house. I have never known Colin to allow anyone to visit more than once, and I attribute much of his improved behaviour to Tomasz living in and setting a benign example. Colin and Emerald sit and watch Neighbours together holding hands, which I think is the extent of the physical relationship.

Colin used most of his allowance to buy Emerald a silver bracelet for her birthday. He has become rather superior towards me, and he and Tomasz have begun to joke that I should be inviting Meera over just as often. But I am quite content with my life as it is. Colin makes regular visits (chauffeured by me or Tomasz) to Emerald's housing facility, and with Tomasz taking a month off over Christmas to be with his wife and family I am becoming reacquainted with my own company at home. I can write my Christmas cards – and this newsletter – in peace. Colin has been invited to a Christmas lunch at Emerald's hostel, which he is very keen to attend.

As for me, prompted by the venerable lady who set up

the flood support group, I will be spending Christmas day with a carol singing group at the Lower Rising Day centre, entertaining senior citizens during their Christmas lunch.

With Christmas wishes,

**Robert**

* * * * *

## Christmas 2003

**15 Paradise View**
**Upley Rising**
**Thameshire**

Dear Friends

I've peeled our jam-stained family organiser off the fridge to check on what we've been up to for the past 12 months. It looks like the nearest this family has got to a normal year since records began.

### January

The New Year's Day storm reduces to shreds the tarpaulins covering our semi-destroyed house, and horizontal rain drenches what's left of our downstairs. It takes nearly a week to dry out the sofa, carpets and dog. We are still waiting for a payout after last year's Golden Jubilee day disaster, but the insurance company's answerphone is experiencing long delays due to customers calling – surprise surprise. While Ant and I spend New Year's Day wading through freezing sludge with mops and buckets, Eleanor and Felipe set off with a collecting box; which turns out to be for the folk who got flooded down the hill in Lower Rising.

Two weeks later I make an emergency trip to A&E with Mackenzie who had been refilling her tippy cup with Ant's turpentine. Three hour wait. No serious injury as far as they can tell.

**February**
I take Eleanor, Felipe, Daniel and the twinnies (aged 13, 13, 11, 3 and 3) to the Stop the War March. There are about a million people and it takes us four hours to get from the Embankment to Hyde Park. We miss most of the speeches. Mackenzie needs the toilet and chooses the biggest protest the country has ever seen to get lost. We search frantically before two policewomen find her. I am reduced to grovelling thanks. The policewomen, who both look about 15, admire my (original 1980s) CND banner. One of them asks what it stands for.

Ant has stayed home on the pretext of minding the dog. He's actually sulking because the prospect of war in Iraq produces a bigger turnout than Chilean human rights protests ever have. Plus he's still in a strop about his Big Hit sculpture being banished from pride of place in the tennis club pavilion to a basement store cupboard. Part of the ongoing vendetta from our vile neighbour, who twisted the arms of the stuffed shirts at the club for unfathomable reasons of his own, probably pure spite. Luckily he and Ant rarely encounter each other or World War Three would have broken out by now.

I put on my smartest clothes and visit the club. I explain that Ant is not a despicable terrorist but a true artist wrestling with his own banishment from the country of his birth. I omit any mention of him acting like a daft twat. The club secretary, who I discover has distant family in Uruguay, writes Ant a letter of apology and offers to reinstate the sculpture. Ant refuses and sends the twins to collect it.

**March**
The insurance money comes through for our house repairs! Work starts; as well as repairing the damage we are pushing the boat out: replacing our prohibited loft windows and adding a posh new extended kitchen. The house is suddenly full of workmen who keep tripping over the dog and over Fraser, who is on formal notice from the nursery for peeing in the sandpit.

Undeterred, I enter our plans for TV's Grand Designs, as the Murder House Reinvented. No reply. Ant and I leaf through catalogues of shiny kitchen units, just like a conventional couple, and I allow myself to imagine an end to spending most of our home life squashed into Ant's studio.

Fraser is reinstated and a week later both twinnies come down with measles, two days before they are due to have their second MMR vaccination. They catch it from the nursery, which I discover harbours unvaccinated toddlers whose parents think the jab will give their darlings two heads. These are adults with university degrees and serious jobs like civil servants or management consultants. I can tell that Fraser and Mackenzie are really poorly as they doze in front of ChuckleVision all day instead of shrieking and/or jumping off the furniture. I am in no rush for them to get better.

My job share is not called Angie for nothing. She

angelically covers for me while I look after the twinnies. She tells me her brother nearly died from measles as a baby and she has always had to look out for him. I take back all my sneery thoughts about her line dancing, or her obsession with tidying up our desk and washing up coffee cups that have only been used once.

Ant gets a call from a friend at Upley Primary inviting him to stand as chair of the PTA as our chronically absent neighbour Charles has finally had the grace to step down. He declines. I tell him that apologies, like opportunities, should be accepted when they are offered. He retorts that at least one person in the family still has principles. We have a major row in front of all the children and the builders. Ant says we are all ganging up on him, including the builders, and storms out.

## April

We get a letter from the council saying that multiple neighbours have complained about our construction works. They are challenging the validity of our planning permission – which translates as 'Your kitchen extension might make my kitchen extension look out of date'.

Building work stops.

Ant installs his reclaimed Big Hit tennis club racket sculpture on our front gate. He announces that controlling your own Art is controlling your own life. It's also a warning to any neighbours who try to come in. Local children start hitting tennis balls at it, then footballs. He refuses to take it down.

Eleanor wins a writing competition for an essay about the fine line between artistic genius and madness.

It's revision season in the library where I work. The study desks fill up with rows of students fiddling with their iPods while staring blankly at illegible notes taken months earlier in a 9am lecture following a heavy night drinking their way through an alcopop multipack. Men in crash helmets appear at my reception desk with a pizza delivery for Patrick in Ancient History or Anishka next to the toilets. There's an exponential increase in (1) the number of textbooks smuggled out; and (2) the volume of illegal alcohol bottles that Angie and I confiscate. We set up a strict stop and search system and enjoy drinks after work on the day we overlap.

## May

We sort out our planning permission problem with the help of our solicitor neighbour Robert who is revealed as a white knight running a free legal advice clinic in his spare time. He was incredibly helpful and I take back every bad thought I ever had about stuffy lawyers. Building work restarts. Very loudly, just as Daniel is working for his SATS (he needs a grade 5 to get into the Queen's Grammar School).

Antonio gets a letter from the South Thameshire Lawn Tennis Club about The Big Hit sculpture on the gate. It points out that as the sculpture was commissioned (and paid for) by the club, it belongs to the club. Ant ignores it.

## June

Daniel's school year goes on the much-coveted Year 6 residential trip to the Isle of Wight. This includes fossil hunting, sailing, a sand sculpture competition and the last night disco.

I get a concerned call afterwards from one of the staff to let me know that Daniel wouldn't take part in any of the fun 'enrichment activities'. He only wanted to be alone with his Gameboy which they had to take away in the end. I ask Daniel about it but he just shrugs and goes back to playing Harvest Moon.

I book new appointments for Daniel with the child psychologist; it's exactly a year since the chimney collapse/corpse episode. I tell Ant he should spend more time bonding with the children since he can't use his studio for work while it's doubling as our kitchen diner. He starts playing Frisbee with them in the back garden using a dinner plate, which Fraser sends spinning through our neighbours' window. I find five more letters from the tennis club stuffed under a pile of papers behind the microwave, requesting then demanding the return of The Big Hit.

## July

The building work is finished at last! After a year of living in a house with no downstairs we move back to our rebuilt, redecorated living room – all traces of the murder mystery removed – and our gleaming new kitchen. It's half the size of the other 12 extensions along our road, but we remind ourselves that size isn't everything, and if we ever felt the need for a Sicilian marble floor or an atrium we could go to a hotel. I stick the jammy family organiser onto the new fridge.

The Big Hit issue is resolved. A retired ballerina called Charlotte Capulet CBE, who is also a member of the tennis club, steps in. She has taken over the Linden Art Gallery in the centre of Upley Rising, where Thameshire's leading lights gather to sip white wine at preview evenings and restock their walls. She offers to display Ant's sculpture in the window, alongside a notice stating it is on loan courtesy of both the Eminent Artist and the South Thameshire Lawn Tennis Club. I tell Ant this is a Home Counties style masterstroke of diplomacy, and he should consider himself lucky given he's been acting like a pillock. He sulks but changes his mind when Ms Capulet telephones him in person and turns on the charm. The sculpture is moved from our front gate to the gallery.

We all go to Upley Rising's Wellspring Festival together, where it's Ant's turn to lose the twinnies. After being spotted trying to untie the well's safety rope they make their way unaided to the missing children's tent where I am doing my regular shift. They claim that Ant abandoned them deliberately, though this could be a ploy to get sympathy and sweets.

Daniel inexplicably gets top grades in every subject in his SATS and we all treat him with new respect. Eleanor and Felipe both say that their own school reports were delayed – then left on the bus – then eaten by the dog – then got destroyed by fire. I find the reports crumpled up at the bottom of their backpacks. They don't make happy reading. I tell them they need to get their acts together; they get all mouthy with me, saying that their father doesn't so why should they.

**August**
Angie and I get a promotion. The Head Librarian says he regards us as a model job share. He refers to our impressive distribution of skills, by which he means me doing all the filing while Angie has volunteered to do the dreaded accounts which are supposed to be his job. We get regraded and a modest pay rise.

We celebrate with a real holiday – abroad! Two blissful weeks in Majorca. We all get sunburnt except for Ant and Felipe, but it's worth it. We dare to feel like a normal family.

When we get back, Angie covers my work for another

week so I can spend time with the children over the holidays. I agree to stand in for her while she goes to the regional line dancing finals in Reading. I lecture the family on the advantages of mutual cooperation.

## September

Back to school. Daniel starts at the Queen's Grammar. All you can see as he sets off for the bus stop is a giant backpack with a tiny pair of legs underneath. Eleanor and Felipe are unhelpful: they refuse to walk with him, mooching along as if their minds are on something far more elevated than getting to school on time. They have started leaving their school shirts untucked and wearing their ties shortened to about two inches. Daniel comes home alone on his first day, and the twins arrive two hours later as they both got detentions. When I ask why I just get monosyllabic answers. Queen's Grammar is number one in the league table for Thameshire and has parents circling its catchment area like wolves, but my 13-year-olds in Year 9 can only speak in words of one syllable. Do you want chips? Ace. Have you done your homework? Grunt.

## October

The twins start to take their homework seriously, probably to impress Daniel. This leads to computer wars, with everyone fighting for time on our state-of-the-art (seven years ago) Compaq which has sat mostly ignored in the corner of our living room. Now it's the centre of attention with teachers setting tasks that need computer time. The living room becomes a battleground. I set up a strict rota, then discover Felipe is using his slot to chat with friends on something called MSN messenger, and Eleanor is writing to our MP about the flood damage in Lower Rising.

## November

Ant gets a paid job – his first since 1995. He is curator at the Linden Gallery, employed by Charlotte Capulet, the retired ballerina/tennis club member who has very long legs and a liking for Ant. She offers him the chance to bring a 'cutting contemporary edge' to her collections. Ant accepts, and transitions seamlessly from the studio (where not much has been going on all year), through the war zone that is our living room, to the Zen-like serenity of Upley Rising's select lakeside gallery. How does he do it?

## December

I'm writing this in my own 30-minute slot on the computer. My parents have announced that they can't wait to see our new kitchen extension and they are coming for Christmas with my sister Gill and her daughter Saffron (previously known as Cousin Shrub), who will be home from uni where she is studying psychology. Saffron wants to use us as her first-year field study. That makes 11 of us for Christmas, plus their new puppy, our dog and cat. Ant tells me there is a Christmas exhibition at the gallery and he won't have much time to help as he'll be working all hours under the watchful eye of the elegant Ms Capulet.

Festive Greetings to you all,

*Alison, Antonio, Eleanor, Felipe, Daniel, Fraser, Mackenzie, and Hector and Salvador*

\* \* \* \* \*

# December 2003

Paradise House, Paradise View
Upley Rising, Thameshire

### Paradise House Christmas News

# Hiya Peeps,

Here we are again, one year on or is it two? Losing track of time is the new hobby, nothing to do with the booze, which you may like to note I've put a cap on lately. It's this single parent lark. Running around like a headless chicken, that's me, one minute it's cheering Max on in the tennis club under-16s finals, the next it's My Darling Clementine's pony pampering birthday party, keeping all the balls in the air alongside the need to bring in the readies on a regular basis. I dunno if I'm coming or going half the time, I always thought the nanny did everything but as she reminds me at every opportunity she didn't sign up to work 24/7 and I should consider myself lucky that she covers when I'm away on business. For a tidy bit of overtime I might add. So gone are my weekends putting the old plates of meat up to watch the footie, gone are my evenings out with the boys, and gone is my sweet Caroline.

What I want to know is, what on earth are Fathers for Justice playing at? Risking their lives climbing up cranes dressed as Spiderman because they want to spend more time with their kids: are they off their rockers? They'll give the rest of us a bad name.

Mind you as single parent families go I think I've done OK this year. Earned my fair share of a very acceptable Christmas bonus at STEAL after clinching a couple of tricky deals – one while on the dog and bone in the checkout queue at the supermarket, no mean feat negotiating a six-figure contract hands-free, the phone jammed between your ear and shoulder while you're juggling with plastic bags and credit cards, watching the cashier nearly fall off her chair when you mention three million quid while she counts out the change. And no need to dress as Spiderman neither.

I've had to cut back on the travelling to be around more at home, which suits me fine, having to take your shoes off every time you go through airport security, even in business class, is nuts. The kids have been great, they don't act like they miss their mum at all. Stiff upper lip I told Maxie, which has been useful as he's added the bagpipes to his instrument repertoire this year. As well as winning the tennis club tournament he also comes up trumps getting first prize in the school photo competition with a telephoto shot of Robbie Williams who was staying in the same hotel as us at half term. And now he's writing for his school's student rag, laying the ground for his Oxbridge CV.

Clementine has got so many friends I can't keep up, they're all called Emily or Chloe, she's at someone's birthday party every weekend; you can't start with networking too early I told her which is just as well as being academic isn't top of her priorities. She's sharp though, I took her to the office with me on Take your Daughter to Work Day and while we were in a meeting she managed to unearth someone's private coke stash which was a sticky moment. What with my business trips and everything else to remember we got a bit behind on the private tutoring, the end result being that she started at Thameshire Community School this year instead of Queen's Grammar like her brother. She's fine with it though, said Daddy I really want to go there, it's much more cool, though what she knows about cool at going on 12 beats me. Anyway she's doing fine and still on the books of three modelling agencies, so no worries on that score.

Being a single bloke in your 40s isn't like it was 20 years ago. Apart from the kids there's the nanny, the cleaner and the gardener to keep tabs on though sometimes it feels like it's the other way round. I'm steering clear of chatting up the ladies after my recent experiences. No need to go into detail, suffice it to say I made one small error of judgement when I was grief stricken and ended up losing My Beautiful Wife. Helena, who was responsible for the whole palaver, didn't stick around either – she was just using me for her own evil ends, which included milking me and everyone in her female spider orbit for cash, and now she's shacked up with some US TV star in Malibu with more dough than either of them know what to do with. Leaving me on my lonesome here in Upley Rising, the gothic clock tower capital of England.

Ho hum. I can't sell the house as Caroline is co-owner, and I can't sell our place in France as that's where She is. Painting her toenails by the pool or playing tennis while I'm running around in the rain in the arsehole of the Home Counties. She says she's fled to Provence to be alone with her despair; meaning alone with her Mother and that weirdo pretend stepfather Rupert dropping in every five minutes to top up on a bit of winter sun and empty my drinks cabinet. Better there than here: the last thing I need in Paradise View is an interfering mother-in-law, especially one that likes to put on airs and graces when we all know she was brought up the daughter of a boarding house landlady in Margate, and struck gold when she married a rich businessman, until he scarpered leaving her with a seven-year-old daughter to bring up.

So I do get why my long-suffering beautiful wife carries all that baggage. But if she could just be easier on us both. She only communicates with me via the nanny, whose salary comes out of my bank account, and who she phones with instructions every couple of days. Has Max had his hair cut? Make sure he goes to Cut Above by the pond, not the other place; and don't let Him buy pizzas, Clementine is allergic to them. The kids went out to Provence for the summer holidays, leaving me home alone in the hottest summer for 30 years. I had to take an emergency short break in Mauritius just to get away from the heat in the UK.

So December 2003 finds me staring down the barrel of my second one-parent family Christmas. We're off to my folks for turkey and trimmings. After dinner I'm turning the TV off and getting them to sit down for a round table discussion about setting up a charity, something fitting to preserve the memory of my brother Ditch. Everyone's got different ideas into their heads. Mum wants a statue in Shoreditch High Street, Dad's been talking about a museum of Ditch Wright memorabilia with a memorable entrance fee to match. One or two of the family clan have already started selling merchandise, which has got his record company in a right lather. Something needs to be done before it all gets out of hand. If only my lovely brother could be here to see how much he's missed.

So after this Christmas Day business meeting it's straight to the airport to get Max and Clementine on the plane so they can spend quality time, which means pick up more presents, with their mum. I'll be putting up my feet at home, lighting a fag since there's no one there to tell me not too, getting mildly plastered on a 35-year-old single malt I've been saving up, contemplating West Ham's chances of getting back into the Premier League and watching the box. Sounds great, but do I miss My Beautiful Wife, the lovely Caroline.

Fortunately I think I've concocted a foolproof plan to get her back.

Have a great one everyone!

**Charles X**

\* \* \* \* \*

*December 2004*

*Paradise House, Paradise View,*
*Upley Rising, Thameshire*

   *Christmas News from the Wrights of Paradise View*

*Dear Everyone,*

I feel so privileged and grateful to be back at the helm of this year's Paradise View Christmas News. Life can take us on strange and wondrous journeys and I have arrived at December 2004 in a refreshed and tranquil state of mind: my very own sunlit uplands.

   I expect everyone has been wondering about my mysterious absence. I have spent a whole year in a period of inner reflection, leading a spartan life in our modest *maison de vacances*. The South of France is the best place in the world for contemplation; all that lavender, mellow stone and Evian water, and the home of so many great artists and philosophers. After starting every day with a purifying swim in our 25-metre pool, I read extensive extracts from Voltaire, Sartre and Coco Chanel, whose iconic sense of style I am often told I naturally emulate.

As some of you may know, Charles and I have had a few minor difficulties. These led to us mutually agreeing to spend some time apart, a sort of marital career break. I had felt hurt and betrayed by Charles's behaviour, and needed to be alone for a while to lick my wounds.

During my retreat I came to realise that life is about gliding over obstacles with elegance and poise, not hiding from them. With my new insight I saw that while Charles was desperately trying to cope through his brother's final illness I was so busy being a popular, driven entrepreneur and a devoted working mother that I was absent when he most needed to reach out to me. It was all too understandable that others took advantage of him in his vulnerable state. Now it was time for me to forgive him and move on.

So I came home at the beginning of this year. France is a divine country and perfect for a finite period in one's own gated enclave, but I don't understand how people can live there all the time. No wonder a year in Provence was enough for Peter Mayle. The French just shrug when you ask them anything, the markets smell of cheese and everyone is always kissing everyone's cheeks, even the man who comes to clean the pool, which really is *de trop*. Returning to England was like being greeted by an old friend. In contrast with endless fields of sunflowers in straight lines, Upley Rising looked so pretty, with just a sprinkling of snow on the streets, not enough to be a nuisance. Civilisation is definitely where the shops are open on Sundays and your beautician doesn't try to make conversation. Charles and the children had fastened a huge yellow ribbon to the door, and had got the nanny to blow up dozens of Welcome Home balloons and tie them all over the house. I was overwhelmed at my reception. I hugged the children, in tears, telling them I simply wasn't any good at managing without them, and they reassured me: 'But you don't have to be good at everything, mummy!'

Not that I had much time to relax, there was plenty for me to do. I began by sacking the nanny. Having so much control over Maximilian and Clementine had gone to her head, and she refused to use the concise 50-page instruction manual I had sent to make things easier for her while I was away. The final straw was finding six packets of cigarettes in her room which she claimed Charles must have hidden there. We now have a very pleasant *au pair* from Estonia who is grateful to have the chance to learn English with us.

My most important task was to get Clementine into a better school. I have nothing against state education, Max is thriving at the Queen's Grammar, but Thameshire Community School was a completely inappropriate learning environment for my daughter. The class sizes were so big that the staff didn't have time to see how sensitive Clementine is, and they were too preoccupied with the many students from so-called deprived homes (families that can't afford private school fees but all have three cars parked outside). Her first term report had the effrontery to describe her as uncommunicative and surly when they should have spotted that she was becoming withdrawn from lack of recognition and was pining for her exiled mother.

She was overlooked for class representative just because they wanted to make a point by giving the role to someone brought up in a children's home, then there was a theft and someone accused Clementine, which was ridiculous as her weekly allowance was ten times more than any of her classmates' pocket money. Clementine put on a brave pretence of enjoying the school, and even insisted she wanted to stay there. But it was clear she was a lone gazelle among warthogs, so Mother and I found her a place at Rossetti House, a delightful school which recognises the unique sensitivities of every child, and allows them to flourish in their own space within and beyond the narrow constraints of a set curriculum. Students can study whatever they are drawn to, and if they get stressed by, say, maths they are not forced to study it. Neither are there barbaric practices that could scar them for life, like doing outdoor PE in all weathers.

The Head of Rossetti House was delighted to accept Clem in the middle of the winter term before any more harm was done. Commenting that a beautiful girl like her should make the most of her looks, he is relaxed about her taking time out for her modelling commitments, as long as we keep up the fees.

Maximilian continues his inexorable progress towards becoming Head Boy in three years' time. As well as founding and leading Queen's Grammar's first ever brass band, he has revolutionised the school newsletter, which he edits, by selling advertising space in it and taking a small commission. It's a little goldmine, parents are clamouring to sell their unused exercise bikes and impromptu timeshare purchases in Northern Portugal. We don't know how he finds the time to fit in studying for his ten GCSEs!

Charles is thrilled to have me home again. He has promised to give up smoking for good, and I trust him. He reminded me how Mark Twain explained that giving up smoking was so easy, he could do it thousands of times. For my 45th birthday (can you believe it!) he whisked me away to Bali for a magical week. At work he won STEAL's Empty Desker of the Year award, one of their highest accolades.

My own working world has taken a new turn. I have sold *Upley Itself,* the unique regional magazine which I founded. The Upley Herald wanted to buy it but I accepted a better offer from Thameshire Residential, who market most of the superior properties in our area, so I know its future is assured. Instead I have decided to concentrate on projects which generate love and tranquillity. When Charles begged me to return from my French sojourn he said he had a very special proposition for me.

Soon after I was home, he took me out for a romantic dinner at Le Rossignol Charbonné, one of Thameshire's most intimate triple star restaurants. Over candlelight and oysters he asked if I would consider using my unique skills and experience to create something special: a charitable fund which would work tirelessly to do justice to the memory of his dear brother. He would see my accepting as being in the spirit of us rebuilding our lives together. How could I refuse? So I am proud to announce that I have created the Ditch Wright Philanthropic Foundation. It is a much-needed new charity dedicated to all the many good causes which Ditch held dear.

Quite coincidentally, Charles's parents have come up with a quaint charity idea of their own. I just happened to launch ours first. Thanks to my extensive contacts (my Imperative Events address book has been invaluable) we are already starting to see donations flood in from Ditch's many fans across the globe.

My other creative venture occurred to me while I was deep in thought in France, leafing through a copy of Simone de Beauvoir's essays. Motivated by the wish to share the benefit of my experiences with others, I am writing a book. It is all about the lessons life has taught me, how I have benefitted from them, and how others can too. I am writing it out of love and altruism rather than for commercial success, though I can't wait to see it on the bestseller lists!

In the meantime, our Christmas tree sits at the centre of our living room which I have had redecorated to symbolise our new start as a family. The tree twinkles with simple white lights, the colour of peace. Our happily reunited family is looking forward to a joyous Christmas together.

Wishing you all a very happy Christmas,

*Caroline, Charles, Maximilian and Clementine Wright*

\* \* \* \* \*


## Christmas 2004

**15 Paradise View**
**Upley Rising**
**Thameshire**

Dear Friends

This year life happened while we were making other plans.

**Our twins** became stars of the stage. In their school's Year 9 Easter production, Eleanor somehow landed the lead part of Lady Macbeth and Felipe played Malcolm. They spent weeks learning lines and practising at home, using the twinnies and the dog as props.

**Antonio** was persuaded to make the stage set. He spent every spare moment working on it when he wasn't curating for Charlotte Capulet CBE at the Linden Gallery, and I hardly saw him for weeks. When the curtain went up the audience gasped like a collective goldfish: no Thameshire grammar school production in living memory was set in such a spine-chillingly desolate fortress. Crows flapped overhead as the wind howled through grim battlements, against a backdrop of Scottish moors endlessly receding towards a hellish horizon. At the end, in the luvvy bit when the bouquets are handed out, the Head singled out Ant for praise. She made a speech about us being lucky to have such artistic brilliance in the community, described Ant as a model parent whose family must be very proud of him, and called him on stage from the wings to take a bow.

Just when you are thinking this is getting too cheesy to read on – read on. Ant came on stage and I saw tears rolling down his cheeks. He walked up to the Head, accepted the expensive-looking bottle she was holding out, bowed to the audience, then turned and without warning flung it through the back wall of the set. It exploded onto the jagged ramparts, champagne mixed with broken glass fizzing over the assembled cast. Ant exited (stage left) to dead silence followed by an uneasy ripple of laughter. I heard a parent two rows in front whisper "genius, absolute genius".

Ant didn't come home all night. When I got in from work the next day, he was sitting at the kitchen table, sewing back the ears that Mackenzie had gnawed off her teddy. He said he'd slept at the gallery and he wanted to talk to me later when the children were in bed. I had worked out what was coming and thought through my options. Ant could move in with Ms Capulet CBE as long as I kept all the children and the dog. He could take our old cat, Salvador, who has developed an uncontrollable weeing problem.

But that wasn't it. Ant wanted to talk to me about his father, who he had last seen after Chile's military coup of 1973, being dragged away in the middle of the night in bare feet and pyjamas by the police. Ant was in his early teens. He would never say much about Cristopher: all I knew was that he was an academic who had put his life on the line to call out the brutal military dictatorship, and that after his arrest and disappearance Ant and his mother had fled to England in 1975 for their own safety.

Ant sat fidgeting with the glass eyeballs on Mackenzie's teddy and started to talk. He told me about his home life when he was young. How his father ran hushed secret planning meetings after dusk with the blinds drawn, in their own flat; how he risked his safety to organise demonstrations or get illegal protest pamphlets printed and distributed across Santiago. He knew he was on a government list of suspects but carried on his work regardless. Other dissidents respected him as a charismatic, principled man devoted to the cause. All this was true: but something else, ugly and suppressed was going on. Alone with his wife and son, Cristopher was a violent, abusive tyrant. He had a savage temper and used to clout Ant for the tiniest thing: for laughing too loudly, or breaking a glass, or making a minor mistake in his homework. He ripped up Ant's sketch book, railing at him for indulging in art when there was serious work to be done, then took out his belt and thrashed him, always in places where the bruises wouldn't show.

Ant lived in terror of these attacks – but he was even more anguished about his father's violence towards his mother, which he witnessed over and over again through their apartment walls. He'd sit curled over on his bed, his hands over his ears, trying to close off the sounds that came from their bedroom. Ant and his mother, trapped in their own hidden nightmare within a nightmare regime, had nowhere to turn: Cristopher's friends all revered him and none of them would have believed their story.

When the police pounded on their door in the night and took Cristopher away, Ant, at 13, was traumatised and confused. He knew his father would be tortured in jail but at the same time he was relieved that he had gone. For the first time their home felt like a safe place. He couldn't work out which feelings were right or wrong. His mother, equally conflicted, became a nervous wreck and couldn't talk to him properly. Friends, unknowing, tried to comfort them, even putting themselves at risk to try and get his father released. Then the opportunity came up for him and his mother to leave the country. They never saw Cristopher again and he is presumed long dead.

Ant had been living with this mess in his brain for years. He had told himself he would never have children as he was terrified he might become like his father; then he ended up with five. He loved them all to distraction but deep within his love ran a twisting seam of fear. This was why he had stayed in Scotland after Fraser and Mackenzie were born in the new millennium; and why he couldn't always keep a lid on his anger. Staring down at Mackenzie's teddy, he told me how his art felt like a double-edged sword: on the one hand his unconditional vocation, but at the same time a monster, one that devoured his emotions but always needed more anger to feed it. The final straw was the school Head telling the hall packed with prim and proper Upley Rising parents he was a perfect father. He had snapped.

I'm putting all this in our Christmas News because Ant wants me to. For the past few months he's been getting therapy. He knows it will take time before he can manage his feelings, but one way forward is to be public and open, so he wants everyone to know what's going on.

People have reacted differently. Felipe tiptoes round Ant and bring him cups of tea. Eleanor says if men had to put up with PMT they wouldn't have time for other traumas, then hugs him. Daniel treats him exactly the same as before. My parents said they always knew there must have been something funny going on to judge by his work, before posting him a huge Get Well Soon card. It's a bit like grief; no one knows how to react, so they make a gesture that feels right for them then expect everything to get back to normal. Which it won't, not for a long time.

**News from Ali:** I told Ant I'd be there for him, and to show I meant it I took a week's family leave. When I got back to work, three strange men were rifling through my desk drawers. Before I could say anything my arm was firmly gripped and I was marched to the office of the Principal. It seemed a bit of an overreaction to a few unplanned days off.

Truth is stranger than fiction, as we librarians like to say. My job share, Angie, had disappeared. Without even washing up her last coffee cup. So had our boss, the Head Librarian. Along with a six-figure sum from the college's funds, which had been drip-fed through the library accounts over months. The Head Librarian was discovered to have a criminal record for embezzlement, and Angie's CV contained more holes than Blackburn Lancashire. Her line dancing awards were the only true bit in it.

It didn't take long for the investigators to work out that the chances of me masterminding a financial fraud were as likely as my skiing up Everest. I can't even calculate late book fines: ask my many happy students. I wouldn't know where to start with a criminal scam, though I was a bit worried they'd find out about my stocking up with Tamiflu off a dodgy internet site on the library computer. But after an hour of grilling in the Principal's office, they said they had no further questions, packed up their papers and left.

At this point the Principal sat back in his chair and looked at me directly. "You are now in charge," he said.

"Excuse me?" I looked over my shoulder but the fraud investigators had definitely gone, there were just two of us in the room.

There are many routes to career advancement: a winning interview technique, sheer brilliance, bribery and nepotism. Leapfrogging criminal colleagues is not typical, but it's worked for me. I am finally, at 45, Head Librarian of South Thameshire Further Education College. I know it's only because the governors were too embarrassed to advertise the post; and I did have to ask for 0.3 of an accountant to support me. Ant says I've got imposter syndrome, a term he's picked up from his therapist. Meanwhile there have been reported sightings of Angie and her dastardly accomplice in Panama and Australia.

**Summer holidays**: None this year, as I had to throw

myself into my new executive role. We let the twins (now 14) go to the Wellspring Festival on their own for the first time. When they came home Eleanor was looking flushed and holding hands with Max, the boy next door, and Felipe was failing to conceal a bottle-shaped item rolled up in his terrorist scarf. They disappeared into the world of chaos that used to be their bedrooms. Ant didn't see much of them all summer.

**Meanwhile …** the twinnies started primary school in September. I warned Upley Primary they might need to up their insurance policy. We think that Daniel has started in Year 8 but it's hard to be sure as he too spends most of his time in his room. Calling him down for supper doesn't work, we've found it's easier to leave a tray of food outside the door.

**Lucky break:** In November we won the Lottery! Justice at last, after ten years of shelling out £1 a week for zilch. We won enough to take us all on a dream holiday, and I brought home a stack of brochures from the travel agent. I organised a family vote – whereupon I learnt that democracy can be a fickle friend. The vote went unanimously (apart from yours truly) in favour of buying every member of the family their own personal computer.

So I'm finishing off this newsletter in the deserted echo chamber of a living room that used to be the beating heart of our family life. Ant is in the studio researching Chilean cousins on the World Wide Web as part of his therapy. The twins and Daniel are upstairs doing homework (they say) in their bedrooms. The twinnies have been quiet for too long and I need to go and check.

I almost miss Angie, who I picture basking in the sunshine somewhere in the Southern Hemisphere. As for Christmas, we had been planning to go to my parents. I was looking forward to putting my feet up at theirs now that I'm working full time, aka all the hours god sends. Mum and Dad retired this year after a combined 79 years in the same textile company where they met. They started sounding a bit shifty soon after, then last month they announced that they've sold up the family home in Rockbury and moved to a bungalow on the East Coast. With one, very small, spare bedroom. I'm trying not to take it personally – when I complained they pointed out I always hated the house and left home as soon as I could.

Festive Greetings to you all,

*Alison, Antonio, Eleanor, Felipe, Daniel, Fraser, Mackenzie, and Hector and Salvador*

\* \* \* \* \*

### 14 Paradise View, Upley Rising, Thameshire

### Christmas 2004

It feels strange to be writing this newsletter in a house devoid of Christmas decorations. The space in the corner of the living room usually reserved for our brightly lit tree is occupied by my packed suitcases; in two days' time I will be on my way to the airport, and the removal van will have completed its work at 14 Paradise View.

This year began with my usual routine. Drafting trusts at Coburn Briggs on weekdays; Tuesday and Thursday evenings spent dispensing pro bono advice from the Thameshire Advice office above the shops in Lower Rising. Rehearsals with the Rising Voices; cooking with

Colin and his companion Emerald at weekends. Gardening if it was fine or tinkering with railway layouts on rainy Sundays. In March, Colin and I joined the Friends of Upley Rising Station Restoration Society. Every Sunday night I sat down at my home computer to read and answer my social e-mails.

In May, Tomasz, Colin's carer, asked to talk to me. I had noticed him making more calls than usual, and being uncharacteristically absent-minded. He told me that he planned to bring his wife and children over to England. They were finding it hard to continue living apart, he missed her, and he wanted his children to have the benefit of an English education and go to university here. I said I would consider having them all to live in my house, but privately the prospect of it being filled with a noisy family which was not my own was unappealing. Tomasz too wanted to make other plans; I learned for the first time that he has a master's degree in behavioural science, and was hoping to set up in freelance practice.

When I asked Tomasz to give me a few weeks to interview new carers, he paused, stroking the St Christopher's medallion he wears, before suggesting that Colin might benefit from living in a supported living hostel. He ventured that it could be good for Colin to have a wider community around him where he could socialise more. I said I would give it some thought. As soon as he had left the room I contacted a care agency to start looking for a permanent replacement carer.

My other ongoing preoccupation was Thameshire Advice. Our service had continued to gain in popularity, to the extent that I would regularly turn up on a Tuesday evening to find a ragged line outside the door squabbling about who had got there first. We had expanded to six volunteer advisers and we were still struggling to cope with the numbers; the problems people have, and cannot solve, are seemingly endless.

Rajiv, our health services adviser, proposed that we apply for a grant for a coordinator. The idea of someone manning a front desk to organise proper appointments, match the right client with the right adviser, and mollify the more difficult customers, was appealing. I began working with him on the process. During one of our discussions Rajiv mentioned that he loved singing and I invited him to try for my singing group, the Rising Voices, which is always on the lookout for more male singers. My concerns that he would experience the same reaction as Meera when she was my guest at the Upley Society were unfounded; he was welcomed warmly, and added to the tea-making rota almost before he had got in the door.

We were sitting in the Thameshire Advice office above the shops one peerless June evening; really an evening for being outside. I was ploughing through the endless forms that are required for the meagrest of subsidies from the public purse, when I noticed Rajiv looking at me intently; then he asked me what was on my mind. I found myself telling him in detail about my dilemma for Colin's future. Rajiv is a very good listener, letting me do most of the speaking before offering a few thoughtful comments. We sat quietly talking for some time. The room fell silent around us; the strong evening sun was streaming in, showing up the shabbiness of the walls. A slab of sunlight drifted down over the metal filing cabinet and the dusty potted plant sitting on its top. I began to feel disconnected from the words we were exchanging. Instead it gradually became clear to me that I felt deeply drawn to Rajiv; and as the conversation took a different turn then faltered, I realised to my amazement and joy that he reciprocated my feelings.

At the age of 54 I am astonished and grateful that love has entered my life. Rajiv is an extraordinary person: quiet, considered, intelligent and non-judgemental. He spends his days fielding demands from irascible senior doctors, or lobbying for money to spend on dialysis machines and MRI scanners. He makes a point of getting onto the wards to find out what matters to patients and staff. He laughs off my facial scarring, distracting me with tales of stomach-turning sights he encounters every working day. When we sing alongside each other at the Rising Voices, and I hear his clear tenor chiming with my own bass, I experience a sense of harmony so profound that I cannot find the words to describe it. We are unconditional companions.

My dear friend and colleague Meera has been more than understanding about our relationship. She claims she saw the whole thing coming and persuaded Rajiv to join Thameshire Advice. She has gone to great lengths to quell certain reactions from some quarters in their family; fortunately they know me well already, which helps. At Coburn Briggs, once word got out, there was an interesting range of responses to the change in circumstance of the old bachelor partner. My name was removed from the radio advertisements we run, then reinstated. Unsubtle jokes were made about dark horses, and bow tie wearing. Inexplicably I am asked for advice on matters of décor or the flower arrangement that is replaced weekly on the front desk.

Colin has accepted Rajiv into our lives with no fuss; his attention is mainly elsewhere these days.

There are two kinds of people: those who believe they are immortal and have all the time in the world ahead of them; and others, who have looked death in the eye and blinked. My experience of surviving a major bomb attack places me in the latter category. Rajiv and I want to spend as much of our lives together as we can, our time already being limited by our working hours. Rajiv proposed that we should share a home, and with Tomasz's departure date becoming closer, I was forced to make a decision about my family circumstances and my future with him and with Colin.

I decided that it was not an option for us to live together in my own house: my parents' wisteria-clad marital home where I spent my childhood and where a framed oil painting of my grandfather still hung on the wall. A fresh start was called for. Having initially resisted Tomasz's suggestion, I began to see that allowing Colin to try outside care was not just serendipitous but the right decision for him. It was obvious how happy he was whenever I took him to visit Emerald at her hostel, where he had also made other friends. While I was trying to force myself to take the logical next step, fate intervened in the form of a telephone call from the hostel's manager. She informed me that a room had unexpectedly become available at the same place; I needed to let her know within a few days if Colin would like to take it. The hostel is a modern, pleasant house, where the residents are supervised with a light touch by caring staff; it could not be further removed from the ill-fated Grey Willows home where he previously had such a disastrous experience.

After two trial runs, Colin was thrilled to become a full-time resident. He has his own large room with a television and his display cabinet safely under lock and key. However his soldier collection sits mostly untouched; he has been spending more and more time chatting in the communal living room. On the day in early September when I left him there permanently, I reached out to shake his hand. As I did so Emerald appeared, beaming, with some of her friends. Colin was off without a glance back, leaving me standing alone in the empty doorway to his room.

Seeing his contentment, and with Tomasz having moved on, I felt safe to put 14 Paradise View on the market.

It has been sold to an enthusiastic couple who will be moving in on December 16th. I offered to put up some of my Christmas decorations to welcome them, but they are adamant that they prefer to bring their own. I am going to live with Rajiv in his house on the edge of Upley Rising, which has a small garden in need of care. It is not far to visit Colin regularly. The 45-minute walk uphill in the mornings to Coburn Briggs will be good for my health.

I have picked out a few pieces of furniture which the incoming people had admired on their viewings, and which I am leaving for them; but many of the house's contents have gone to auction. I have kept back some favourite pieces from my mother's china collection, to sit on the window ledges alongside Rajiv's more contemporary choices. I think my mother would have enjoyed the stimulating contrast. The painting of my great-grandfather now hangs in the Upley Society's Churchill Room, and I sent my grandfather's portrait to one of my cousins who felt he had been overlooked in my parents' wills; I have distributed some of the other items within the wider family. I hope they will enjoy them. I have donated some of my model railway collection to the Friends of Upley Rising Station, but the Clapham layout is going into safe storage until we can find somewhere for it.

As I sat down to write this Christmas newsletter, for the first time I questioned my eagerness for this annual task. I wondered if my motivation was enthusiasm or duty, and where the line falls between the two. I looked at the premium stationery paper in front of me waiting for the wet ink to sink in, its lustre drying alongside my initial verve. (Habit, or obstinacy, makes me cling to the calligraphic form for this annual exercise, rather than using the word processor. Rajiv calls it fogeyish.)

The letter will soon be completed, photocopied 46 times, folded with its accompanying cards into envelopes which will be addressed and stamped with one of the Christmas stamps I make sure to purchase in advance every year. I will place them into the red post box at the top of Paradise View for collection by the post van at exactly 5pm. I imagine the envelopes being delivered all over the country, with a number travelling across the world to Asia, South Africa, Australia and even Japan. Reaching old friends from university or school, not seen for many years. Do you really want to hear about my visit to Glyndebourne, the small interplays of office politics, or my newfound romance? Do you follow my little quips? I picture Barney (BSc in mathematics), now a longtime banker in Hong Kong, leaving my letter unopened on the table as he departs for a last-minute rush at the office; or Archie (third class natural sciences degree, almost sent down for selling psychedelic mushrooms in the college bar), currently living in Perth, glancing through the first few lines over morning coffee, chuckling, before his wife calls him away to get on and clean the barbecue.

So this may well be my last Christmas newsletter. I have taken a two-month sabbatical; more time off than I have had in many years. Rajiv and I leave for India tomorrow. We fly to Bangalore, from where we will be touring. He can't wait to show me his grandparents' hometown, the colours and scents of the markets, the temples, Indian classical music. I have insisted that we include a trip on the Nilgiri Mountain Railway from Mettupalayam to Ootacamund. Rajiv has agreed, though he gently jibes about the mixed legacy of the empire, and I realise that I still have a great deal to learn.

With Christmas wishes,

**Robert**

# PART EIGHT 2005–2007:

# ALI, CAROLINE

## Christmas 2005

**15 Paradise View**
**Upley Rising**
**Thameshire**

Dear Friends

Apologies, our family news is a bit rushed this year. Being full-time Head Librarian at a county further education college is an existential challenge. I asked for extra resources and they sent me on a time management course. Now I've got a list for everything and I've even started to think in bullet points.

- Family update: Felipe and Eleanor are 15, Daniel is 13, Fraser and Mackenzie are Five Alive. Our dog Hector is eight and Salvador the cat has morphed into an unquantifiable state of motionless cat infinity, sustained entirely by sleep and vets' bills.

- Biggest social event this year: The twins' 15th birthday party which they persuaded their gullible parents to let them have at home alone. 40 friends invited, 120 turned up. Eleanor wore an item resembling her Make Poverty History wristband as a skirt. Felipe spent twice as long as Eleanor choosing what to wear, his mind on the big new love of his life, Alima. We could hear the party from the Thai restaurant in the High Street where we had gone for a romantic meal out. So could the rest of Upley Rising. Neighbours called the police at 10pm, 11pm and 11.30pm, when the party was closed down.

- **Fallout** from party: (1) Eleanor refused food for a month after her on/off boyfriend Max ditched her in front of the 120 party guests, snogged Alima all over our new sofa then went home with her. (2) Felipe got a month's detention for beating up Max at school. (3) Vanessa has stopped speaking to me after having the twinnies sleep over the night of the party – an offer she claims to have no memory of making. (4) The parents of two teenaged party guests we found impersonating a sleeping octopus on the floor of Ant's studio the day after the party are beyond furious, and got us delisted from the school parents' Quiz Night (the most terrifying punishment they could think up).
*Note to self: must improve interpersonal skills.*

- **Cultural Triumph** of the year: Ant's solo exhibition at Charlotte Capulet CBE's Linden Gallery. The show consisted of Ant sitting on a metal folding chair all day, staring at the wall opposite. Said wall was blank but every 47 seconds flickering images of Chile in the 1970s, interspersed with the streets of Upley Rising running with blood, were projected onto it in short bursts. Billed as an Artist's Introspective, The Upley Herald publicised it as a major retrospective. Both of which were true.

- **Fallout** from exhibition: (1) The Upley Society and the South Thameshire Lawn Tennis Club, joint exhibition sponsors, asked for their funding back due to 'pernicious implications for Upley Rising's integrity'. (2) Charlotte Capulet CBE regretfully 'lets Ant go'. She says she'll always be his biggest fan but she can't turn a profit selling blank walls to angry customers. (I am secretly not unhappy that he is no longer spending time there.) (3) Ant's therapist says the exhibition was a major step forward in his recovery.

- **Holidays:** (1) A family trip to Glastonbury – the first since 1989 for Ant and me. We got our tent up in time to see it swamped by the biggest thunderstorm since Noah's flood. Mackenzie was swept away – Daniel identified her hand sticking up holding a lolly just as she was disappearing under the mud at the bottom of the field. Fraser had to be pulled offstage by security men at the Babyshambles set. We never found out what the twins did as they had their own tent in a different field, and forgot to turn on their new mobile phones, but they both said it was wicked.

- **Holidays:** (2) The twins went on Duke of Edinburgh silver expeditions. It's supposed to be a challenge, and it was: finding sanity-defying sums of cash for so-called essential survival gear. Essential for the survival gear companies, that is. I tell the twins how where I grew up we wore T-shirts and trainers outside all winter and it didn't do us any harm.

- **Holidays:** (3) None, as we spent the rest of our fund on Ant's therapy sessions.

- Daniel: His worried form teacher contacted us. Daniel doesn't speak to anyone at school and spends lessons staring into space. We pointed out he always gets reasonable grades and probably likes the peace and quiet of school compared to home. She said that the only time he spoke all term was in PSHE where in sharing time he spoke about having a close encounter with a corpse. He was spooking the others, PSHE was supposed to be about relationship education. We agreed to book more appointments with the child psychologist.

*Note to self: research therapists offering two-family member discount bundles.*

- **More troubles**: Felipe got stopped by the police for buying cider underage. He had got away with it in the shop because he looks older than his age, but some sneak shopped him and he was lucky to get off with a caution. He said he was only doing it as a favour for someone else, but wouldn't say any more; Eleanor defended him. We know they were hiding something but extracting information from twin 15-year-olds makes a job with the Spanish Inquisition look cushy. We suspect the hand of our Nasty Next-door Neighbours; the runaway wife eventually came back and has been strangely polite, which for some reason makes my blood run cold.

- Work-life balance: I allocated diary time to (1) spend more time with the family; (2) start running again.

I promised myself I would do both, just as soon as I had got my quarterly report for the governors done, finalised the budget submission, completed five staff appraisals and evaluated the library's health and safety compliance processes. I can't remember the last time I held a reaL book in my hands.

- **Other family news**: My parents, newly retired and downsized, stopped over on their way from their precious Yorkshire ('nowhere on Earth like it') to board a three-week transatlantic cruise. Mum went upstairs to read the twinnies a bedtime story and amazed us by keeping them silent and spellbound for at least 40 minutes. The following week, with Mum and Dad 1,000 miles away playing deck quoits, we started getting angry calls from parents of other five-year-olds in their class; Mum had read them a school sex education manual that Daniel had chucked out of his bedroom, and the twinnies were giving graphic demonstrations every day during break.

- **Fallout** from above: We are playground pariahs again – not that I have time to notice.

**Summary of the year**: I think I've cracked this senior management lark. It's got nothing to do with sitting round shiny boardroom tables in a crisp white shirt, blagging about forecasts and steamrollering everyone else's opinions. It's much easier than that: you just treat everyone the same way you do your kids. Decide your priorities then tell the staff what needs doing and if it doesn't get done you take it off their pocket money/wages. They soon get the idea. A ruthless manager born to multi-task, that's me. Oh, and if Ant is struggling at home I just delegate that to the therapist since we're paying her so much already.

Ant is doing our Christmas this year. The college Principal has asked me to put together a VIP project application. I'll have to work all through the Christmas break but I don't mind – it makes a change to finally feel a valued part of a bigger picture.

Festive Greetings to you all,

*Alison, Antonio, Eleanor, Felipe, Daniel, Fraser, Mackenzie, and Hector and Salvador*

\* \* \* \* \*

*December 2005*

*Paradise House, Paradise View,*
*Upley Rising, Thameshire*

*Christmas News from the Wrights of Paradise View*

*Dear Everyone,*

My book, *Rising Up: Finding Your Personal Pedestal and Staying On it Without Wobbling* was published this year, to rapturous reviews. The Lady praised it as 'a brisk, no stilettos barred wellbeing guide – it reads like leaving the window open on a freezing cold day'. Bathrooms Monthly said, 'Nothing about pedestals that we cover, but who's objecting to a free review copy?' and it even got a mention in Time Out: 'A merciless landgrab at the meaning of life from the pampered perspective of outer London's leafiest suburb. Caroline Wright is to wellbeing literature what Harold Shipman was to medicine.'

As an introverted only child, I never dared to dream that one day I would appear on the glossy dustjacket of my very own published work. But now, rows of me smile out radiantly from Upley Rising's Vellum Bookshop window, looking like a mixture of Diana and Madonna or so I'm told.

My book promotes my simple philosophy: Every woman should be unafraid to place herself upon her own pedestal. On your personal marble podium you are elevated above anything life throws at you. The world becomes serene and problems shrink to insignificance. Others will look up to you and respect you. From your pedestal it is so much easier to emanate love and tranquillity – and so much harder for others to compete with you. The world becomes yours for the asking.

As the blurb on the back cover says, you can read Aristotle in ancient Greek and toil through 750 pages of Kant – or you can gain a refreshing new philosophy of life in less than 200 pages from Thameshire's 'sage of the suburbs', Caroline Wright!

As well as publishing my own book I am proud to have spent much of the year campaigning and fundraising for the Ditch Wright Philanthropic Foundation, the charity I founded in memory of my beloved brother-in-law. We have been busy raising eye-watering sums of money. Our son Maximilian's 24-hour non-stop tuba performance outside the local hospital was just one of our many heroic efforts this year.

But cake sales and charity balls aside, I have had to draw on every last ounce of Pedestal Power (as I call it in my book) to support Charles through an unexpected tribulation.

His family have persisted with a spurious, unfounded claim that our worthy cause, the Ditch Wright Philanthropic Foundation, was plagiarising their own Ditch Wright Charitable Foundation. They have become difficult and unpleasant, spreading unfounded rumours about me and the incredibly hard work I have undertaken in Ditch's name. It is obvious that with my events management experience and Charles's global contacts network we are far better able to promote the good work that Ditch would have wanted. But Charles's family can't see reason and have continued to bombard him with threats.

I had to ban Charles from speaking to his parents, which is so hard for him given that he has already lost a beloved brother. To prevent him succumbing to temptation to go and visit his mother and father, who are getting quite elderly, I sent him on a sabbatical: a charity climb up Mount Kilimanjaro. Not only did this raise over £5,000 (thanks to all of you who donated – it's still not too late), it also kept him far away from London and his parents for two whole months. As a bonus, he really had to give up smoking as part of his training. That's Pedestal Power for you!

Our children are both thrilled that their mother has written a real book. Max has had a busy year studying for 12 GCSEs, winning our club's teenage tennis challenge as part of his route to the 2012 Olympics, and generally being the most sought-after boy in his class, which isn't surprising given how handsome he has become. We literally have young women queuing up at our door, all claiming to be his latest girlfriend. Charles has a tendency to call whichever girl Max has in tow by the wrong name, which all too often leads to tears, and me having to sit the poor thing down and console her with pieces of advice from my book. I've sold quite a few copies that way.

In a tumultuous year of book signings and charity event appearances it was inevitable, even in our family, that something would get overlooked.

One Sunday morning in September I was surprised to find one of Max's girlfriends helping herself to herbal tea in the kitchen at breakfast time. When she turned round I screamed; and here I have to confess I nearly wobbled on my personal pedestal. The strange girl, with straight black hair, wearing a silver nose stud and squeezed into ripped and faded jeans, was our daughter Clementine. Unrecognisable, looking like she'd wandered into our house from one of those gloomy posters about homeless teenagers.

Going through her bedroom to find the hidden hair dye I was even more horrified to uncover four bottles of cider secreted under her pink satin duvet cover. They were large bottles, of a disgusting cheap brand that looked brash and incongruous in our lovely home.

As a caring parent I realised it was time for a mature, compassionate mother-daughter heart to heart.

First I got Clem to take responsibility for her actions by flushing away the black hair dye and giving the disgusting jeans to charity. Then I spelt out to her that if she didn't tell me what was going on her allowance would be suspended indefinitely. Clementine broke down into sobs and confessed that our neighbour's son had told her that the corner shop sold lovely apple juice, and had persuaded her to give him the money to buy it for her as they sold it to him for a special price.

A call to the police soon sorted things out there. We have a completely dysfunctional family living next door, a blot on our lovely road; they are fortunate that I took the initiative to sort things out; the mother's brain is completely addled from having too many children.

Clementine's beautiful blonde curls will take months to grow again. We can't think what possessed her to change her appearance, but at least we got a term's fees back from her school, Rossetti House, whom we pay to provide an all-round education; the money will cover her lost modelling sessions.

As I say in my book, you have to learn to sway with the wind on a pedestal and shoulder the adversities life may bring with a shrug and a smile before moving on. We are off to Austria for a magical ski trip over Christmas, where Clementine can keep her hair covered under a fur hat, and where as a published author I will feel at home on the slopes with the rich and famous.

To save anyone the embarrassment of asking, you can purchase a copy of *Rising Up: Finding Your Own Personal Pedestal and Staying On it Without Wobbling* from Narcissus Publishing Ltd, or you can actually buy it from the internet, through the Amazon Booksellers for £18.99. I have attached a free preview extract for you to enjoy over your Christmas break. And you can send donations in memory of Ditch to me direct by cheque in the post, made out to Caroline Wright, Chief Executive, the Ditch Wright Philanthropic Foundation.

Wishing Everyone a very Happy Christmas,

*Caroline, Charles, Maximilian and Clementine Wright*

*Caroline's Top Tips for finding your own personal pedestal and staying on it without wobbling*

- *Every woman belongs on a pedestal. But why wait for someone to put you there? Build your own, climb onto it (gracefully, if you are wearing a tight skirt) and defend your position against all comers. It won't take long before everyone will know that's where you belong.*

- *Take a few of your favourite possessions with you onto your pedestal. Possessions are more reliable than people. Marriages may come and go but your favourite silk dress is always your friend.*

- *But never let your possessions go stale, throw them off the pedestal first; old belongings are as bad for the soul as mouldy food is for the body.*

- *The previous tip does not apply to diamonds.*

- *Did you know that most people never look up? Your pedestal is the perfect place to watch what is going on unobserved, whether it is the gardener leaving work early or your partner smoking in secret. You can intervene in a gracious but assertive manner. Remember what Gandhi said: forgiveness is the attribute of the strong.*

\* \* \* \* \*

# Christmas 2006

**15 Paradise View**
**Upley Rising**
**Thameshire**

## Dear Friends

I've always hated lemons. Sour, acidic imposters pretending to be fruit. Never, ever, tell me that I should be making lemonade.

In March an email thudded into my inbox at work. As Head Librarian I had got used to receiving dozens of emails every day, most of them pointless messages from distant college staff copying in everyone from the finance department to student services, just because they could broadcast with a single click. But this one was different.

The college Principal informed me – along with 325 other staff – that South Thameshire Further Education College was about to be subsumed into a new, Greater Thameshire Enhanced Further Education Academy. All services provided from my college building would be transferred to a glittering new edifice being built on the site of our sister institution, North Thameshire Further Education College. This unparalleled opportunity for the county was happening courtesy of a newly won £30 million government grant. (This was the same project I had spent weeks slaving over on unpaid overtime, though vital details, like the actual names of the colleges, had now been replaced.) The message concluded that he – the current Principal – was delighted to announce he had been appointed to preside over the newly created Academy. Efficiency savings would be made by combining job functions but we were welcome to reapply for our own posts.

I knew my counterpart Head Librarian at North Thameshire College: a smooth-talking American with an Information Science masters from Yale and a string of connections on both sides of the Atlantic. It took me precisely three nano seconds to make a decision about my chances of becoming the new Head Librarian for Enhanced Further Education. I took the redundancy.

And that's it: 22 years of dedicated service to further education reduced to one flimsy P45. The scruffy 1960s redbrick campus where I spent so many happy hours has been sold to developers who are turning it into a retail park. 'My' library: cluttered, comfortable, with threadbare carpets and leaky windows, is being regenerated on a new site into a brightly lit, state-of-the-art information centre with no dark corners for despairing students to contemplate the meaning of life or finalise illicit drug deals.

We put most of my redundancy cash into the new decorating business which Ant agreed to start, as we had to find a regular source of income and were completely out of other ideas. Where normal people breathe, Upley Rising citizens namedrop, and two people had already employed him so they could tell their friends that their walls were painted by an award-winning artist – though it turned out one of them was expecting a mural. We invested in a van with the strapline 'Cortinez Quality Home Decorating'. The work started to roll in, Ant came home every night covered in paint but that was nothing new. But after a few weeks the jobs started to dwindle, and soon there were none. I did a bit of undercover investigation in the twinnies' school playground, where most other parents had no idea who I was. The problem wasn't Ant. The same customers who claimed that quality workmanship was more important than price had found quotes from two local Lithuanian firms (who were following Ant's van round Upley Rising in unmarked vehicles) too tempting. Maybe they needed the money they saved for tennis club fees or for their children's private tutors. Ant tried lowering his prices but the Lithuanian builders slashed theirs to even more. I suppose they have to make a living too.

But by June we were out of business.

At 45 Ant and I found ourselves at home all day, like a retired couple only without the pension or the free prescriptions. And we were skint. The Job Centre staff tried to be helpful but had problems seeing the difference between a catering assistant and a Head Librarian. Ant and I decided to take a constructive approach to life. He started researching art grants again, while I focused on managing the children and overcoming feelings of hopelessness.

We sold the van and paid for Eleanor and Felipe to go to Newquay after their GCSEs. Having ignored Ant and me for the best part of two years the twins suddenly reacquired the art of speech, just for long enough to plead that absolutely <u>everyone</u> has to spend a week in Newquay after their exams, or they will be cast out from the tribe and left to starve in the social wilderness for eternity. They had both got more A grades than they had a right to deserve so we relented. Off they went on the strict condition that they would phone every night. No calls came, and I was on the point of driving all the way to Cornwall in the dark to knock on caravan doors, when we got one text at 3am: 'We R having gr8 time lol.'

In early July Daniel disappeared. At first we didn't notice. He's always either at school or holed up in his room, so he's never really with us anyway. But when we got a call from the school because we hadn't reported him sick, I checked his bedroom and there was no Daniel. This was a few weeks short of his 14$^{th}$ birthday. Since he doesn't do friends, we called everyone in his class ('Daniel who?') then the police. Starting to panic, we pasted up dozens of Missing posters. Four different neighbours responded at once: to complain that smudgy mugshots of a boy in a sweatshirt and trainers lowered the tone of the wrought-iron lampposts in Paradise View. So much for hugging a hoodie. Felipe said Daniel had told him he was born into the wrong family. Fraser asked if he could have Daniel's bedroom. Vanessa reassured us Daniel would be fine, and came round to make me endless mugs of tea. Two hideous days and nights dragged by. Ant started organising search parties. I stayed at home, sitting staring at the undrunk tea. On day three, just as the police were finally about to put out a national alert, Daniel came walking up the road. He looked just like the boy in the posters in his grey hoodie and jeans, carrying his backpack; but nobody noticed him until he got to our door. He might as well have been invisible.

He wouldn't – still won't – talk about where he'd been or what happened to him. Despite being quizzed by the police, his psychotherapist and a social worker. All he'll say is that no harm came to him. His lost three days have taken at least three years off my life expectancy.

The year continued in the same vein, with both Antonio and me being sucked into then spat out of projects. I threw myself into this year's Wellspring Festival, only to discover that the inconceivable has happened: a management takeover. Let me be clear – we are talking about a ritual ceremony of mythological proportions that has been unchanged for over 300 years. Now I was sent a terse email telling me my services weren't required, which didn't make sense. I'd become a regular fixture with my guitar in the missing children's tent. Children lose their parents on purpose to come and hear my version of All Along the Watchtower.

I couldn't believe it when I found out that my apex predator neighbour Caroline – who had treated the festival like cheap entertainment laid on for the lower classes, until she reinvented herself as some sort of suburban power guru – had charmed her way onto the committee. She sidelined the lovely Astrantia who has run things for over 30 years, packed the committee with her stuck-up friends and got herself elected as chair. The days of relaxed gatherings in Astrantia's jumbled kitchen, where festival planning came together organically over herbal tea and home-made flapjacks, were replaced by formal meetings with agendas, held at the tennis club. How could Caroline Wright possibly understand the chilled festival vibe? I couldn't believe my eyes when I saw her wafting along at the front of the Wellspring procession in a kaftan, chatting away with the chief Druid like they'd been best mates for ever.

I should have guessed she'd have an ulterior motive. She created, and appointed herself head of, a new audition process for next year's Upley Maiden. Which will no doubt quite coincidentally give the role to her own daughter.

While I was being sacked from the Wellspring, Antonio's submission for the Refugees and Displaced Persons Art Prize was rejected. Prompted by his therapist (who has started accepting charcoal sketches of the state of the inside of Ant's mind instead of cash) he had spent nearly a year working up a darkly beautiful, complex piece. He called it Distant Love, and it actually brought a lump to my throat. His first major artwork for a long time, it's about multiple layers of longing, for his lost Chile and his vanished father/son relationship.

But according to the Prize small print he no longer qualified as a refugee, having built a life and a career (hollow laugh) in this country. The letter of refusal explained that since Antonio had come to the UK in the 1970s many more waves of displaced persons have arrived in the UK, bringing their own new forms of tortured creative output. These merited priority. I said they have a point: we may be starving, but we are starving in a leafy Home Counties suburb with our children at one of the best schools in the country and our very own kitchen extension. Shuffling our His and Hers piles of CVs on the kitchen table, Ant said he feels more of an outsider than ever.

It's hard living in a place like this when you haven't got any money. By June, summertime in Upley Rising was in full swing. People were employing extra gardeners, ferrying their children to taekwondo, replacing their wardrobe collections, organising May balls. After a morning spent weeding our back garden veg patch I went out in my gardening clothes to stock up on food from the Reduced to Tears shelf in the Coop. I found myself pausing to gaze through the windows of the Rising Bean, where I didn't even have the cash to drop in for a coffee. As I stood there someone tapped me on the arm and tried to press a pound coin into my hand in exchange for the copy of the Big Issue I had just bought down the road.

Our holiday this year was a trip to Hull for my niece Saffron's Masters graduation in psychology (she got a distinction for her dissertation on the distorting impact of the extended family). My sister Gill asked us all to come as our parents were away on a month's trip seeing the sights of China. None of us recognised Saffron – formerly Cousin Shrub – who had dyed her hair blue and cut off her famous fringe. We could see her face for the first time since she was a baby. I was even more shocked when I saw Gill, who hadn't told us about her breast cancer diagnosis. We all cried and hugged. Saffron, mascara running down her cheeks, said it was OK and took notes for her PhD proposal. The twinnies went round the graduation celebration marquee drinking dregs from the champagne glasses and both were sick.

As the autumn term started we settled into the routine that people living with zero money in a posh area normally lead. We pretended we were walking everywhere because it was healthier. The twins (now in the 6th form, doing nine AS levels between them) turned into mature and resourceful human beings. Felipe informed his new girlfriend he's a feminist and is cool about her paying for him. Eleanor told everyone she's given all her possessions to the world's poor. Daniel never goes out (not counting his three-day disappearance) and doesn't eat much. The twinnies deal with poverty in the same way they approach life in general, by yelling at things/people or jumping up and down on them. It's just as well they've never shown any interest in violin lessons or ballet classes.

It's amazing how inventive you can be when you've got no money, without actually breaking the law. Our TV licence expired just as the air crash in Neighbours was happening. I wasn't prepared to add another criminal record to the family so creative thinking was required. There's a TV in the dentist's waiting room; I managed to sneak past the receptionist at broadcast time three afternoons in a row before she got suspicious and twigged that I wasn't really there to collect my son. It must be a first, being expelled from your own dentist.

But still no work. Three weeks ago I was sitting at the computer looking up remote contacts on Friends Reunited just in case someone I never spoke to at school 30 years ago might be on the lookout for a senior librarian rather than a post-divorce get-together. The phone rang. It was Gill. My Mum, on a day trip with her step class friends to an outlet mall near Grimsby, had collapsed without warning. She'd suffered a major stroke.

I told you it was a year of lemons. Here I am, writing this year's Christmas news in the intensive care stroke unit at Scunthorpe General Hospital. Mum hasn't recovered consciousness and no one knows if she will or what brain damage there might be. She's plugged into that many wires and tubes she looks like one of her own pieces of crochet. Even with her eyes closed there's a tinge of smugness in her expression, which Saffron would say is my own Freudian projection.

Gill can't get up here easily as her clients don't get it when their social worker has family issues, then there's her radiotherapy sessions. One upside of long-term unemployment is that I've got unlimited time to sit at a hospital bedside. And to look after my dad, who's pretending he can manage perfectly well but he's completely distracted; last night I caught him heating up a tin of dog food for supper.

Ant sends news bulletins from home to cheer me up. Last week he called to say Salvador our cat had died. Finally. He had crept away to find somewhere to be alone. Our neighbours' emo daughter Clementine appeared at our door appropriately all in black, holding a rigid grey object which she thrust into Mackenzie's arms: "I found this. My mother says to keep your dead animals out of our back garden." Daniel came out of his room for the first time in weeks and organised a cat funeral in our veg patch.

I tell everything to Mum but get no reaction. Even a flickering eyelid would be something. Holding her hand I notice that her fingernails must be growing as the peach polish from her latest manicure is slowly advancing away from the cuticles. The nursing staff are run off their feet and haven't got time to comb her hair or put Radio 2 on the radio Dad brought in.

This will be another Christmas newsletter that doesn't get sent.

The steady bleep of the monitor sounds like silence. I've got more time to think than I've had for years. My thoughts keep skipping to the twinnies; I miss Mackenzie mixing glue with sugar because we can't afford honey, or collecting Fraser from classmates' houses where he's turned up uninvited for tea after school because it's better food than at home. I miss Daniel's invisible presence from behind his bedroom door, and the twins coming home an hour after their 11pm deadline, not texting as they can't afford the phone credits. So they say. I miss Ant promising that the next grant application will be The One, then chucking another unidentifiable repurposed object out of the studio. I need to get a job. How can a senior information services manager and an award-winning artist who's displayed work at the Royal Academy find themselves living on the poverty line? Invisibly, surrounded by people whose lives are made meaningful by baby grand pianos, potted olive trees and professions where the Christmas bonuses are bigger than some small countries' economies?

It just keeps slipping away, this fantasy called normal family life. It's all around: on advertising hoardings and in TV sitcoms. But for us it's like one of the new bus stops in the centre of Upley Rising, with flashing signs that say your bus will arrive in two minutes. When you blink it's changed to 27 minutes, then 35 minutes – always just edging out of reach. I thought this was going to be the year when everything worked out, but the lemons just keep coming.

Festive Greetings to you all,

*Alison, Antonio, Eleanor, Felipe, Daniel, Fraser, Mackenzie and Hector*

\* \* \* \* \*

## December 2006

*Paradise House, Paradise View,*
*Upley Rising, Thameshire*

*Christmas News from the Wrights of Paradise View*

## Dear Everyone,

2006 has been another fabulous year in the Wright household.

Charles was promoted to Director of Extracurricular Negotiations when his company STEAL was bought by a genuine Russian billionaire, who quickly spotted his potential. He's travelling to Moscow and St Petersburg now, which is so much more exotic than New York, and my wardrobe is overflowing with fur. I don't have any problems with this as the poor animals lead miserable lives anyway and must be grateful to be dead by the time they make the coats.

We decided to celebrate Charles's new role with a winter holiday; Charles wanted to go skiing but I really couldn't cope with another suntan stopping in a straight line across my neck, so Thailand it had to be.

I have spent the year building on the success of my book (*Rising Up: Finding Your Personal Pedestal and Staying On it Without Wobbling*), which has recently been translated into Welsh and Esperanto. Wanting to find new ways to sprinkle the fairy dust of my new philosophy, I considered standing for Thameshire Council in the local elections, but as Mother Theresa said, politics is just showbusiness for ugly people. Then I realised that what people really wanted was not a second edition of my book, but a personification of my Pedestal Power philosophy: something they could touch and feel. So this spring I launched my latest venture.

The Caroline Wright Wellbeing Emporium is a select retail establishment located on Upley Rising's most exclusive street, between the bridal boutique and the artisan loaves bakery. The billionaire who owns STEAL had quite a few spare roubles in need of a temporary home, so he has invested in my project, in a charming gesture of faith.

It is so rewarding to bring a shaft of sunlight into the humdrum lives of Upley Rising residents; to offer a temporary escape from the daily ennui of Montessori school runs and gym circuits. My Emporium is a welcome haven. Customers are greeted by the gentle chime of Tibetan bells as they open the door and enter a softly lit world suffused with the fragrance of lotus blossom candles. They can browse undisturbed for these and other luxury items that resonate with the teachings in my book, their minds calmed by the gentle burbling of indoor water features. Everything they see, hear and smell is for sale. It's so inspirational to think that a small child lovingly creating a hand-loomed silk rug in faraway Nepal can transform mundane abodes here in Thameshire. My clients can even make an appointment for a private coaching session with me, where I advise them which of my products will enhance their life experience. As I tell them, a Caroline Wright gold leaf facemask feels as good as owning your own private island.

It's hardly surprising that my Emporium has proved a huge success. And one triumph led to another, something I had not foreseen.

One of my most loyal customers is the shy Baron, the unsung member of the House of Lords who runs Upley Rising's endearing Wellspring Festival. He's a genuine aristocrat – one who inherited his title, rather than having to buy his way in on merit. We struck up a real friendship this year; I think he is rather lonely. He doesn't get to Westminster very often, only to claim his expenses. He loves to come in and shop for essential oils, and we gossip like old friends.

During one of these little chats he poured out his heart to me about the direction the Wellspring Festival had taken. Over the years, organising it had changed from a Zen process which unfolded like an origami swan, to a series of squabbly sessions dominated by argumentative committee members who turned up to meetings wearing scruffy zip-up fleeces covered in dog hairs. There was endless wrangling over tedious details like recycling points and expensive facilities for lost children. They had lost sight of the festival's original spiritual ethic, with the Upley Maiden at its heart symbolising youth, innocence and seasonal renewal as she emerges from the well anew every summer. A commitment which should have been a fulfilling vocation was becoming needlessly stressful for the poor man.

The Baron went on to mention how much money the festival made. Before I knew it I had given him a summary of my CV covering my experience organising global world summits for Imperative Events and generating multimillion dollar sales for the LavishUs Corporation.

And here I am, chairing the committee that runs this country's most unique celebration of rural life! I feel privileged to be the custodian of such a precious jewel in our national heritage. I have thrown myself into my new role, putting together a top team of like-minded associates. We plan to remodel the festival into a pastoral celebration fit for the 21st century. This year, being new, we barely scratched the surface; but I will ensure that next year's Wellspring is a sensation.

* * * * *

We were thrilled, if not surprised, when Maximilian passed at least 15 GCSEs, all grade A*. He and his tutor worked incredibly hard for this moment. While most of his year group went off for a rowdy celebration in Newquay, we paid for him and a few of his friends to spend a smart weekend in London's Claridge's hotel, giving them a taste of the lifestyle they can look forward to in the future.

Max also came with us on this year's summer holiday to Madagascar, before volunteering to spend three weeks doing an unpaid internship for STEAL to gain valuable work experience. Now he is a busy sixth former, doing

A levels in Music, Russian, History and Philosophy – in between tennis tournaments, partying and the school orchestra.

Meanwhile, our fragile flower of a daughter Clementine has had another difficult year, poor lamb. Where Max sails through life, Clem wades. Coping with two high achiever parents and a gifted brother cannot be easy for her. She took to playing truant from her very expensive school, and on several occasions our *au pair* has had to extricate her from a group of so-called friends who congregate after school on the steps of Upley Rising's clock tower. The police are very unhelpful and maintain it is for parents to manage their own children, despite the huge sums we taxpayers shower on our police force.

I have certainly done my best. I confiscated Clementine's hair straighteners for good, before sending her to spend the summer holidays with Mother in the healthy fresh air of Rupert's 2,000-acre Scottish estate, which Mother said would be cheaper and more practical than a rehabilitation clinic. Mother complained that Clementine wouldn't eat anything, which is probably because they have a habit of serving food that is so fresh it is still twitching, and Clem has a delicate stomach. Clem claimed that Rupert patrols the corridors of the house at night with a shotgun, occasionally howling. To rekindle her motivation in life, I have encouraged her to apply for the role of next year's Wellspring Festival Maiden.

You might wonder how I fill my time when I am not organising national festivals, signing copies of my book or visiting ethical trade fairs to pick out replica ivory netsuke for my Emporium. The answer is of course championing the Ditch Wright Philanthropic Foundation. This year our loving memorial to my dear brother-in-law has burgeoned: we have introduced a Ditch Wright South Thameshire Lawn Tennis Club Trophy, and a Ditch Wright range of sacred pyramid crystals. But I am sad to report that Charles's family persist in battling on with their own copycat project, the Ditch Wright Charitable Foundation, and are even threatening to take us to court. Charles agrees with me that their behaviour is outrageous, but he is conflicted. It is hard for him to pit himself against his father, especially one whose collection of sharpened knives hangs on his living room wall as a reminder of the reputation he once commanded on the streets of East London.

It is truly terrible to see a family ripped apart like this. I constantly have to shred letters addressed to Charles and marked private and confidential, but I think his family may have been getting to him at work despite my having a word with his secretary. And though I try to rise above the mêlée, some of the unspeakable threats left on our answerphone aimed at me have given me sleepless nights. Most unforgivably, Charles's parents have stopped sending our children birthday and Christmas presents.

However I am made of stronger stuff; resilience has always been my watchword and I am confident we will work through this little difficulty. And on a much brighter note, here is the news you will all have been waiting for!

Next year will be not just our 20th wedding anniversary and the 150th anniversary of our Tennis Club, but my darling husband's 50th birthday! Enclosed with this newsletter is your invitation to a SURPRISE Half Century celebration for Charles next September. Anyone who breathes a word to him will be deleted from my address book forever.

Save the date, and start planning your Court of Henry

VIII themed costume now!

Wishing everyone a very Happy Christmas,

*Caroline, Charles, Maximilian and Clementine Wright*

## December 2007

*Paradise House, Paradise View,*
*Upley Rising, Thameshire*

*Christmas News from the Wrights of Paradise View*

## Dear Everyone,

Choosing the highlights of the Wright family year is always a dilemma, but this year the order is dictated by protocol. I shall start at the very top.

**Caroline has a very royal audience**

The pinnacle of a year which has been one long pinnacle was my invitation to Buckingham Palace. I was beyond thrilled to receive a formal request to spend an afternoon with Her Majesty in the sylvan privacy of her own back garden. It was a moment I had dreamed of all my life.

Charles and I were asked to arrive three hours early, which gave us the opportunity to take in the beauty of the grounds. Other people started to appear; I hadn't realised the Queen had invited quite so many other guests as well as Charles and me – but then if I owned 39 acres in the heart of Central London I too would relish the chance to entertain on a grand scale.

You could feel the air quivering with anticipation as we all lined up along the lawns for our very special audience. Charles and I were accidentally placed in the back row, from where I got my first glimpse of our gracious monarch. She wore a tasteful shade of buttercup yellow, was crownless and with one of her signature handbags on her arm (it has to be said, Princess Margaret always had the sharper fashion sense). As I stood on tiptoe to see Her Majesty pausing near us to chat with some foreign dignitary, Charles gallantly put his hands round my slender waist and lifted me above the assembled masses; and The Queen looked up, bestowing on me the kindest, most beautiful smile. There was a true moment of empathetic connection, as she recognised that what she and I have in common is a tiny stature but a big presence. Also, I think she must have recognised me from the cover of my book, a few complimentary copies of which I had thoughtfully sent her in advance. Then a uniformed usher appeared from nowhere, tapped Charles on the arm – a touch too hard for a social event – and commanded him to put me down – as if I was some sort of weapon!

Later, while we were standing in the line of people hoping for a word with Sir David Attenborough, who should join us but His Royal Highness Prince Charles! He's much more attractive in real life than in the magazines, and surprisingly knowledgeable; he'd even heard of Upley Rising's Wellspring Festival, and took a great interest in my Emporium. He'll make a marvellous monarch one day in the very distant future.

It was a day whose memory I shall treasure forever.

**Max goes to Oxford!**
We are all thrilled at the prospect of Maximilian taking up

his place at Oxford University.

Becoming Head Boy at one of the country's top schools would have been enough for most boys his age to sit back and wait for the university offers to flood in – but not for our perfectionist son.

Max spent many hours working on a unique personal statement exploring the parallels between his being Head Boy at the Queen's Grammar and his grandfather masterminding one of London's most famous East End gangs. He explained how it would be a misconception to think of his grandfather's profession as criminal, since it took directionless young men and gave them a true sense of purpose, as well as making them economically useful. He asked the copywriting team at Charles's company to read it over, and they sent it back unchanged saying that it defied improvement. Max had his interview for a music scholarship (majoring in tuba studies) just last week. He touched the tutors' hearts with a speech describing how his beloved Uncle Ditch, whose untimely death was such a blow to him in his formative years, had appeared to him in a dream and played him a new song called To Oxford You Must Go.

We are expecting Max's offer to come through early in the new year, and Charles has sent the college a discreet Christmas cash donation as an advance thank you.

It's not all serious study though for our genius son – we can hardly keep up with Max's social life. He celebrated outstanding summer AS level results with a week in Ibiza, and landed a coveted ticket to the Glastonbury Festival through a friend. A group of them shared a yurt in the VIP area. He's been so busy he's hardly had time to use the car we bought him for his 17th birthday.

## Charity triumph

The most touching moment of the year was seeing my strong, stoic husband hugging his own father and sobbing with happiness at their reconciliation.

Not long after my audience with Her Majesty the Queen we had an unexpected visit from several of Charles's cousins. They arrived without warning one rainy Saturday, sent on behalf of his estranged parents. The cousins had obviously put a lot of thought into making an impression, arriving dressed to kill and accompanied by four huge bodyguards. It was rather over the top for Upley Rising, which is hardly known for its high crime rate. We all sat on the cream leather sofas in our spacious extension: in deference to the seriousness of the occasion I did not ask any of our visitors to take their shoes off, and they declined my offer of coffee.

We had a frank conversation. The cousins explained that Charles's parents were deeply offended because they thought that the Buckingham Palace garden party invitation was mistakenly addressed, and should have been sent to Charles's father (who has the same initials as me; he is Charles Percival, I am Caroline Penelope) at the Ditch Wright Charitable Foundation, instead of to me at the Ditch Wright Philanthropic Foundation. As if the Palace could make such an elementary error, or as if I wouldn't have passed the invitation on if I had spotted that the envelope was addressed to a charity with an almost identical name!

Putting to good use the listening skills I honed through my many business successes, and noticing one of the cousins distractedly making deep scratches on my Italian glass coffee table with the pointed bezel of his large gold signet ring, I realised how truly hurt Charles's parents were. When the security men got up and began pacing up and down in their muddy boots on my white carpet, I realised it was time to heal the wounds.

In the spirit of unity and forgiveness, Charles and I have agreed to combine the two Foundations. The new organisation is called the Shoreditch Wright Family Trust. I am in charge of charitable income for the whole of Thameshire while his family look after the other bits of the world. In a further gesture of harmony, I am donating a share of the royalties from my book *(Rising Up: Finding Your Own Personal Pedestal and Staying On it Without Wobbling)* to the new Trust, in return for publicity on the new joint charity website. Charles and I are both thrilled that the family differences have been resolved in a way that Ditch would have wanted.

This realignment in my responsibilities will allow me to devote more time to expanding my Emporium, starting with branches all over Thameshire before multiplying nationally.

It should also put a stop to any more nosy letters from the Charity Commission snooping into the money we spent on last year's modest winter family getaway in Phuket.

### Caroline rescues a national treasure

2007 has seen me back doing what I have always excelled at: managing extraordinary events. I have had a fabulous time leading Upley Rising's Wellspring Festival committee. After three centuries of dropping maidens down the same well, year after year, the annual festivities were looking stale and tired. My events management experience was exactly what the Festival needed to give it a new lease of life.

In fact I did such a good job raising its profile that the

Baron, whose family has held the feudal rights to hold the festival every year since 1735, received an offer to buy it! He came into my Emporium to share his dilemma. Should he take the much-needed cash, or plough on with the Wellspring through his twilight years, as all his ancestors had done down the centuries? The poor man was torn between the responsibilities inherent to his lineage and his natural desire for freedom from his weighty burden, not to mention the temptation of a healthy bank account.

I sold him a Himalayan sound bath so he could clear his mind and tune in to his deepest inner feelings.

Thanks to my efforts (Pedestal Power in action again) the Baron has been rescued from genteel poverty and is able to live a lifestyle more suited to his title; he has gone to Las Vegas where he intends to meditate and live in harmony with nature. The Wellspring Festival is now under the caring ownership of something called a Hedge Fund. With such a pastoral name we can be sure its future is in safe hands. The professional businessmen who are its new proprietors are delighted for me to continue running the management committee, and I am looking forward to next year's festival being an even bigger success.

### Clementine spreads her wings

As for this year's Wellspring Festival, one of my proudest moments of the year was witnessing our daughter Clementine steal the show. The secret dream of every young girl in Upley Rising is to be chosen as the Festival's maiden. Clem's selection as this year's new style Upley Princess (my cutting-edge new committee decided to update the title, as 'maiden' sounds so old-fashioned) followed a scrupulously fair process in which I as committee chair made sure to take a back seat. By sheer coincidence the two other finalists had to drop out. One got a nasty stomach bug just before the audition, the day after Clem had invited her to our house for tea. I had organised a taxi to make sure the other girl, who sadly has a disability, arrived on time but it somehow got hopelessly lost and she arrived after the judging process had finished.

Clementine's victory was well deserved. She has gone through such a challenging time as a teenager exploring her identity. And I need not have worried; she threw herself into the event with true determination. The years I spent grooming her for modelling shoots paid off; without boring you with the details, I will just say that she gave a showstopping performance that left spectators gasping. She may not be academic like her brilliant brother, but I have come to realise that she has other talents in droves; indeed Charles remarked how much she is starting to remind him of his dear departed brother. She certainly took the Wellspring Festival in her stride; she did it her way, and people will talk about the 2007 Upley Princess for a long time to come.

### Charles's half century

Charles has fulfilled his lifetime ambition to become a board director before the age of 50.

In February he was appointed to the board of STEAL. He loves all the perks, especially open access to the boardroom drinks cabinet, a BMW upgrade every year, and recommending his own annual bonuses. But he finds the day-to-day detail, like reading long reports and sacking staff, very tedious. He's been so busy we found it hard to fit in our usual three holidays this year: we just managed a month in our French retreat, where we have planted a vineyard so that we can market our own wine label, and a quick long weekend in Dubai.

We have both been so immersed in life as Upley Rising's premier power couple (The Upley Herald's phrase, not mine!) that unfortunately I had to cancel the little party I had planned to celebrate Charles's 50th birthday in September. By the time I found a moment to send out repeat invitations to those of you who somehow missed them in last year's Wright Family Christmas News, by complete coincidence many of you had made other plans for the exact same date. Apologies to those of you who had already invested in your Anne Boleyn or Cardinal Wolsey costumes. I am sure you will be able to put them to good use!

You will be relieved to hear that Charles didn't miss out on celebrating his 50th in style. The Russian billionaire who owns STEAL kindly freed up his superyacht for the occasion so off we all flew for a sumptuous celebration with vodka and caviar in Cannes harbour.

## A proper family Christmas in Paradise

We are looking forward to a family Christmas in Paradise View. We will have Mother with us this year. She and Rupert have decided to go their separate ways. Mother says she'd had enough of draughty Scottish castles where you have to shoot your own dinner and it takes an hour and a half to drive to the nearest Unwins as the butler refuses to part with the key to the wine cellar. Also she's heard on the grapevine that Gordon Brown has a plan to nationalise Scottish mansions.

Mother will be staying with us until she decides on her next move. She has made sure to get a decent financial settlement from Rupert, helped by Clementine's late-night phone call to Childline reporting him for taking pot shots at her from his bedroom window whenever she ventured onto the lawn. I have warned Mother against jumping out of the frying pan into the fire; the other day I noticed her whispering into her mobile phone, and when I happened to glance at it later I was shocked to see an Australian code for the last caller flash up: it was my father. Mother said he had been advising her on ways to invest the settlement cash from Rupert in the stock market, which is apparently having a very good run and is expected to do well in 2008. Perhaps he is finally reforming, and taking a genuine interest in her welfare.

While she was helping me with the Christmas drinks shopping list, Mother had a wonderful idea: she suggested building an Olympic-sized swimming pool in our back garden. No other house in our road has a pool. We will simply have to get the conservation area rules changed, remove a few big old trees and rebuild our extension to incorporate a changing room area. The works will release the artwork gifted to us by our next-door neighbour. What a good investment that was, as he is finally making his name as an artist. The rear aspect of our garden could have been designed with an infinity pool in mind: poised above Upley Rising, flowing seamlessly towards the South Thameshire Lawn Tennis Club. The perfect view from Paradise!

Wishing everyone a very Happy Christmas,

*Caroline, Charles, Maximilian and Clementine Wright*

\* \* \* \* \*

# Christmas 2007

**15 Paradise View**
**Upley Rising**
**Thameshire**

## Dear Friends

Spoiler alert: this year's Christmas news has a happy ending. Be prepared for shocking scenes of the Pickthwaite-Cortinez family dancing ecstatically round the living room and hugging each other.

### Eleanor and Felipe

Somehow our twins are nearly 18. Old enough to vote, get a job, be kicked out of the nest. Mind, they can still show the other twins in the family how to throw a proper tantrum; and they still act with infuriating twin-ness, Felipe communicating secret information to Eleanor just by flashing a look, or Eleanor finishing a sentence that no one heard Felipe start.

This year, with A levels coming up, they've been fitting in the odd bit of schoolwork between parties (there's a big 18th every other week for someone); asking for lifts; doing Saturday jobs (Eleanor at Oxfam, Felipe at the Screen on the Up cinema); asking for lifts; watching every episode of Skins; and asking for lifts. Eleanor is doing Maths, Psychology and Economics. Felipe is doing Art, Graphic Design and Spanish. Ant and I have been summoned to various school open evenings to discuss university options. As we stand in the queue for the careers adviser, other parents rushing round clutching shiny prospectuses charge up to us. 'Is this the Oxbridge queue?' ... then seeing it's Ant and me: 'Oh no, it can't be, sorry …' and move on.

## My parents

While I was away in Yorkshire, Eleanor and Felipe were stars at home, helping Ant with everything. I spent the first six weeks of the year staying with my dad while Mum was sunk in a deep coma at Scunthorpe General hospital's stroke unit. I visited Mum and looked after Dad, who stumbled through every day in a daze. We made grim plans for the worst: going through paperwork, discussing how Dad would manage on his own long term. Stroke victims can stay unconscious for weeks, months, even years, or die at any time. But I couldn't be away from the family indefinitely. I said goodbye to Mum on a freezing, grey February afternoon. As I was leaving the room, I glanced back. Mum opened her eyes, looked straight at me and said: "Isn't it about time you got married?"

That was the beginning of the beginning. She came home a month later, shuffling slowly round the bungalow with the help of a frame. She still finds speech difficult which Dad says is an improvement on the way things were before. But by September she was well enough to stand in the queue for three hours outside their local Northern Rock branch, set on withdrawing her Silver Saver's cash in case the run on the bank threatened her cruise savings. Proving her physiotherapist right that there's nothing like an incentive to get you moving.

In the meantime my sister Gill took a sabbatical after she got over her breast cancer. She's just turned 50 which she's celebrated by travelling the world on her own. So far we've had postcards from Thailand, India, Namibia and the Seychelles.

The day after Mum opened her eyes again I got back to Upley Rising following a nine-hour train journey from hell – thanks to staff shortages, unheated carriages, a signal operator's strike and a missed connection at Crewe. I was numb with cold in my worn-out winter coat and had lost a glove. I could hardly turn my key in the front door. When I eventually got in I thought it was the wrong house.

Room after room was clean, tidy and warm. It was like the scene in The Little Princess where the orphan comes in starving from the snow to find her freezing garret transformed with a crackling fire and a feast laid out. Felipe and Eleanor were in the kitchen cooking spaghetti bolognese for supper with the radio on, singing along to Beyoncé. A huge Welcome Back banner was strung across the hallway. Hector was curled up in front of the fireplace with tinsel (left over from Christmas) round his collar. Mackenzie and Fraser rushed up and gave me sticky hugs and a giant home-made card. Even Daniel emerged from his bedroom and smiled.

## Antonio

Antonio appeared in a clean white shirt and jeans and presented me with a glass of Prosecco and a bunch of black and silver resin tulips. He had broken the habit of a lifetime and remembered it was Valentine's Day.

Ant is a changed person. He is also an international contemporary artist of distinction – it's official. While I was away he received an invitation from the Chilean equivalent of our Arts Council. He's been rediscovered as an 'artist from the lost years' and awarded a major prize for being an overseas champion of Chilean art. The prize included an invitation to meet the President at a big reception after the awards ceremony. Ant decided that he was ready to go back. Various cousins he'd been emailing wanted to meet up with him. It was a big step. His therapist, jubilant, has started writing scholarly articles about him.

We were all over the moon for Ant. He wanted the whole family to go with him to Santiago but I wouldn't hear of him spending most of the prize money that way. He wouldn't even receive it until the ceremony, and we were still totally and utterly skint – just a value pasta bag away from penury. We decided to pool our pathetic holiday fund so he could go to the presentation in December.

## Home
Ant's invitation sat on the mantelpiece of our (rebuilt) fireplace while we got on with everyday life as the impoverished embarrassment of Paradise View. Looking for a job in a library that isn't closing down, I got some freelance archiving work for the Upley Society, an institution which I had heard of but thought was extinct. Its purpose, as far as I can tell, is to conserve Upley Rising in aspic – there are still portraits of Queen Victoria on its walls – and pretend that the 21$^{st}$ century is a temporary aberration which will go away if the desiccated old men that run it just keep their heads in the sand and their eyes closed. They'd have got a shock if they opened them at this year's Wellspring Festival.

Upley Rising's very own pagan suburban ritual, which spits in the face of health and safety by hurling a teenage girl down a well every summer, and which we'd strangely grown to love, has undergone a sanitised makeover. I first assumed it must all be the work of my neighbour who already had a stranglehold over the organising committee and whose daughter, Clementine, had as predicted been elected this year's Upley Maiden. But Vanessa found out from her friend who clerks for the town council that it had changed hands altogether. Astrantia's brother, the robed Druid who led the procession every summer, had undergone a mid-life crisis, sold the ownership and disappeared overseas: rumour has it he's leading a hermit's life in a cave in the Greek mountains. Astrantia was so upset she wouldn't talk about it, or to him; the feudal rights to hold the Wellspring procession and festival having been in her family for generations. So much for peace, love and the magic of tradition.

The new owners are a shady group of investors who Vanessa's contact, who did some digging, says are registered in the Cayman Islands. We were so furious that we decided not to go along this year, but there were howls of protest from Mackenzie and Fraser who sobbed that everyone in their class was going and there was going to be a bouncy castle and we'd promised to take them.

As we walked with the usual crowds down the High Street we thought we'd come to the wrong event. Instead of the torchlit procession to the Market Square there was a series of boring carnival floats advertising local businesses. Police were patrolling the streets making sure that nobody was drinking anything stronger than Fanta. My old missing children's tent had been outsourced to Group 4 who were running it from a Portakabin alongside St John's Ambulance. The car park where I had famously choreographed collisions as a volunteer was full of officious traffic wardens sticking tickets on windscreens.

The square dominated by an enormous stall branded Caroline's Emporium Products, selling 'licenced festival fun' along with wristbands entitling the wearer to a metal seat on a small grandstand erected for the occasion. We declined – and stared in horror at the place where the Well, into whose depths generations of Upley Maidens have been sunk, should be. In its place – completely concealing it – was a gross pink plastic podium arrangement, with 'Upley Princess 2007' in glittery letters strung across the front. On the podium sat a huge pink and yellow throne, looking like a giant slice of Battenberg cake. The team of cider-fuelled teenage boys who have pulled the maiden out of the well for the last 300 years had been replaced by a couple of leery men in suits waiting to slip a silk sash over the new princess's bosom.

We were about to give up and go home in disgust. But we needn't have worried. The day was saved by Clementine herself, who made her entrance standing at the prow of a building society sponsored float, shrouded in a long white hooded cloak.

The float came to a halt in the square. Stepping down, Clementine ignored the plastic podium, and strode straight past the leery waiting men to the gothic clock tower. She mounted the stone steps, where she turned to face the square and flung off her cloak. In place of the frothy floral garb beloved of Upley Maidens down the centuries, she was wearing a few shreds of frayed black fabric held together with safety pins. Oh, and she'd completely shaved her head. ("It's Britney!" breathed Eleanor.) As one of the leery men, confused, stepped forward with the sash, Clem produced a set of steel handcuffs and snapped them shut over her wrists, locking them to the railings round the clock tower. "Let the Up Rising begin!" she shouted. Everyone cheered. The teenage boys who had been banned from pulling the well ropes this year appeared out of nowhere and invaded the pink podium; three of them made for the throne and plonked themselves on it together, and the Princess Crown which one of them had grabbed on the way caught the plastic causing the whole thing to collapse. The other boys showered Clem and anyone in reach with cider. Everyone cheered again. The fire crew, who were eating burgers in the car park, took an hour to get through the crowds and arrived with everything except bolt cutters, so Clem stayed chained to the railings for most of the afternoon.

She and Ant have struck up a friendship and she has told her parents she intends to go to art college. In the meantime she has single-handedly kept the spirit of the Wellspring Festival alive, for the time being at least.

## Daniel

That leaves Daniel. Our invisible middle child who never attracts attention – if you don't count his three-day disappearance last year.

Daniel's school report this year was the standard set of lukewarm comments about him being bright but not fulfilling his potential. As usual we didn't do much about it, just putting it down to his being the youngest in his year; we were preoccupied with the twins' university applications. August 30th was Daniel's birthday – the last in his year to turn 15. He hadn't wanted a party so we made sure there was a cake on the table with his presents when he wandered downstairs at about midday. We asked him what he'd like to do for the rest of the day. He thought for a minute then asked if we could speak to his financial adviser.

So we said yes – it was his birthday after all. Here comes the bombshell. Daniel had just been offered a jaw-dropping sum of money. For a computer game that he's been sitting upstairs creating for the past two years. Don't ask me to explain what it's about – it involves an imaginary universe and leaps through wormholes into various dimensions. He sent it to a nerdy development company who were so intrigued they asked him to come in for discussions (remember that three-day disappearance …). Then a big Japanese company got involved, who decided it's the best thing they've seen since something Felipe is addicted to called Call of Duty. They've signed Daniel up and commissioned a whole series of sequel games from him. All these negotiations were done by email and text; the nerdy developers never bothered to ask his age, and the powers that be at the Japanese company didn't twig that they were dealing with a schoolboy. At some point they all realised Daniel is under 18 and our son thought he'd better get round to telling us about it.

This is the bit where we all danced round the living room.

So Ant and I are the parents of a child prodigy. I know Christmas newsletters are the seasonal soapbox for wunderkinds who effortlessly achieve the highest violin grades known to mankind, followed by scholarships to Harvard. Daniel has bypassed mainstream education to design something that neither of us understands and that will earn him more than the rest of the family combined. But he's not old enough to manage the money, so we are his trustees and we can spend it for him. On anything, say the rules, that enriches the quality of his home life.

We went to see our bank manager – the same one who treats us like something he's found on the sole of his shoe – and asked him to open a new account. When he saw how much we were paying in he turned a weird shade of puce and virtually lay down on the carpet for us to walk over him on our way out.

In Upley Rising money doesn't just talk, it gossips, tattles and broadcasts. We've had an invitation out of the blue to join the South Thameshire Lawn Tennis Club and we have both been asked to become governors at the Queen's Grammar School. Filling out the form to say yes, I listed our address as The Murder House, Paradise View. The murderer may never have been identified, but has definitely left a legacy.

Daniel is unphased and unchanged. He doesn't want any designer versions of his usual hoodie and trainers. He still spends most of the time in his bedroom. On Saturday nights while we're sitting watching Strictly eating pizza with the twinnies, he's in his room working on Galactic Corpse Frenzy (did I mention the name of his game?) or building Lego palaces as downtime. He makes rare guest appearances in the kitchen to pick at scraps from the fridge. Felipe, Eleanor, Mackenzie and Fraser are collectively awestruck – being twins seems to make them immune from sibling envy.

**The twinnies**
Not much to add about Mackenzie and Fraser this year except they have become minor celebrities at school and are the most popular kids in the playground. Fraser has given up fighting to sell advance bits of information about Daniel's game, and Mackenzie trades promises of audiences with him for sweets.

**Ali**
I am still jobless. This means I'm actually working harder than ever: I spend most of my time trying to manage Daniel's income. The financial adviser wants me to put it into some American property fund but my parents say it'll

be better off in the Northern Rock, which is back in their good books again. Who should I believe?

I don't need to work now but I can't kick the habit. I'm a librarian and that's that. Cut me open and you'll find ISBN numbers stamped all the way through. I've been headhunted to work part time at the prison library. (Nice people round here don't often mention it, but HM Prison Thameshire is just north of Upley Rising.) I pointed out that I'm an academic librarian used to working with people intent on getting a degree, and they said that was exactly what they needed. That put me in my place and I'm going to give it a go.

My biggest achievement this year was gasping my way through all of 5k in Upley Rising's very own park run. Vanessa and I came last behind all the teachers, quantity surveyors, estate agents, dentists and parents with buggies. But we can only improve.

## Christmas

We are all travelling FIRST CLASS to Santiago for three weeks (Saffron will combine housesitting Hector with writing her thesis) to see Ant awarded his prize. Since news leaked out he's started receiving more commissions than he can manage, which means he can charge serious prices. Not that he's in it for the money. It'll be summer in Chile, so when Ant isn't gladhanding local bigwigs or meeting his long-lost cousins, we'll all be sunning ourselves by the sea. Chile has nearly 3,000 miles of sandy beach to die for, says Eleanor, so no fighting over deckchair space for us. We can't wait.

Though Felipe is grousing about having to leave some girl he's just met, and Mackenzie and Fraser are furious that they've had to turn down a once-in-a-lifetime opportunity to play both halves of the donkey in the school nativity play.

This family is still a work in progress.

Festive Greetings to you all,

*Alison, Antonio, Eleanor, Felipe, Daniel, Fraser, Mackenzie and Hector*

\* \* \* \* \*

Printed in Great Britain
by Amazon